ANOTHER WORLD

ANOTHER WORLD
A Science Fiction Anthology

Edited, with introduction and commentary by
Gardner Dozois

Follett Publishing Company Chicago

Acknowledgment is made for permission to reprint the following material:

"The Oldest Soldier" by Fritz Leiber. Copyright © 1960 by Mercury Press, Inc. Reprinted by permission of the author and his agent, Robert P. Mills, Ltd.

"After the Myths Went Home" by Robert Silverberg. Copyright © 1969 by Mercury Press, Inc. Reprinted by permission of the author and the author's agents, Scott Meredith Literary Agency, Inc., 845 Third Avenue, New York, N.Y. 10022.

"The Stars Below" by Ursula K. Le Guin. Copyright © 1974, 1975 by Ursula K. Le Guin. Reprinted by permission of the author and the author's agent, Virginia Kidd.

"Straw" by Gene Wolfe. Copyright © 1974 by UPD Publishing Corporation. Reprinted by permission of the author and the author's agent, Virginia Kidd.

"On the Gem Planet" by Cordwainer Smith. Copyright © 1963 by Galaxy Publishing Corp. Reprinted by permission of the author and the author's agents, Scott Meredith Literary Agency, Inc., 845 Third Avenue, New York, N.Y. 10022.

"Beam Us Home" by James Tiptree, Jr. Copyright © 1969 by Universal Publishing and Distributing Corp. Reprinted by permission of the author and his agent, Robert P. Mills, Ltd.

"The Barbarian" by Joanna Russ. Copyright © 1968 by Damon Knight. Reprinted by permission of the author.

"Among the Hairy Earthmen" by R.A. Lafferty. Copyright © 1966 by Galaxy Publishing Corp. Reprinted by permission of the author and the author's agent, Virginia Kidd.

"Man in the Jar" by Damon Knight. Copyright © 1957 by Galaxy Publishing Corp. Reprinted by permission of the author.

"Old Hundredth" by Brian W. Aldiss. Copyright © 1960 by Brian W. Aldiss. Reprinted by permission of the author and the author's agents, Georges Borchardt, Inc.

"The Signaller" by Keith Roberts. Copyright © 1966 by Keith Roberts. Reprinted by permission of the author and the author's agents, Wallace, Aitken & Sheil, Inc.

International Standard Book Number: 0-695-40695-7 Titan Binding
International Standard Book Number: 0-695-80695-5 Trade Binding

Library of Congress Catalog Card Number: 76-19885

123456789/828180797877   8/00/994

Jacket by Carlos Ochagavia

For
Susan Casper,
who
taught me the
value
of π

CONTENTS

The editor would like to thank the following people for their help and support: Virginia Kidd, Robert Silverberg, David G. Hartwell, Susan Casper, Kirby McCauley, Fred Fisher of the Hourglass SF bookstore in Philadelphia, and Tom Whitehead and his staff from the Special Collections Department of the Paley Library at Temple University.

INTRODUCTION

EVEN TODAY, people still occasionally ask, "Why do you read science fiction?" This is not always an easy question to answer in an increasingly time-clocked, think-tanked, buttoned-down world. After all, SF won't help you balance your budget, lose weight, attain nirvana, play the stock market, find a Perfect Mate, or get an exciting, high-paying job as a computer programmer.

So why read the stuff?

Let's attack that hairy old animal from the flank, obliquely, and see if we can pull it down.

I grew up in New England, an odd corner of the country where cultural dinosaurs linger on long after they've died everywhere else, and as a result my childhood is filled with memories that a person of my generation shouldn't have: working steam trains in operation along the North Shore, scissor-grinder men on bicycle carts, stealing slivers of ice from trucks in the summer, televisionless houses, automobiles that did not fall apart immediately after purchase.

It's possible that I may also be one of the last people

to have undergone the scorn and opprobrium traditionally heaped on people who read science fiction. That doesn't happen much today, especially not among young people. An SF writer going onto a college campus today is greeted as a celebrity, or at least as a curiosity. He or she is invited into the faculty lounge for bad coffee and surrounded by kids who are actually *encouraged* by their teachers to read SF, and they ask him some pretty intelligent questions. The same thing applies when an SF writer visits a high school, except that the kids are even more avid and the questions even more intelligent. But when I was a boy, admitting that you read SF was tantamount to admitting that you had lice or ringworm. It took real devotion to keep reading the stuff in the face of constant adverse pressure from parents, teachers, friends, neighbors, from the whole community, in fact. But I did. I ate it up in ton lots with no discrimination whatsoever. And when I started trying to write, SF stories were what I scribbled in my dime-store notebook at night, sometimes writing with a flashlight under the covers, ducking everything and pretending to be asleep when I heard my parents coming. They did not approve of me wasting my time writing, and they especially did not approve of my reading SF, that "mind-rotting junk." But I kept reading SF. The ban slowed my consumption of it not at all, even if I had to smuggle it into the house and hide it the way kids hide grass today. And it made me high in an oddly similar way.

Edgar Rice Burroughs, A. Merritt, H. Rider Haggard, Doc Smith, H.G. Wells! Boy, did I love it! The wind that whistled across the dead sea bottoms of Barsoom blew also through my bedroom, although the roses on the wallpaper did not stir as it passed. The molten sunlight of enchanted Africa shone upon my room throughout the New England winter; Tharks and dinosaurs came to call; Lemuria rose again in the aspect of our weed-overgrown backyard. I flew the Skylark. I was the Invisible Man. And the key and the conduit for all this magic were the lurid paperbacks that were sold to me like contraband by disdainful drugstore proprietors.

It was the magic that drew me first, the lure of fantastic places and heroic deeds, the dark thrill of Mystery and Distance. Eventually I learned that the best SF was also full of ideas, concepts, codifications, insights into the workings of the world, and that, far from being dry or boring, it was even *more* exciting, more magical, more full of the "sense of wonder." I came eventually to agree with Vonnegut's Mr. Rosewater that SF writers were almost the only ones who "really notice what machines do to us, what wars do to us, what cities do to us, what big, simple ideas do to us . . . the only ones zany enough to agonize over time and distances without limit."

And yet, for all of that, SF has kept its magic. The best SF is seldom stuffy or pretentious or arrogant in that particularly purblind way that excludes automatically the validity of ideas and viewpoints other than your own. SF is one of the few remaining forms of literature—perhaps the only remaining form—that is entertaining in the full sense of the word, producing both intellectual and emotional excitement, molding magic and rationality, producing healthy hybrids of "escapist entertainment" and "relevancy" that satisfy both the emotions and the mind. The most profound and mind-stretching of stories are apt to be full of excitement, mystery, action, humor. The most lighthearted of romps or the most fast-paced adventure tale is still likely to contain something to make you think, to wonder, to reconsider your values and ideas, to make you suddenly sit bolt upright, covered in cold sweat.

This anthology demonstrates the full range of modern SF, its strength, its eclecticism, its vitality, its ability to conjure up new worlds and new lives, and, more importantly, to make us live in those worlds and through those lives as naturally as if they were our own, without losing any of the

wonder, joy, terror, or beauty of the experience. Here is
life on another world, in another place, another time. Here
is what it is like to wear an alien skin. Here are new
concepts, new vistas, magic: a far future society conjures up
all the gods and devils and heroes of the distant past with
disastrous results; a young semaphore Signalman faces
elves, isolation, and a lonely winter death in a twentieth-
century England that never was; a self-styled coward,
inadvertently caught up in a universe-wide time war, must
match wills with a monster in nighttime Chicago; a per-
secuted astronomer looks into his soul to find wonders as
vast as the stars; a barbarian adventuress has a deadly
battle of wits with a seemingly omnipotent time-traveler; an
intelligent sloth and a mutated baluchitherium roam a
haunted future Earth from which humans have forever departed; a boy keeps a lifelong secret that he hopes will take
him to the stars; in an alternate Dark-Age Europe, sword-
wielding mercenaries travel the countryside in hot-air bal-
loons seeking war and employment; an alien bellhop must
deal with his most deadly customer; children from the stars
assume human form and play at war and statesmanship with
real nations for pawns; an interplanetary wanderer, with
his own life at stake, must decide the fate of an immortal
horse on a world where precious gems are more common
than dirt.

SF is alive—still growing, still changing, still vital. That's
the answer to the question, "Why read science fiction?" It's
alive in a world of dead art, dead minds, dead institutions;
it's a bright-eyed, irreverent little animal scurrying through
a petrified landscape of old dead trees; it's unashamedly
potent and prolific in a world that grows increasingly
weary and sterile; it dares to raise its voice in boisterous
joy, sorrow, and anger in a place full of sour silence and
dead echoes.

Gardner Dozois

THE OLDEST SOLDIER

Fritz Leiber

Hugo- and Nebula-winner Fritz Leiber has long been recognized as one of the modern masters of science fiction. It is less widely known that he is also a master of the macabre, perhaps the foremost modern practitioner of the suspense and supernatural horror tale.

Here he adroitly mingles both genres in a chilling tale of preternatural cat and mouse: a bizarre rearguard action fought through the shadowed streets of nighttime Chicago, where the flap and scurry above you might be wind-blown trash or the beating of dark wings; where the smoldering red pinpoints behind you might be car taillights or cigarette butts or the hungry eyes of something alien and evil.

○ THE ONE we called the Leutnant took a long swallow of
his dark Lowensbrau. He'd just been describing a battle of
infantry rockets on the Eastern Front, the German and
Russian positions erupting bundles of flame.

Max swished his paler beer in its green bottle and his eyes
got a faraway look and he said, "When the rockets killed
their thousands in Copenhagen, they laced the sky with fire
and lit up the steeples in the city and the masts and bare
spars of the British ships like a field of crosses."

"I didn't know there were any landings in Denmark,"
someone remarked with an expectant casualness.

"This was in the Napoleonic wars," Max explained. "The
British bombarded the city and captured the Danish fleet.
Back in 1807."

"Vas you dere, Maxie?" Woody asked, and the gang
around the counter chuckled and beamed. Drinking at a
liquor store is a pretty dull occupation and one is grateful
for small vaudeville acts.

"Why bare spars?" someone asked.

"So there'd be less chance of the rockets setting the
launching ships afire," Max came back at him. "Sails burn
fast and wooden ships are tinder anyway—that's why ships
firing red-hot shot never worked out. Rockets and bare spars
were bad enough. Yes, and it was Congreve rockets made
the 'red glare' at Fort McHenry," he continued unruffled,
"while the 'bombs bursting in air' were about the earliest
precision artillery shells, fired from mortars on bomb
ketches. There's a condensed history of arms in the American anthem." He looked around smiling.

"Yes, I was there, Woody—just as I was with the South
Martians when they stormed Copernicus in the Second
Colonial War. And just as I'll be in a foxhole outside
Copeybawa a billion years from now while the blast waves
from the battling Venusian spaceships shake the soil and
roil the mud and give me some more digging to do."

This time the gang really snorted its happy laughter and

Woody was slowly shaking his head and repeating, "Copen-hagen and Copernicus and—what was the third? Oh, what a mind he's got," and the Leutnant was saying, "Yah, you vas there—in books," and I was thinking, *Thank God for all the screwballs, especially the brave ones who never flinch, who never lose their tempers or drop the act, so that you never do quite find out whether it's just a gag or their solemnest belief. There's only one person here takes Max even one percent seriously, but they all love him because he won't ever drop his guard. . . .*

"The only point I was trying to make," Max continued when he could easily make himself heard "was the way styles in weapons keep moving in cycles."

"Did the Romans use rockets?" asked the same light voice as had remarked about the landings in Denmark and the bare spars. I saw now it was Sol from behind the counter.

Max shook his head. "Not so you'd notice. Catapults were their specialty." He squinted his eyes. "Though now you mention it, I recall a dogfoot telling me Archimedes faked up some rockets powered with Greek fire to touch off the sails of the Roman ships at Syracuse—and none of this romance about a giant burning glass."

"You mean," said Woody, "that there are other gazebos besides yourself in this fighting-all-over-the-universe-and-to-the-end-of-time racket?" His deep whiskey voice was at its solemnest and most wondering.

"Naturally," Max told him earnestly. "How else do you suppose wars ever get really fought and refought?" '

"Why should wars ever be refought?" Sol asked lightly. "Once ought to be enough."

"Do you suppose anybody could time-travel and keep his hands off wars?" Max countered.

I put in my two cents' worth. "Then that would make Archimedes' rockets the earliest liquid-fuel rockets by a long shot."

Max looked straight at me, a special quirk in his smile. "Yes, I guess so," he said after a couple of seconds. "On this planet, that is."

The laughter had been falling off, but that brought it back and while Woody was saying loudly to himself, "I like that refighting part—that's what we're all so good at," the Leutnant asked Max with only a moderate accent that fit North Chicago, "And zo you aggshually have fought on Mars?"

"Yes, I have," Max agreed after a bit. "Though that ruckus I mentioned happened on our moon—expeditionary forces from the Red Planet."

"Ach, yes. And now let me ask you something—"

I really mean that about screwballs, you know. I don't care whether they're saucer addicts or extrasensory perception bugs or religious or musical maniacs or crackpot philosophers or psychologists or merely guys with a strange dream or gag like Max—for my money they are the ones who are keeping individuality alive in this age of conformity. They are the ones who are resisting the encroachments of the mass media and motivation research and the mass man. The only really bad thing about crack pottery and screwballistics (as with dope and prostitution) is the coldblooded people who prey on it for money. So I say to all screwballs: Go it on your own. Don't take any wooden nickels or give out any silver dimes. Be wise and brave—like Max.

He and the Leutnant were working up a discussion of the problems of artillery in airless space and low gravity that was a little too technical to keep the laughter alive. So Woody up and remarked, "Say, Maximillian, if you got to be in all these wars all over hell and gone, you must have a pretty tight schedule. How come you got time to be drinking with us bums?"

"I often ask myself that," Max cracked back at him. "Fact is, I'm on a sort of unscheduled furlough, result of a transportation slip-up. I'm due to be picked up and returned

to my outfit any day now—that is, if the enemy underground doesn't get to me first."

It was just then, as Max said that bit about enemy underground, and as the laughter came, a little diminished, and as
Woody was chortling "Enemy underground now. How do
you like that?" and as I was thinking how much Max had
given me in these couple of weeks—a guy with an almost
poetic flare for vivid historical reconstruction, but with more
than that . . . it was just then that I saw the two red eyes low
down in the dusty plate-glass window looking in from the
dark street.

Everything in modern America has to have a big plate-
glass display window, everything from suburban mansions,
general managers' offices and skyscraper apartments to bar-
ber shops and beauty parlors and ginmills—there are even
gymnasium swimming pools with plate-glass windows
twenty feet high opening on busy boulevards—and Sol's
dingy liquor store was no exception; in fact I believe there's
a law that it's got to be that way. But I was the only one of
the gang who happened to be looking out of this particular
window at the moment. It was a dark windy night outside
and it's a dark untidy street at best and across from Sol's are
more plate-glass windows that sometimes give off very odd
reflections, so when I got a glimpse of this black formless
head with the two eyes like red coals peering in past the
brown pyramid of empty whiskey bottles, I don't suppose it
was a half second before I realized it must be something
like a couple of cigarette butts kept alive by the wind, or
more likely a freak reflection of taillights from some car
turning a corner down street, and in another half second it
was gone, the car having finished turning the corner or the
wind blowing the cigarette butts away altogether. Still, for
a moment it gave me a very goosey feeling, coming right on
top of that remark about an enemy underground.

And I must have shown my reaction in some way, for
Woody, who is very observant, called out, "Hey, Fred, has

that soda pop you drink started to rot your nerves—or are
even Max's friends getting sick at the outrageous lies he's
been telling us?"

Max looked at me sharply and perhaps he saw something
too. At any rate he finished his beer and said, "I guess I'll be
taking off." He didn't say it to me particularly, but he kept
looking at me. I nodded and put down on the counter my
small green bottle, still one-third full of the lemon pop I
find overly sweet, though it was the sourest Sol stocked. Max
and I zipped up our Windbreakers. He opened the door and
a little of the wind came in and troubled the tanbark
around the sill. The Leutnant said to Max, "Tomorrow
night we design a better space gun;" Sol routinely advised
the two of us, "Keep your noses clean;" and Woody called,
"So long space soldiers." (And I could imagine him saying
as the door closed, "That Max is nuttier than a fruitcake and
Freddy isn't much better. Drinking soda pop—ugh!")

And then Max and I were outside leaning into the wind,
our eyes slitted against the blown dust, for the three-block
trudge to Max's pad—a name his tiny apartment merits
without any attempt to force the language.

There weren't any large black shaggy dogs with red eyes
slinking about and I hadn't quite expected there would be.

Why Max and his soldier-of-history gag and our out-
wardly small comradeship meant so much to me is something that goes way back into my childhood. I was a lonely
timid child, with no brothers and sisters to spar around with
in preparation for the battles of life, and I never went
through the usual stages of boyhood gangs either. In line
with those things I grew up into a very devout liberal and
"hated war" with a mystical fervor during the intermission
between 1918 and 1939—so much so that I made a point
of avoiding military services in the second conflict, though
merely by working in the nearest war plant, not by the
arduously heroic route of out-and-out pacifism.

But then the inevitable reaction set in, sparked by the liberal curse of being able, however, belatedly, to see both sides of any question. I began to be curious about and cautiously admiring of soldiering and soldiers. Unwillingly at first, I came to see the necessity and romance of the spearmen—those guardians, often lonely as myself, of the perilous camps of civilization and brotherhood in a black hostile universe . . . necessary guardians, for all the truth in the indictments that war caters to irrationality and sadism and serves the munition makers and reaction.

I commenced to see my own hatred of war as in part only a mask for cowardice, and I started to look for some way to do honor in my life to the other half of the truth. Though it's anything but easy to give yourself a feeling of being brave just because you suddenly want that feeling. Obvious opportunities to be obviously brave come very seldom in our largely civilized culture, in fact they're clean contrary to safety drives and so-called normal adjustment and good peacetime citizenship and all the rest, and they come mostly in the earliest part of a man's life. So that for the person who belatedly wants to be brave it's generally a matter of waiting for an opportunity for six months and then getting a tiny one and muffing it in six seconds.

But however uncomfortable it was, I had this reaction to my devout early pacifism, as I say. At first I took it out only in reading. I devoured war books, current and historical, fact and fiction. I tried to soak up the military aspects and jargon of all ages, the organization and weapons, the strategy and tactics. Characters like Tros of Samothrace and Horatio Hornblower became my new secret heroes, along with Heinlein's space cadets and Bullard and other brave rangers of the spaceways.

But after a while reading wasn't enough. I had to have some real soldiers and I finally found them in the little gang that gathered nightly at Sol's liquor store. It's funny but liquor stores that serve drinks have a clientele with more character and comradeship than the clienteles of most bars —perhaps it is the absence of juke-boxes, chromium plate, bowling machines, trouble-hunting, drink-cadging women, and—along with those—men in search of fights and forget-fulness. At any rate, it was at Sol's liquor store that I found Woody and the Leutnant and Bert and Mike and Pierre and Sol himself. The casual customer would hardly have guessed that they were anything but quiet souses, certainly not soldiers, but I got a clue or two and I started to hang around, making myself inconspicuous and drinking my rather sym-bolic soda pop, and pretty soon they started to open up and yarn about North Africa and Stalingrad and Anzio and Korea and such and I was pretty happy in a partial sort of way.

And then about a month ago Max had turned up and he was the man I'd really been looking for. A genuine soldier with my historical slant on things—only he knew a lot more than I did, I was a rank amateur by comparison—and he had this crazy appealing gag too, and besides that he actu-ally cottoned to me and invited me on to his place a few times, so that with him I was more than a tavern hanger-on. Max was good for me, though I still hadn't the faintest idea of who he really was or what he did.

Naturally Max hadn't opened up the first couple of nights with the gang, he'd just bought his beer and kept quiet and felt his way much as I had. Yet he looked and felt so much the soldier that I think the gang was inclined to accept him from the start—a quick stocky man with big hands and a leathery face and smiling tired eyes that seemed to have seen everything at one time or another. And then on the third or fourth night Bert told something about the Battle of the Bulge and Max chimed in with some things he'd seen there, and I could tell from the looks Bert and the Leutnant exchanged that Max had "passed"—he was now the ac-cepted seventh member of the gang, with me still as the tolerated clerical-type hanger-on, for I'd never made any secret of my complete lack of military experience.

Not long afterwards—it couldn't have been more than one or two nights—Woody told some tall tales and Max started matching him and that was the beginning of the time-and-space-soldier gag. It was funny about the gag. I suppose we just should have assumed that Max was a history nut and liked to parade his bookish hobby in a picturesque way—and maybe some of the gang did assume just that—but he was so vivid yet so casual in his descriptions of other times and places that you felt there had to be something more and sometimes he'd get such a lost, nostalgic look on his face talking of things fifty million miles or five hundred years away that Woody would almost die laughing, which was really the sincerest sort of tribute to Max's convincingness.

Max even kept up the gag when he and I were alone together, walking or at his place—he'd never come to mine —though he kept it up in a minor-key sort of way, so that it sometimes seemed that what he was trying to get across was not that he was the Soldier of a Power that was fighting across all of time to change history, but simply that we men were creatures with imaginations and it was our highest duty to try to feel what it was really like to live in other times and places and bodies. Once he said to me, "The growth of consciousness is everything, Fred—the seed of awareness sending its roots across space and time. But it can grow in so many ways, spinning its web from mind to mind like the spider or burrowing into the unconscious darkness like the snake. The biggest wars are the wars of thought."

But whatever he was trying to get across, I went along with his gag—which seems to me the proper way to behave with any other man, screwball or not, so long as you can do it without violating your own personality. Another man brings a little life and excitement into the world, why try to kill it? It is simply a matter of politeness and style.

I'd come to think a lot about style since knowing Max. It doesn't matter so much what you do in life, he once said to me—soldiering or clerking, preaching or picking pockets—so long as you do it with style. Better fail in a grand style than succeed in a mean one—you won't enjoy the successes you get the second way.

Max seemed to understand my own special problems without my having to confess them. He pointed out to me that the soldier is trained for bravery. The whole object of military discipline is to make sure that when the six seconds of testing come every six months or so, you do the brave thing without thinking, by drilled second nature. It's not a matter of the soldier having some special virtue or virility the civilian lacks. And then about fear. All men are afraid, Max said, except a few psychopathic or suicidal types and they merely haven't fear at the conscious level. But the better you know yourself and the men around you and the situation you're up against (though you can never know all of the last and sometimes you have only a glimmering), then the better you are prepared to prevent fear from mastering you. Generally speaking, if you prepare yourself by the daily self-discipline of looking squarely at life, if you imagine realistically the troubles and opportunities that may come, then the chances are you won't fail in the testing. Well, of course I'd heard and read all those things before, but coming from Max they seemed to mean a lot more to me. As I say, Max was good for me.

So on this night when Max had talked about Copenhagen and Copernicus and Copeybawa and I'd imagined I'd seen a big black dog with red eyes and we were walking the lonely streets hunched in our jackets and I was listening to the big clock over at the University tolling eleven . . . well, on this night I wasn't thinking anything special except that I was with my screwball buddy and pretty soon we'd be at his place and having a nightcap. I'd make mine coffee.

I certainly wasn't expecting anything.

Until, at the windy corner just before his place, Max suddenly stopped.

Max's junky front room-and-a-half was in a smoky brick building two flights up over some run-down stores. There is a rust-flaked fire escape on the front of it, running past the old-fashioned jutting bay windows, its lowest flight a counter-balanced one that only swings down when somebody walks out onto it—that is, if a person ever had occasion to.

When Max stopped suddenly, I stopped too of course. He was looking up at his window. His window was dark and I couldn't see anything in particular, except that he or somebody else had apparently left a big black bundle of something out on the fire escape and—it wouldn't be the first time I'd seen that space used for storage and drying wash and whatnot, against all fire regulations, I'm sure.

But Max stayed stopped and kept on looking.

"Say, Fred," he said softly then, "how about going over to your place for a change? Is the standing invitation still out?"

"Sure Max, why not," I replied instantly, matching my voice to his. "I've been asking you all along."

My place was just two blocks away. We'd only have to turn the corner we were standing on and we'd be headed straight for it.

"Okay then," Max said. "Let's get going." There was a touch of sharp impatience in his voice that I'd never heard there before. He suddenly seemed very eager that we should get around that corner. He took hold of my arm.

He was no longer looking up at the fire escape, but I was. The wind had abruptly died and it was very still. As we went around the corner—to be exact as Max pulled me around it—the big bundle of something lifted up and looked down at me with eyes like two red coals.

I didn't let out a gasp or say anything. I don't think Max realized then that I'd seen anything, but I was shaken. This time I couldn't lay it to cigarette butts or reflected taillights, they were too difficult to place on a third-story fire escape. This time my mind would have to rationalize a lot more inventively to find an explanation, and until it did I would have to believe that something . . . well, alien . . . was at large in this part of Chicago.

Big cities have their natural menaces—hold-up artists, hopped-up kids, sick-headed sadists, that sort of thing—and you're more or less prepared for them. You're not prepared for something . . . alien. If you hear a scuttling in the basement you assume it's rats and although you know rats can be dangerous you're not particularly frightened and you may even go down to investigate. You don't expect to find bird-catching Amazonian spiders.

The wind hadn't resumed yet. We'd gone about a third of the way down the first block when I heard behind us, faintly but distinctly, a rusty creaking ending in a metallic jar that didn't fit anything but the first flight of the fire escape swinging down to the sidewalk.

I just kept walking then, but my mind split in two—half of it listening and straining back over my shoulder, the other half darting off to investigate the weirdest notions, such as that Max was a refugee from some unimaginable concentration camp on the other side of the stars. If there were such concentration camps, I told myself in my cold hysteria, run by some sort of supernatural SS men, they'd have dogs just like the one I'd thought I'd seen . . . and, to be honest, thought I'd *see* padding along if I looked over my shoulder now.

It was hard to hang on and just walk, not run, with this insanity or whatever it was hovering over my mind, and the fact that Max didn't say a word didn't help either.

Finally, as we were starting the second block, I got hold of myself and I quietly reported to Max exactly what I thought I'd seen. His response surprised me.

"What's the layout of your apartment, Fred? Third floor, isn't it?"

"Yes. Well . . ."

"Begin at the door we'll be going in," he directed me.

"That's the living room, then there's a tiny short open hall, then the kitchen. It's like an hour-glass, with the living room and kitchen the ends, and the hall the wasp waist. Two doors open from the hall: the one to your right (figuring from the living room) opens into the bathroom; the one to your left, into a small bedroom."

"Windows?"

"Two in the living room, side by side," I told him. "None in the bathroom. One in the bedroom, onto an air shaft. Two in the kitchen, apart."

"Back door in the kitchen?" he asked.

"Yes. To the back porch. Has glass in the top half of it. I hadn't thought about that. That makes three windows in the kitchen."

"Are the shades in the windows pulled down now?"

"No."

Questions and answers had been rapid-fire, without time for me to think, done while we walked a quarter of a block. Now after the briefest pause Max said, "Look, Fred, I'm not asking you or anyone to believe in all the things I've been telling as if for kicks at Sol's—that's too much for all of a sudden—but you do believe in that black dog, don't you?" He touched my arm warningly. "No, don't look behind you!"

I swallowed. "I believe in him right now," I said.

"Okay. Keep on walking. I'm sorry I got you into this, Fred, but now I've got to try to get both of us out. *Your* best chance is to disregard the thing, pretend you're not aware of anything strange happened—then the beast won't know whether I've told you anything, it'll be hesitant to disturb you, it'll try to get at me without troubling you, and it'll even hold off a while if it thinks it will get me that way. But it won't hold off forever—it's only imperfectly disciplined. *My* best chance is to get in touch with head-quarters—something I've been putting off—and have them pull me out. I should be able to do it in an hour, maybe less. You can give me that time, Fred."

"How?" I asked him. I was mounting the steps to the vestibule. I thought I could hear, very faintly, a light pad-padding behind us. I didn't look back.

Max stepped through the door I held open and we started up the stairs.

"As soon as we get in your apartment," he said, "you turn on all the lights in the living room and kitchen. Leave the shades up. Then start doing whatever you might be doing if you were staying up at this time of night. Reading or typing, say. Or having a bite of food, if you can manage it. Play it as naturally as you can. If you hear things, if you feel things, try to take no notice. Above all, don't open the windows or doors, or look out of them to see anything, or go to them if you can help it—you'll probably feel drawn to do just that. Just play it naturally. If you can hold them . . . it . . . off that way for half an hour or so—until midnight, say—if you can give me that much time, I should be able to handle my end of it. And remember, it's the best chance for you as well as for me. Once I'm out of here, you're safe."

"But you—" I said, digging for my key, "—what will you —?"

"As soon as we get inside," Max said, "I'll duck in your bedroom and shut the door. Pay no attention. Don't come after me, whatever you hear. Is there a plug-in in your bedroom? I'll need juice."

"Yes," I told him, turning the key. "But the lights have been going off a lot lately. Someone has been blowing the fuses."

"That's great," he growled, following me inside.

I turned on the lights and went in the kitchen, did the same there and came back. Max was still in the living room, bent over the table beside my typewriter. He had a sheet of light-green paper. He must have brought it with him. He was scrawling something at the top and bottom of it. He straightened up and gave it to me.

"Fold it up and put it in your pocket and keep it on you the next few days," he said.

It was just a blank sheet of cracklingly thin light-green paper with "Dear Fred" scribbled at the top and "Your friend, Max Bournemann" at the bottom and nothing in between.

"But what—?" I began, looking up at him.

"Do as I say!" He snapped at me. Then, as I almost flinched away from him, he grinned—a great big comradely grin.

"Okay, let's get working," he said, and he went into the bedroom and shut the door behind him.

I folded the sheet of paper three times and unzipped my Windbreaker and tucked it inside the breast pocket. Then I went to the bookcase and pulled at random a volume out of the top shelf—my psychology shelf, I remembered the next moment—and sat down and opened the book and looked at a page without seeing the print.

And now there was time for me to think. Since I'd spoken of the red eyes to Max there had been no time for anything but to listen and to remember and to act. Now there was time for me to think.

My first thoughts were: *This is ridiculous! I saw something strange and frightening, sure, but it was in the dark, I couldn't see anything clearly, there must be some simple natural explanation for whatever it was on the fire escape. I saw something strange and Max sensed I was frightened and when I told him about it he decided to play a practical joke on me in line with that eternal gag he lives by. I'll bet*

*right now he's lying on my bed and chuckling, wondering
how long it will be before I—*

The window beside me rattled as if the wind had suddenly
risen again. The rattling grew more violent—and then it
abruptly stopped without dying away, stopped with a feeling
of tension, as if the wind or something more material
were still pressing against the pane.

And I did not turn my head to look at it, although (or
perhaps because) I knew there was no fire escape or other
support outside. I simply endured that sense of a presence
at my elbow and stared unseeingly at the book in my hands,
while my heart pounded and my skin froze and flushed.

I realized fully then that my first skeptical thoughts had
been the sheerest automatic escapism and that, just as I'd
told Max, I believed with my whole mind in the black dog.
I believed in the whole business insofar as I could imagine it.
I believed that there are undreamed of powers warring in
this universe. I believed that Max was a stranded time-
traveller and that in my bedroom he was now frantically
operating some unearthly device to signal for help from
some unknown headquarters. I believed that the impossible
and the deadly was loose in Chicago.

But my thoughts couldn't carry further than that. They
kept repeating themselves, faster and faster. My mind felt
like an engine that is shaking itself to pieces. And the
impulse to turn my head and look out the window came to
me and grew.

I forced myself to focus on the middle of the page where
I had the book open and start reading.

*Jung's archetypes transgress the barriers of time and
space. More than that: they are capable of breaking the
shackles of the laws of causality. They are endowed with
frankly mystical "prospective" faculties. The soul itself,
according to Jung, is the reaction of the personality to
the unconscious and includes in every person both male*

and female elements, the animus and anima, as well as
the persona or the person's reaction to the outside
world. . . .

I think I read that last sentence a dozen times, swiftly at
first, then word by word, until it was a meaningless jumble
and I could no longer force my gaze across it.

Then the glass in the window beside me creaked.

I laid down the book and stood up, eyes front, and went
into the kitchen and grabbed a handful of crackers and
opened the refrigerator.

The rattling that muted itself in hungry pressure followed.
I heard it first in one kitchen window, then the other, then in
the glass in the top of the door. I didn't look.

I went back in the living room, hesitated a moment
beside my typewriter, which had a blank sheet of yellow
paper in it, then sat down again in the armchair beside the
window, putting the crackers and the half carton of milk on
the little table beside me. I picked up the book I'd tried to
read and put it on my knees.

The rattling returned with me—at once and peremptorily,
as if something were growing impatient.

I couldn't focus on the print any more. I picked up a
cracker and put it down. I touched the cold milk carton and
my throat constricted and I drew my fingers away.

I looked at my typewriter and then I thought of the blank
sheet of *green* paper and the explanation for Max's strange
act suddenly seemed clear to me. Whatever happened to
him tonight, he wanted me to be able to type a message
over his signature that would exonerate me. A suicide note,
say. Whatever happened to him . . .

The window beside me shook violently, as if at a terrific
gust.

It occurred to me that while I must not look out of the
window as if expecting to see something (that would be the
sort of give-away against which Max warned me) I could

safely let my gaze slide across it—say, if I turned to look at the clock behind me. Only, I told myself, I mustn't pause or react if I saw anything.

I nerved myself. After all, I told myself, there was the blessed possibility that I would see nothing outside the taut pane but darkness.

I turned my head to look at the clock.

I saw *it* twice, going and coming back, and although my gaze did not pause or falter, my blood and my thoughts started to pound as if my heart and mind would burst.

It was about two feet outside the window—a face or mask or muzzle of a more gleaming black than the darkness around it. The face was at the same time the face of a hound, a panther, a giant bat, and a man—in between those four. A pitiless, hopeless man-animal face alive with knowledge but dead with a monstrous melancholy and a monstrous malice. There was the sheen of needlelike white teeth against black lips or dewlaps. There was the dull pulsing glow of eyes like red coals.

My gaze didn't pause or falter or go back—yes—and my heart and mind didn't burst, but I stood up then and stepped jerkily to the typewriter and sat down at it and started to pound the keys. After a while my gaze stopped blurring and I started to see what I was typing. The first thing I'd typed was:

the quick red fox jumped over the crazy black dog . . .

I kept on typing. It was better than reading. Typing I was doing something, I could discharge. I typed a flood of fragments: "Now is the time for all good men—", the first words of the Declaration of Independence and the Constitution, the Winston Commercial, six lines of Hamlet's "To be or not to be," without punctuation, Newton's Third Law of Motion, "Mary had a big black—"

In the middle of it all the face of the electric clock that I'd looked at sprang into my mind. My mental image of it had been blanked out until then. The hands were at quarter to twelve.

Whipping in a fresh yellow sheet, I typed the first stanza of Poe's "Raven," the Oath of Allegiance to the American Flag, the lost-ghost lines from Thomas Wolfe, the Creed and the Lord's prayer, "Beauty is truth; truth, blackness—"

The rattling made a swift circuit of the windows—though I heard nothing from the bedroom, nothing at all—and finally the rattling settled on the kitchen door. There was a creaking of wood and metal under pressure.

I thought: *You are standing guard. You are standing guard for yourself and for Max.* And then the second thought came: *If you open the door, if you welcome it in, if you open the kitchen door and then the bedroom door, it will spare you, it will not hurt you.*

Over and over again I fought down that second thought and the urge that went with it. It didn't seem to be coming from my mind, but from the outside. I typed Ford, Buick, the names of all the automobiles I could remember, Overland Moon, I typed all the four-letter words, I typed the alphabet, lower case and capitals. I typed the numerals and punctuation marks, I typed the keys of the keyboard in order from left to right, top to bottom, then in from each side alternately. I filled the last yellow sheet I was on and it fell out and I kept pounding mechanically, making shiny black marks on the dull black platen.

But then the urge became something I could not resist. I stood up and in the sudden silence I walked through the hall to the back door, looking down at the floor and resisting, dragging each step as much as I could.

My hands touched the knob and the long-handled key in the lock. My body pressed the door, which seemed to surge against me, so that I felt it was only my counter-pressure that kept it from bursting open in a shower of splintered glass and wood.

Far off, as if it were something happening in another universe, I heard the University clock tolling **One** . . . two . . .

And then, because I could resist no longer, I turned the key and the knob.

The lights all went out.

In the darkness the door pushed open against me and something came in past me like a gust of cold black wind with streaks of heat in it.

I heard the bedroom door swing open.

The clock completed its strokes. Eleven . . . twelve . . .

And then . . .

Nothing . . . nothing at all. All pressures lifted from me. I was aware only of being alone, utterly alone. I knew it, deep down.

After some . . . minutes, I think, I shut and locked the door and I went over and opened a drawer and rummaged out a candle, lit it, and went through the apartment and into the bedroom.

Max wasn't there. I'd known he wouldn't be. I didn't know how badly I'd failed him. I lay down on the bed and after a while I began to sob and, after another while, I slept.

Next day I told the janitor about the lights. He gave me a funny look.

"I know," he said. "I just put in a new fuse this morning. I never saw one blown like that before. The window in the fuse was gone and there was a metal sprayed all over the inside of the box."

That afternoon I got Max's message. I'd gone for a walk in the park and was sitting on a bench beside the lagoon, watching the water ripple in the breeze when I felt something burning against my chest. For a moment I thought I'd dropped my cigarette butt inside my windbreaker. I reached in and touched something hot in my pocket and jerked it out. It was the sheet of green paper Max had given me. Tiny threads of smoke were rising from it.

I flipped it open and read, in a scrawl that smoked and grew blacker instant by instant:

Thought you'd like to know I got through okay. Just in time. I'm back with my outfit. It's not too bad. Thanks for the rearguard action.

The handwriting (thought-writing?) of the blackening scrawl was identical with the salutation above and the signature below.

And then the sheet burst into flame. I flipped it away from me. Two boys launching a model sailboat looked at the paper flaming, blackening, whitening, disintegrating . . .

I know enough chemistry to know that paper smeared with wet white phosphorus will burst into flame when it dries completely. And I know there are kinds of invisible writing that are brought out by heat. There are those general sorts of possibility. Chemical writing.

And then there's thoughtwriting, which is nothing but a word I've coined. Writing from a distance—a literal telegram.

And there may be a combination of the two—chemical writing activated by thought from a distance . . . from a great distance.

I don't know. I simply don't know. When I remember that last night with Max, there are parts of it I doubt. But there's one part I never doubt.

When the gang asks me, "Where's Max?" I just shrug.

But when they get to talking about withdrawals they've covered; rearguard actions they've been in, I remember mine. I've never told them about it, but I never doubt that it took place.

AFTER THE MYTHS WENT HOME

Robert Silverberg

*In spite of our modern pretense of cooled-out logical prag-
matism and think-tank rationality, we still need myths.
In fact, in a world where most of the age-old props—
religion, morality, tradition, culture, family—have been
knocked out from under us we may need them more
urgently than ever. Denied the traditional gods and heroes
and demons of the past, we instinctively endeavor to replace them with a pantheon of our own devising, rough-
hewing our myths out of whatever archetypical material
comes most readily to hand: JFK, Evel Knievel,* Jaws,
Marilyn Monroe, the Beatles, James Bond, and the God-
father.

*Here Hugo- and Nebula-winner Robert Silverberg—
SF's most acidulous and elegant satirist—examines an effete
future society that has forgotten the value of myth, although
they are able to crank out gods and heroes to order in any
desired quantity, a society that has made the possibly fatal
mistake of confusing the substance with the show.*

○ For a while in those years we were calling great ones out of the past, to find out what they were like. This was in the middle twelves—12400 to 12450, say. We called up Caesar and Antony, and also Cleopatra. We got Freud and Marx and Lenin into the same room and let them talk. We summoned Winston Churchill, who was a disappointment (he lisped and drank too much), and Napoleon, who was magnificent. We raided ten millennia of history for our sport.

But after half a century of this we grew bored with our game. We were easily bored, in the middle twelves. So we started to call up the myth people, the gods and the heroes. That seemed more romantic, and this was one of Earth's romanticist eras we lived in.

It was my turn to serve as curator of the Hall of Man, and that was where they built the machine, so I watched it going up from the start. Leor the Builder was in charge. He had made the machines that called the real people up, so this was only slightly different, no real challenge to his talents. He had to feed in another kind of data, full of archetypes and psychic currents, but the essential process of reconstruction would be the same. He never had any doubt of success.

Leor's new machine had crystal rods and silver sides. A giant emerald was embedded in its twelve-angled lid. Tinsel streamers of radiant platinum dangled from the bony struts on which it rose.

"Mere decoration," Leor confided to me. "I could have made a simple black box. But brutalism is out of fashion."

The machine sprawled all over the Pavilion of Hope on the north face of the Hall of Man. It hid the lovely flickermosaic flooring, but at least it cast lovely reflections into the mirrored surfaces of the exhibit cases. Somewhere about 12570, Leor said he was ready to put his machine into operation.

We arranged the best possible weather. We turned the

winds, deflecting the westerlies a bit and pushing all clouds far to the south. We sent up new moons to dance at night in wondrous patterns, now and again coming together to spell out Leor's name. People came from all over Earth, thousands of them, camping in whisper-tents on the great plain that begins at the Hall of Man's doorstep. There was real excitement then, a tension that crackled beautifully through the clear blue air.

Leor made his last adjustments. The committee of literary advisers conferred with him over the order of events, and there was some friendly bickering. We chose daytime for the first demonstration, and tinted the sky light purple for better effect. Most of us put on our youngest bodies, though there were some who said they wanted to look mature in the presence of these fabled figures out of time's dawn.

"Whenever you wish me to begin—" Leor said.

There were speeches first. Chairman Peng gave his usual lighthearted address. The Procurator of Pluto, who was visiting us, congratulated Leor on the fertility of his inventions. Nistim, then in his third or fourth successive term as Metabolizer General, encouraged everyone present to climb to a higher level. Then the master of ceremonies pointed to me. No, I said, shaking my head, I am a very poor speaker. They replied that it was my duty, as curator of the Hall of Man, to explain what was about to unfold.

Reluctantly I came forward.

"You will see the dreams of old mankind made real today," I said, groping for words. "The hopes of the past will walk among you, and so, I think, will the nightmares. We are offering you a view of the imaginary figures by means of whom the ancients attempted to give structure to the universe. These gods, these heroes, summed up patterns of cause and effect, and served as organizing forces around which cultures could crystallize. It is all very strange for us and it will be wonderfully interesting. Thank you."

Leor was given the signal to begin.

"I must explain one thing," he said. "Some of the beings you are about to see were purely imaginary, concocted by tribal poets, even as my friend has just told you. Others, though, were based on actual human beings who once walked the Earth as ordinary mortals, and who were transfigured, given more-than-human qualities, raised to the pantheon. Until they actually appear, we will not know which figures belong to which category, but I can tell you how to detect their origin once you see them. Those who were human beings before they became myths will have a slight aura, a shadow, a darkness in the air about them. This is the lingering trace of their essential humanity, which no mythmaker can erase. So I learned in my preliminary experiments. I am now ready."

Leor disappeared into the bowels of his machine. A single pure note, high and clean, rang in the air. Suddenly, on the stage looking out to the plain, there emerged a naked man, blinking, peering around.

Leor's voice, from within the machine, said, "This is Adam, the first of all men."

And so the gods and the heroes came back to us on that brilliant afternoon in the middle twelves, while all the world watched in joy and fascination.

Adam walked across the stage and spoke to Chairman Peng, who solemnly saluted him and explained what was taking place. Adam's hand was outspread over his loins. "Why am I naked?" Adam asked. "It is wrong to be naked."

I pointed out to him that he had been naked when he first came into the world, and that we were merely showing respect for authenticity by summoning him back that way.

"But I have eaten the apple," Adam said. "Why do you bring me back conscious of shame, and give me nothing to conceal my shame? Is this proper? Is this consistent? If you want a naked Adam, bring forth an Adam who has not yet eaten the apple. But—"

Leor's voice broke in: "This is Eve, the mother of us all."

Eve stepped forth, naked also, though her long silken hair hid the curve of her breasts. Unashamed, she smiled and held out a hand to Adam, who rushed to her, crying, "Cover yourself! Cover yourself!"

Surveying the thousands of onlookers, Eve said coolly, "Why should I, Adam? These people are naked too, and this must be Eden again."

"This is not Eden," said Adam. "This is the world of our children's children's children's children."

"I like this world," Eve said. "Relax."

Leor announced the arrival of Pan the Goat-footed.

Now, Adam and Eve both were surrounded by the dark aura of essential humanity. I was surprised at this, since I doubted that there had ever been a First Man and a First Woman on whom legends could be based; yet I assumed that this must be some symbolic representation of the concept of man's evolution. But Pan, the half-human monster, also wore the aura. Had there been such a being in the real world?

I did not understand it then. But later I came to see that if there had never been a goat-footed man, there nevertheless had been men who behaved as Pan behaved, and out of them that lusty god had been created. As for the Pan who came out of Leor's machine, he did not remain long on the stage. He plunged forward into the audience, laughing and waving his arms and kicking his cloven hooves in the air. "Great Pan lives!" he cried. "Great Pan lives!" He seized in his arms Milian, the year-wife of Divud the Archivist, and carried her away toward a grove of feather-trees.

"He does me honor," said Milian's year-husband Divud.

Leor continued to toil in his machine.

He brought forth Hector and Achilles, Orpheus, Perseus, Loki, and Absalom. He brought forth Medea, Cassandra,

Odysseus, Oedipus. He brought forth Thoth, the Minotaur, Aeneas, Salome. He brought forth Shiva and Gilgamesh, Viracocha and Pandora, Priapus and Astarte, Diana, Diomedes, Dionysus, Deucalion. The afternoon waned and the sparkling moons sailed into the sky, and still Leor labored. He gave us Clytemnestra and Agamemnon, Helen and Menelaus, Isis and Osiris. He gave us Damballa and Geudenibo and Papa Legba. He gave us Baal. He gave us Samson. He gave us Krishna. He woke Quetzalcoatl, Adonis, Holger Dansk, Kali, Ptah, Thor, Jason, Nimrod, Set.

The darkness deepened and the creatures of myth jostled and tumbled on the stage, and overflowed onto the plain. They mingled with one another, old enemies exchanging gossip, old friends clasping hands, members of the same pantheon embracing or looking warily upon their rivals. They mixed with us, too, the heroes selecting women, the monsters trying to seem less monstrous, the gods shopping for worshipers.

Perhaps we had enough. But Leor would not stop. This was his time of glory.

Out of the machine came Roland and Oliver, Rustum and Sohrab, Cain and Abel, Damon and Pythias, Orestes and Pylades, Jonathan and David. Out of the machine came St. George, St. Vitus, St. Nicholas, St. Christopher, St. Valentine, St. Jude. Out of the machine came the Furies, the Harpies, the Pleiades, the Fates, the Norns. Leor was a romantic, and he knew no moderation.

All who came forth wore the aura of humanity.

But wonders pall. The Earthfolk of the middle twelves were easily distracted and easily bored. The cornucopia of miracles was far from exhausted, but on the fringes of the audience I saw people taking to the sky and heading for home. We who were close to Leor had to remain, of course, though we were surfeited by these fantasies and baffled by their abundance.

An old white-bearded man wrapped in a heavy aura left the machine. He carried a slender metal tube. "This is Galileo," said Leor.

"Who is he?" the Procurator of Pluto asked me, for Leor, growing weary, had ceased to describe his conjured ghosts.

I had to request the information from an output in the Hall of Man. "A latter-day god of science," I told the Procurator, "who is credited with discovering the stars. Believed to have been an historical personage before his deification, which occurred after his martyrdom by religious conservatives."

Now that the mood was on him, Leor summoned more of these gods of science, Newton and Einstein and Hippocrates and Copernicus and Oppenheimer and Freud. We had met some of them before, in the days when we were bringing real people out of lost time, but now they had new guises, for they had passed through the mythmakers' hands. They bore emblems of their special functions, and they went among us offering to heal, to teach, to explain. They were nothing like the real Newton and Einstein and Freud we had seen. They stood three times the height of men, and lightnings played around their brows.

Then came a tall, bearded man with a bloodied head. "Abraham Lincoln," said Leor.

"The ancient god of emancipation," I told the Procurator, after some research.

Then came a handsome young man with a dazzling smile and also a bloodied head. "John Kennedy," said Leor.

"The ancient god of youth and springtime," I told the Procurator. "A symbol of the change of seasons, of the defeat of winter by summer."

"That was Osiris," said the Procurator. "Why are there two?"

"There were many more," I said. "Baldur, Tammuz, Mithra, Attis."

"Why did they need so many?" he asked.

Leor said, "Now I will stop."

The gods and heroes were among us. A season of revelry began.

Medea went off with Jason, and Agamemnon was reconciled with Clytemnestra, and Theseus and the Minotaur took up lodgings together. Others preferred the company of men. I spoke a while with John Kennedy, the last of the myths to come from the machine. Like Adam, the first, he was troubled at being here.

"I was no myth," he insisted. "I lived. I was real. I entered primaries and made speeches."

"You became a myth," I said. "You lived and died and in your dying you were transfigured."

He chuckled. "Into Osiris? Into Baldur?"

"It seems appropriate."

"To you, maybe. They stopped believing in Baldur a thousand years before I was born."

"To me," I said, "you and Osiris and Baldur are contemporaries. You are of the ancient world. You are thousands of years removed from us."

"And I'm the last myth you let out of the machine?"

"You are."

"Why? Did men stop making myths after the twentieth century?"

"You would have to ask Leor. But I think you are right: your time was the end of the age of mythmaking. After your time we could no longer believe such things as myths. We did not *need* myths. When we passed out of the era of troubles, we entered a kind of paradise where every one of us lived a myth of his own, and then why should we have to raise some men to great heights among us?"

He looked at me strangely. "Do you really believe that? That you live in paradise? That men have become gods?"

"Spend some time in our world," I said, "and see for yourself."

He went out into the world, but what his conclusions
were I never knew, for I did not speak to him again. Often
I encountered roving gods and heroes, though. They were
everywhere. They quarreled and looted and ran amok, some
of them, but we were not very upset by that, since it was
how we expected archetypes out of the dawn to act. And
some were gentle. I had a brief love affair with Persephone.
I listened, enchanted, to the singing of Orpheus. Krishna
danced for me.

Dionysus revived the lost art of making liquors, and
taught us to drink and be drunk.

Loki made magics of flame for us.

Taliesin crooned incomprehensible, wondrous ballads to
us.

Achilles hurled his javelin for us.

It was a season of wonder, but the wonder ebbed. The
mythfolk began to bore us. There were too many of them,
and they were too loud, too active, too demanding. They
wanted us to love them, listen to them, bow to them, write
poems about them. They asked questions—some of them,
anyway—that pried into the inner workings of our world,
and embarrassed us, for we scarcely knew the answers. They
grew vicious, and schemed against each other, sometimes
causing perils for us.

Leor had provided us with a splendid diversion. But we
all agreed it was time for the myths to go home. We had
had them with us for fifty years, and that was quite
enough.

We rounded them up, and started to put them back into
the machine. The heroes were the easiest to catch, for all
their strength. We hired Loki to trick them into returning
to the Hall of Man. "Mighty tasks await you there," he told
them, and they hurried thence to show their valor. Loki led
them into the machine and scurried out, and Leor sent them
away, Heracles, Achilles, Hector, Perseus, Cuchulainn, and
the rest of that energetic breed.

After that many of the demonic ones came, and said they were as bored with us as we were with them, and went back into the machine of their free will. Thus departed Kali, Legba, Set, and many more.

Some we had to trap and take by force. Odysseus disguised himself as Breel, the secretary to Chairman Peng, and would have fooled us forever if the real Breel, returning from a holiday in Jupiter, had not exposed the hoax. And then Odysseus struggled. Loki gave us problems. Oedipus launched blazing curses when we came for him. Daedalus clung touchingly to Leor and begged, "Let me stay, brother! Let me stay!" and had to be thrust within.

Year after year the task of finding and capturing them continued, and one day we knew we had them all. The last to go was Cassandra, who had been living alone in a distant island, clad in rags.

"Why did you send for us?" she asked. "And, having sent, why do you ship us away?"

"The game is over," I said to her. "We will turn now to other sports."

"You should have kept us," Cassandra said. "People who have no myths of their own would do well to borrow those of others, and not just as sport. Who will comfort your souls in the dark times ahead? Who will guide your spirits when the suffering begins? Who will explain the woe that will befall you? Woe! Woe!"

"The woes of Earth," I said gently, "lie in Earth's past. We need no myths."

Cassandra smiled and stepped into the machine. And was gone.

And then the age of fire and turmoil opened, for when the myths went home, the invaders came, bursting from the sky. And our towers toppled and our moons fell. And the cold-eyed strangers went among us, doing as they wished.

And those of us who survived cried out to the old gods,
the vanished heroes.

Loki, come!

Achilles, defend us!

Shiva, release us!

Heracles! Thor! Gawain!

But the gods are silent, and the heroes do not come. The
machine that glittered in the Hall of Man is broken. Leor
its maker is gone from this world. Jackals run through our
gardens, and our masters stride in our streets, and we are
made slaves. And we are alone beneath the frightful sky.
And we are alone.

THE STARS BELOW

Ursula K. Le Guin

Of all the decade's new SF writers, Ursula K. Le Guin is not only the most honored—four Hugos, three Nebulas, a Jupiter, and the National Book Award for Children's Literature—but also probably the most widely popular. Her appeal seems to cut across all lines and through all social strata, and she has been hailed by both conservative and avant-garde voices as the most significant and powerful new talent to enter the genre in years.

In "The Stars Below" she relates the grim but oddly beautiful story of an astronomer who, denied the study of the stars, undertakes a strange and perilous journey into the uncharted hinterland of his own soul.

○ THE WOODEN HOUSE and outbuildings caught fire fast,
blazed up, burned down, but the dome, built of lathe and
plaster above a drum of brick, would not burn. What they
did at last was heap up the wreckage of the telescopes, the
instruments, the books and charts and drawings, in the
middle of the floor under the dome, pour oil on the heap,
and set fire to that. The flames spread to the wooden beams
of the big telescope frame and to the clockwork mechanisms. Villagers watching from the foot of the hill saw the
dome, whitish against the green evening sky, shudder and
turn, first in one direction then in the other, while a black
and yellow smoke full of sparks gushed from the oblong
slit: an ugly and uncanny thing to see.

It was getting dark, stars were showing in the east. Orders
were shouted. The soldiers came down the road in single
file, dark men in dark harness, silent.

The villagers at the foot of the hill stayed on after the
soldiers had gone. In a life without change or breadth a
fire is as good as a festival. They did not climb the hill,
and as the night grew full dark they drew closer together.
After a while they began to go back to their villages. Some
looked back over their shoulders at the hill, where nothing
moved. The stars turned slowly behind the black beehive
of the dome, but it did not turn to follow them.

About an hour before daybreak a man rode up the steep
zigzag, dismounted by the ruins of the workshops, and approached the dome on foot. The door had been smashed
in. Through it a reddish haze of light was visible, very dim,
coming from a massive support-beam that had fallen and
had smoldered all night inward to its core. A hanging, sour
smoke thickened the air inside the dome. A tall figure
moved there and its shadow moved with it, cast upward on
the murk. Sometimes it stooped, or stopped, then blundered
slowly on.

The man at the door said: "Guennar! Master Guennar!"

The man in the dome stopped still, looking towards the

door. He had just picked up something from the mess of wreckage and half-burnt stuff on the floor. He put this object mechanically into his coat pocket, still peering at the door. He came towards it. His eyes were red and swollen almost shut, he breathed harshly in gasps, his hair and clothes were scorched and smeared with black ash.

"Where were you?"

The man in the dome pointed vaguely at the ground.

"There's a cellar? That's where you were during the fire? By God! Gone to ground! I knew it, I knew you'd be here." Bord laughed, a little crazily, taking Guennar's arm. "Come on. Come out of there, for the love of God. There's light in the east already."

The astronomer came reluctantly, looking not at the grey east but back up at the slit in the dome, where a few stars burned clear. Bord pulled him outside, made him mount the horse, and then, bridle in hand, set off down the hill leading the horse at a fast walk.

The astronomer held the pommel with one hand. The other hand, which had been burned across the palm and fingers when he picked up a metal fragment still red-hot under its coat of cinders, he kept pressed against his thigh. He was not conscious of doing so, or of the pain. Sometimes his senses told him, "I am on horseback," or, "It's getting lighter," but these fragmentary messages made no sense to him. He shivered with cold as the dawn wind rose, rattling the dark woods by which the two men and the horse now passed in a deep lane overhung by teasel and briar; but the woods, the wind, the whitening sky, the cold were all remote from his mind, in which there was nothing but a darkness shot with the reek and heat of burning.

Bord made him dismount. There was sunlight around them now, lying long on rocks above a river valley. There was a dark place, and Bord urged him and pulled him into the dark place. It was not hot and close there but cold and silent. As soon as Bord let him stop he sank down, for his knees would not bear; and he felt the cold rock against his seared and throbbing hands.

"Gone to earth, by God!" said Bord, looking about at the veined walls, marked with the scars of miners' picks, in the light of his lanterned candle. "I'll be back; after dark, maybe. Don't come out. Don't go farther in. This is an old adit, they haven't worked this end of the mine for years. May be slips and pitfalls in these old tunnels. Don't come out! Lie low. When the hounds are gone, we'll run you across the border."

Bord turned and went back up the adit in darkness. When the sound of his steps had long since died away, the astronomer lifted his head and looked around him at the dark walls and the little burning candle. Presently he blew it out. There came upon him the earth-smelling darkness, silent and complete. He saw green shapes, ocherous blots drifting on the black; these faded slowly. The dull, chill black was balm to his inflamed and aching eyes, and to his mind.

If he thought, sitting there in the dark, his thoughts found no words. He was feverish from exhaustion and smoke inhalation and a few slight burns, and in an abnormal condition of mind; but perhaps his mind's workings, though lucid and serene, had never been normal. It is not normal for a man to spend twenty years grinding lenses, building telescopes, peering at stars, making calculations, lists, maps and charts of things which no one knows or cares about, things which cannot be reached, or touched, or held. And now all he had spent his life on was gone, burned. What was left of him might as well be, as it was, buried.

But it did not occur to him, this idea of being buried. All he was keenly aware of was a great burden of anger and grief, a burden he was unfit to carry. It was crushing his mind, crushing out reason. And the darkness here seemed to relieve that pressure. He was accustomed to the dark, he had lived at night. The weight here was only rock, only earth. No granite is so hard as hatred and no clay so cold as cruelty. The earth's black innocence enfolded him. He lay down within it, trembling a little with pain and with relief from pain, and slept.

Light waked him. Count Bord was there, lighting the candle with flint and steel. Bord's face was vivid in the light: the high color and blue eyes of a keen huntsman, a red mouth, sensual and obstinate. "They're on the scent," he was saying. "They know you got away."

"Why . . ." said the astronomer. His voice was weak; his throat, like his eyes, was still smoke-inflamed. "Why are they after me?"

"Why? Do you still need telling? To burn you alive, man! For heresy!" Bord's blue eyes glared through the steadying glow of the candle.

"But it's gone, burned, all I did."

"Aye, the earth's stopped, all right, but where's their fox? They want their fox! But damned if I'll let them get you."

The astronomer's eyes, light and wide-set, met his and held. "Why?"

"You think I'm a fool," Bord said with a grin that was not a smile, a wolf's grin, the grin of the hunted and the hunter. "And I am one. I was a fool to warn you. You never listened. I was a fool to listen to you. But I liked to listen to you. I liked to hear you talk about the stars and the courses of the planets and the ends of time. Who else ever talked to me of anything but seed corn and cow dung? Do you see? And I don't like soldiers and strangers, and trials and burnings. Your truth, their truth, what do I know about the truth? Am I a master? Do I know the courses of the stars? Maybe you do. Maybe they do. All I know is you have sat at my table and talked to me. Am I to watch you burn? God's fire, they say; but you said the stars are the fires of God. Why do you ask me that, 'Why?' Why do you ask a fool's question of a fool?"

"I am sorry," the astronomer said.

"What do you know about men?" the count said. "You
thought they'd let you be. And you thought I'd let you
burn." He looked at Guennar through the candlelight, grin-
ning like a driven wolf, but in his blue eyes there was a
glint of real amusement. "We who live down on the earth,
you see, not up among the stars . . ."

He had brought a tinderbox and three tallow candles,
a bottle of water, a ball of peas-pudding, a sack of bread.
He left soon, warning the astronomer again not to venture
out of the mine.

When Guennar woke again a strangeness in his situation
troubled him, not one which would have worried most
people hiding in a hole to save their skins, but most dis-
tressing to him: he did not know the time.

It was not clocks he missed, the sweet banging of the
church bells in the villages calling to morning and evening
prayer, the delicate and willing accuracy of the timepieces
he used in his observatory and on whose refinement so many
of his discoveries had depended; it was not the clocks he
missed, but the great clock.

Not seeing the sky, one cannot know the turning of the
earth. All the processes of time, the sun's bright arch and
the moon's phases, the planet's dance, the wheeling of the
constellations around the pole star, the vaster wheeling of
the seasons of the stars, all these were lost, the warp on
which his life was woven.

Here there was no time.

"O my God," Guennar the astronomer prayed in the darkness under ground, "how can it offend you to be praised?
All I ever saw in my telescopes was one spark of your glory,
one least fragment of the order of your creation. You could
not be jealous of that, my Lord! And there were few
enough who believed me, even so. Was it my arrogance in
daring to describe your works? But how could I help it,

Lord, when you let me see the endless fields of stars? Could
I see and be silent? O my God, do not punish me any more,
let me rebuild the smaller telescope. I will not speak, I will
not publish, if it troubles your holy Church. I will not say
anything more about the orbits of the planets or the nature
of the stars. I will not speak, Lord, only let me see!"

"What the devil, be quiet, Master Guennar. I could hear
you halfway up the tunnel," said Bord, and the astronomer
opened his eyes to the dazzle of Bord's lantern. "They've
called the full hunt up for you. Now you're a necromancer.
They swear they saw you sleeping in your house when they
came, and they barred the doors; but there's no bones in
the ashes."

"I was asleep," Guennar said, covering his eyes. "They
came, the soldiers. . . . I should have listened to you. I
went into the passage under the dome. I left a passage there
so I could go back to the hearth on cold nights, when it's
cold my fingers get too stiff, I have to go warm my hands
sometimes." He spread out his blistered, blackened hands
and looked at them vaguely. "Then I heard them overhead. . . ."

"Here's some more food. What the devil, haven't you
eaten?"

"Has it been long?"

"A night and a day. It's night now. Raining. Listen,
Master: there's two of the black hounds living at my house
now. Emissaries of the Council, what the devil, I had to
offer hospitality. This is my county, they're here, I'm the
count. It makes it hard for me to come. And I don't want
to send any of my people here. What if the priests asked
them, 'Do you know where he is? Will you answer to God
you don't know where he is?' It's best they don't know. I'll
come when I can. You're all right here? You'll stay here?
I'll get you out of here and over the border when they've
cleared away. They're like flies now. Don't talk aloud like

that. They might look into these old tunnels. You should go farther in. I will come back. Stay with God, Master."

"Go with God, count."

He saw the color of Bord's blue eyes, the leap of shadows up the rough-hewn roof as he took up the lantern and turned away. Light and color died as Bord, at the turning, put out the lantern. Guennar heard him stumble and swear as he groped his way.

Presently Guennar lighted one of his candles and ate and drank a little, eating the staler bread first, and breaking off a piece of the crusted lump of peas-pudding. This time Bord had brought him three loaves and some salt meat, two more candles and a second skin bottle of water, and a heavy duffle cloak. Guennar had not felt cold. He was wearing the coat he always wore on cold nights in the observatory and very often slept in, when he came stumbling to bed at dawn. It was a good sheepskin, filthy from his rummagings in the wreckage in the dome and scorched at the sleeve-ends, but it was as warm as ever, and was like his own skin to him. He sat inside it eating, gazing out through the sphere of frail yellow candlelight to the darkness of the tunnel beyond. Bord's words, "You should go farther in," were in his mind. When he was done eating he bundled up the provisions in the cloak, took up the bundle in one hand and the lighted candle in the other, and set off down the side-tunnel and then the adit, down and inward.

After a few hundred paces he came to a major cross-tunnel, off which ran many short leads and some large rooms or stopes. He turned left and presently passed a big stope in three levels. He entered it. The farthest level was only about five feet under the roof, which was still well timbered with posts and beams. In a corner of the backmost level, behind an angle of quartz intrusion which the miners had left jutting out as a supporting buttress, he made his new camp, setting out the food, water, tinderbox, and candles where they would come under his hand easily in the dark, and laying the cloak as a mattress on the floor, which was of a rubbly, hard clay. Then he put out the candle, already burned down by a quarter of its length, and lay down in the dark.

After his third return to that first side-tunnel, finding no sign that Bord had come there, he went back to his camp and studied his provisions. There were still two loaves of bread, half a bottle of water, and the salt meat, which he had not yet touched; and four candles. He guessed that it might have been six days since Bord had come, but it might have been three, or eight. He was thirsty, but dared not drink, so long as he had no other supply.

He set off to find water.

At first he counted his paces. After a hundred and twenty he saw that the timbering of the tunnel was askew, and there were places where the rubble fill had broken through, half filling the passage. He came to a winze, a vertical shaft, easy to scramble down by what remained of the wooden ladder, but after it, in the lower level, he forgot to count his steps. Once he passed a broken pick handle; farther on he saw a miner's discarded headband, a stump of candle still stuck in the forehead socket. He dropped this into the pocket of his coat and went on.

The monotony of the walls of hewn stone and planking dulled his mind. He walked on like one who will walk forever. Darkness followed him and went ahead of him.

His candle burning short spilled a stream of hot tallow on his fingers, hurting him. He dropped the candle, and it went out.

He groped for it in the sudden dark, sickened by the reek of its smoke, lifting his head to avoid that stink of burning. Before him, straight before him, far away, he saw the stars.

Tiny, bright, remote, caught in a narrow opening like the slot in the observatory dome: an oblong full of stars in blackness.

He got up, forgetting about the candle, and began to run towards the stars.

They moved, dancing, like the stars in the telescope field when the clockwork mechanism shuddered or when his eyes were very tired. They danced, and brightened.

He came among them, and they spoke to him.

The flames cast queer shadows on the blackened faces and brought queer lights out of the bright, living eyes.

"Here, then, who's that? Hanno?"

"What were you doing up that old drift, mate?"

"Hey, who is that?"

"Who the devil, stop him—"

"Hey, mate! Hold on!"

He ran blind into the dark, back the way he had come. The lights followed him and he chased his own faint, huge shadow down the tunnel. When the shadow was swallowed by the old dark and the old silence came again he still stumbled on, stooping and groping so that he was oftenest on all fours or on his feet and one hand. At last he dropped down and lay huddled against the wall, his chest full of fire.

Silence, dark.

He found the candle end in the tin holder in his pocket, lighted it with the flint and steel, and by its glow found the vertical shaft not fifty feet from where he had stopped. He made his way back up to his camp. There he slept; woke and ate, and drank the last of his water; meant to get up and go seeking water again; fell asleep, or into a doze or daze, in which he dreamed of a voice speaking to him.

"There you are. All right. Don't startle. I'll do you no harm. I said it wasn't no knocker. Who ever heard of a knocker as tall as a man? Or who ever seen one, for that matter. They're what you *don't* see, mates, I said. And what we did see was a man, count on it. So what's he doing in the mine, said they, and what if he's a ghost, one of the lads that was caught when the house of water broke in the old south adit, maybe, come walking? Well then, I said, I'll

go see that. I never seen a ghost yet, for all I heard of them.
I don't care to see what's not meant to be seen, like the
knocker folk, but what harm to see Temon's face again, or
old Trip, haven't I seen 'em in dreams, just the same, in the
ends, working away with their faces sweating same as life?
Why not? So I come along. But you're no ghost, no miner.
A deserter you might be, or a thief. Or are you out of your
wits, is that it, poor man? Don't fear. Hide if you like.
What's it to me? There's room down here for you and me.
Why are you hiding from the light of the sun?"

"The soldiers . . ."

"I thought so."

When the old man nodded, the candle bound to his forehead set light leaping over the roof of the stope. He squatted
about ten feet from Guennar, his hands hanging between his
knees. A bunch of candles and his pick, a short-handled,
finely shaped tool, hung from his belt. His face and body,
beneath the restless star of the candle, were rough shadows,
earth-colored.

"Let me stay here."

"Stay and welcome! Do I own the mine? Where did you
come in, eh, the old drift above the river? That was luck to
find that, and luck you turned this way in the crosscut, and
didn't go east instead. Eastward this level goes on to the
caves. There's great caves there; did you know it? Nobody
knows but the miners. They opened up the caves before I
was born, following the old lode that lay along here sun-
ward. I seen the caves once, my dad took me, you should see
this once, he says. See the world underneath the world. A
room there was no end to. A cavern as deep as the sky, and
a black stream falling into it, falling and falling till the light
of the candle failed and couldn't follow it, and still the water
was falling on down into the pit. The sound of it came up
like a whisper without an end, out of the dark. And on
beyond that there's other caves, and below. No end to
them, maybe. Who knows? Cave under cave, and glittering

with the barren crystal. It's all barren stone, there. And all worked out, here, years ago. It's a safe enough hole you chose, mate, if you hadn't come stumbling in on us. What was you after? Food? A human face?"

"Water."

"No lack of that. Come on, I'll show you. Beneath here in the lower level there's all too many springs. You turned the wrong direction. I used to work down there, with the damned cold water up to my knees, before the vein ran out. A long time ago. Come on."

The old miner left him in his camp, after showing him where the spring rose and warning him not to follow down the watercourse, for the timbering would be rotted and a step or sound might bring the earth down. Down there all the timbers were covered with a deep glittering white fur, saltpeter perhaps, or a fungus: it was very strange, above the oily water. When he was alone again Guennar thought he had dreamed that white tunnel full of black water, and the visit of the miner. When he saw a flicker of light far down the tunnel, he crouched behind the quartz buttress with a great wedge of granite in his hand: for all his fear and anger and grief had come down to one thing here in the darkness, a determination that no man would lay hand on him. A blind determination, blunt and heavy as a broken stone, heavy in his soul.

It was only the old man coming, with a hunk of dry cheese for him.

He sat with the astronomer, and talked. Guennar ate up the cheese, for he had no food left, and listened to the old man talk. As he listened the weight seemed to lift a little, he seemed to see a little farther in the dark.

"You're no common soldier," the miner said, and he replied, "No, I was a student once," but no more, because he dared not tell the miner who he was. The old man knew all the events of the region; he spoke of the burning of the

Round House on the hill, and of Count Bord. "He went off
to the city with them, with those black-gowns, to be tried,
they do say, to come before their council. Tried for what?
What did he ever do but hunt boar and deer and foxen? Is
it the council of the foxen trying him? What's it all about,
this snooping and soldiering and burning and trying? Better
leave honest folk alone. The count was honest, as far as the
rich can be, a fair landlord. But you can't trust them, none
of such folk. Only down here. You can trust the men who
go down into the mine. What else has a man got down here
but his own hands and his mates' hands? What's between
him and death, when there's a fall in the level or a winze
closes and he's in the blind end, but their hands, and their
shovels, and their will to dig him out? There'd be no silver
up there in the sun if there wasn't trust between us down
here in the dark. Down here you can count on your mates.
And nobody comes but them. Can you see the owner in his
lace, or the soldiers, coming down the ladders, coming down
and down the great shaft into the dark? Not them! They're
brave at tramping on the grass, but what good's a sword
and shouting in the dark? I'd like to see 'em come down
here. . . ."

The next time he came another man was with him, and
they brought an oil lamp and a clay jar of oil, as well as
more cheese, bread, and some apples. "It was Hanno thought
of the lamp," the old man said. "A hempen wick it is, if she
goes out blow sharp and she'll likely catch up again. Here's
a dozen candles, too. Young Per swiped the lot from the
doler, up on the grass."

"They all know I'm here?"

"*We* do," the miner said briefly. "*They* don't."

Some time after this, Guennar returned along the lower,
westleading level he had followed before, till he saw the
miners' candles dance like stars; and he came into the stope
where they were working. They shared their meal with him.
They showed him the ways of the mine, and the pumps, and

the great shaft where the ladders were and the hanging
pulleys with their buckets; he sheered off from that, for the
wind that came sucking down the great shaft smelled to him
of burning. They took him back and let him work with
them. They treated him as a guest, as a child. They had
adopted him. He was their secret.

There is not much good spending twelve hours a day in a
black hole in the ground all your life long if there's nothing
there, no secret, no treasure, nothing hidden.

There was the silver, to be sure. But where ten crews of
fifteen had used to work these levels and there had been no
end to the groan and clatter and crash of the loaded buckets
going up on the screaming winch and the empties banging
down to meet the trammers running with their heavy carts,
now one crew of eight men worked: men over forty, old
men, who had no skill but mining. There was still some
silver there in the hard granite, in little veins among the
gangue. Sometimes they would lengthen an end by one foot
in two weeks.

"It was a great mine," they said with pride.

They showed the astronomer how to set a gad and swing
the sledge, how to go at granite with the finely balanced and
sharp-pointed pick, how to sort and "cob," what to look
for, the rare bright branchings of the pure metal, the crumbling rich rock of the ore. He helped them daily. He was in
the stope waiting for them when they came, and spelled one
or another on and off all day with the shovel work, or
sharpening tools, or running the ore-cart down its grooved
plank to the great shaft, or working in the ends. There they
would not let him work long; pride and habit forbade it.
"Here, leave off chopping at that like a woodcutter. Look:
this way, see?" But then another would ask him, "Give me
a blow here, lad, see, on the gad, that's it."

They fed him from their own coarse meager meals.

In the night, alone in the hollow earth, when they had
climbed the long ladder up "to grass" as they said, he lay

and thought of them, their faces, their voices, their heavy, scarred, earth-stained hands, old men's hands with thick nails blackened by bruising rock and steel; those hands, intelligent and vulnerable, which had opened up the earth and found the shining silver in the solid rock. The silver they never held, never kept, never spent. The silver that was not theirs.

"If you found a new vein, a new lode, what would you do?"

"Open her, and tell the masters."

"Why tell the masters?"

"Why, man! We gets paid for what we brings up! D'you think we does this damned work for love?"

"Yes."

They all laughed at him, loud, jeering laughter, innocent. The living eyes shone in their faces blackened with dust and sweat.

"Ah, if we could find a new lode! The wife would keep a pig like we had once, and by God I'd swim in beer! But if there's silver they'd have found it; that's why they pushed the workings so far east. But it's barren there, and worked out here, that's the short and long of it."

Time stretched behind him and ahead of him like the dark drifts and crosscuts of the mine, all present at once, wherever he with his small candle might be among them. When he was alone now the astronomer often wandered in the tunnels and the old stopes, knowing the dangerous places, the deep levels full of water, adept at shaky ladders and tight places, intrigued by the play of his candle on the rock walls and faces, the glitter of mica that seemed to come from deep inside the stone. Why did it sometimes shine out that way? as if the candle found something far within the shining broken surface, something that winked in answer and occulted, as if it had slipped behind a cloud or an unseen planet's disc.

"There are stars in the earth," he thought. "If one knew how to see them."

Awkward with the pick, he was clever with machinery; they admired his skill, and brought him tools. He repaired pumps and windlasses; he fixed up a lamp on a chain for "young Per" working in a long narrow deadend, with a reflector made from a tin candleholder beaten out into a curved sheet and polished with fine rockdust and the sheepskin lining of his coat. "It's a marvel," Per said. "Like daylight. Only, being behind me, it don't go out when the air gets bad, and tell me I should be backing out for a breath."

For a man can go on working in a narrow end for some time after his candle has gone out for lack of oxygen.

"You should have a bellows rigged there."

"What, like I was a forge?"

"Why not?"

"Do ye ever go up to the grass, nights?" asked Hanno, looking wistfully at Guennar. Hanno was a melancholy, thoughtful, soft-hearted fellow. "Just to look about you?"

Guennar did not answer. He went off to help Bran with a timbering job; the miners did all the work that had once been done by crews of timberers, trammers, sorters, and so on.

"He's deathly afraid to leave the mine," Per said, low.

"Just to see the stars and get a breath of the wind," Hanno said, as if he was still speaking to Guennar.

One night the astronomer emptied out his pockets and looked at the stuff that had been in them since the night of the burning of the observatory: things he had picked up in those hours which he now could not remember, those hours when he had groped and stumbled in the smoldering wreckage, seeking . . . seeking what he had lost. . . . He no longer thought of what he had lost. It was sealed off in his mind by a thick scar, a burn-scar. For a long time this scar in his mind kept him from understanding the nature of the objects now ranged before him on the dusty stone floor of the mine: a wad of papers scorched all along one side; a round piece of glass or crystal; a metal tube; a beautifully worked wooden cogwheel; a bit of twisted blackened copper etched with fine lines; and so on, bits, wrecks, scraps. He put the papers back into his pocket, without trying to separate the brittle half-fused leaves and make out the fine script. He continued to look at and occasionally to pick up and examine the other things, especially the piece of glass.

This he knew to be the eyepiece of his ten-inch telescope. He had ground the lens himself. When he picked it up he handled it delicately, by the edges, lest the acid of his skin etch the glass. Finally he began to polish it clean, using a wisp of fine lambswool from his coat. When it was clear, he held it up and looked at and through it at all angles. His face was calm and intent, his light wide-set eyes steady.

Tilted in his fingers, the telescope lens reflected the lamp flame in one bright tiny point near the edge and seemingly beneath the curve of the face, as if the lens had kept a star in it from the many hundred nights it had been turned toward the sky.

He wrapped it carefully in the wisp of wool and made a place for it in the rock niche with his tinderbox. Then he took up the other things one by one.

During the next weeks the miners saw their fugitive less often while they worked. He was off a great deal by himself: exploring the deserted eastern regions of the mine, he said, when they asked him what he did.

"What for?"

"Prospecting," he said with the brief, wincing smile that gave him a very crazy look.

"Oh, lad, what do you know about that? She's all barren

there. The silver's gone; and they found no eastern lode. You might be finding a bit of poor ore or a vein of tin-stone, but nothing worth the digging."

"How do you know what's in the earth, in the rock under your feet, Per?"

"I know the signs, lad. Who should know better?"

"But if the signs are hidden?"

"Then the silver's hidden."

"Yet you know it is there, if you knew where to dig, if you could see into the rock. And what else is there? You find the metal, because you seek it, and dig for it. But what else might you find, deeper than the mine, if you sought, if you knew where to dig?"

"Rock," said Per. "Rock, and rock, and rock."

"And then?"

"And then? Hellfire, for all I know. Why else does it get hotter as the shafts go deeper? That's what they say. Getting nearer hell."

"No," the astronomer said, clear and firm. "No. There is no hell beneath the rocks."

"What is there, then, underneath it all?"

"The stars."

"Ah," said the miner, floored. He scratched his rough, tallow-clotted hair, and laughed. "There's a poser," he said, and stared at Guennar with pity and admiration. He knew Guennar was mad, but the size of his madness was a new thing to him, and admirable. "Will you find 'em then, the stars?"

"If I learn how to look," Guennar said, so calmly that Per had no response but to heft his shovel and get back to loading the cart.

One morning when the miners came down they found Guennar still sleeping, rolled up in the battered cloak Count Bord had given him, and by him a strange object, a contraption made of silver tubing, tin struts and wires beaten from old headlamp-sockets, a frame of pick handles carefully carved and fitted, cogged wheels, a bit of twinkling glass. It was elusive, makeshift, delicate, crazy, intricate.

"What the devil's that?"

They stood about and stared at the thing, the lights of their headlamps centering on it, a yellow beam sometimes flickering over the sleeping man as one or another glanced at him.

"He made it, sure."

"Sure enough."

"What for?"

"Don't touch it."

"I wasn't going to."

Roused by their voices, the astronomer sat up. The yellow beams of the candles brought his face out white against the dark. He rubbed his eyes and greeted them.

"What would that be, lad?"

He looked troubled or confused when he saw the object of their curiosity. He put a hand on it protectively, yet he looked at it himself without seeming to recognize it for a while. At last he said, frowning and speaking in a whisper, 'It's a telescope."

"What's that?"

"A device that makes distant things clear to the eye."

"How come?" one of the miners asked, baffled. The astronomer answered him with growing assurance. "By virtue of certain properties of light and lenses. The eye is a delicate instrument, but it is blind to half the universe—far more than half. The night sky is black, we say: between the stars is void and darkness. But turn the telescope-eye on that space between the stars, and lo, the stars! Stars too faint and far for the eye alone to see, rank behind rank, glory beyond glory, out to the uttermost boundaries of the universe. Beyond all imagination, in the outer darkness, there is light: a great glory of sunlight. I have seen it. I have

seen it, night after night, and mapped the stars, the beacons
of God on the shores of darkness. And here too there is
light! There is no place bereft of the light, the comfort and
radiance of the creator spirit. There is no place that is out-
cast, outlawed, forsaken. There is no place left dark. Where
the eyes of God have seen, there light is. We must go farther,
we must look farther! There is light if we will see it. Not
with eyes alone, but with the skill of the hands and the
knowledge of the mind and the heart's faith is the unseen
revealed, and the hidden made plain. And all the dark
earth shines like a sleeping star."

He spoke with that authority which the miners knew
belonged by rights to the priests, to the great words priests
spoke in the echoing churches. It did not belong here, in the
hole where they grubbed their living, in the words of a
crazy fugitive. Later on, one talking to another, they shook
their heads, or tapped them. Per said, "The madness is growing in him," and Hanno said, "Poor soul, poor soul!" Yet
there was not one of them who did not, also, believe what
the astronomer had told them.

"Show me," said old Bran, finding Guennar alone in a
deep eastern drift, busy with his intricate device. It was Bran
who had first followed Guennar, and brought him food, and
led him back to the others.

The astronomer willingly stood aside and showed Bran
how to hold the device pointing downward at the tunnel
floor, and how to aim and focus it, and tried to describe its
function and what Bran might see: all hesitantly, since he
was not used to explaining to the ignorant, but without
impatience when Bran did not understand.

"I don't see nothing but the ground," the old man said
after a long and solemn observation with the instrument.
"And the little dust and pebbles on it."

"The lamp blinds your eyes, perhaps," the astronomer
said with humility. "It is better to look without light. I can
do it because I have done it for so long. It is all practice—

like placing the gads, which you always do right, and I always do wrong."

"Aye. Maybe. Tell me what you see—" Bran hesitated. He had not long ago realized who Guennar must be. Knowing him to be a heretic made no difference but knowing him to be a learned man made it hard to call him "mate" or "lad." And yet here, and after all this time, he could not call him Master. There were times when, for all his mildness, the fugitive spoke with great words, gripping one's soul, times when it would have been easy to call him Master. But it would have frightened him.

The astronomer put his hand on the frame of his mechanism and replied in a soft voice, "There are . . . constellations."

"What's that, constellations?"

The astronomer looked at Bran as if from a great way off, and said presently, "The Wain, the Scorpion, the Sickle by the Milky Way in summer, those are constellations. Patterns of stars, gatherings of stars, parenthoods, semblances . . ."

"And you see those here, with this?"

Still looking at him through the weak lamplight with clear brooding eyes, the astronomer nodded, and did not speak, but pointed downward, at the rock on which they stood, the hewn floor of the mine.

"What are they like?" Bran's voice was hushed.

"I have only glimpsed them. Only for a moment. I have not learned the skill; it is a somewhat different skill. . . . But they are there, Bran."

Often now he was not in the stope where they worked, when they came to work, and did not join them even for their meal, though they always left him a share of food. He knew the ways of the mine now better than any of them, even Bran, not only the "living" mine but the "dead" one, the abandoned workings and exploratory tunnels that ran eastward, ever deeper, towards the caves. There he was most often; and they did not follow him.

When he did appear amongst them and they talked with him, they were more timid with him, and did not laugh.

One night as they were all going back with the last cartload to the main shaft, he came to meet them, stepping suddenly out of a crosscut to their right. As always he wore his ragged sheepskin coat, black with the clay and dirt of the tunnels. His fair hair had gone grey. His eyes were clear. "Bran," he said, "come, I can show you now."

"Show me what?"

"The stars. The stars beneath the rock. There's a great constellation in the stope on the old fourth level, where the white granite cuts down through the black."

"I know the place."

"It's there: underfoot, by that wall of white rock. A great shining and assembly of stars. Their radiance beats up through the darkness. They are like the faces of dancers, the eyes of angels. Come and see them, Bran!"

The miners stood there, Per and Hanno with backs braced to hold the cart from rolling: stooped men with tired, dirty faces and big hands bent and hardened by the grip of shovel and pick and sledge. They were embarrassed, compassionate, impatient.

"We're just quitting. Off home to supper. Tomorrow," Bran said.

The astronomer looked from one face to another and said nothing.

Hanno said in his hoarse gentle voice, "Come up with us, for this once, lad. It's dark night out, and likely raining; it's November now; no soul will see you if you come and sit at my hearth, for once, and eat hot food, and sleep beneath a roof and not under the heavy earth all by yourself alone!"

Guennar stepped back. It was as if a light went out, as his face went into shadow. "No," he said. "They will burn out my eyes."

"Leave him be," said Per, and set the heavy ore-cart moving towards the shaft.

"Look where I told you," Guennar said to Bran. "The mine is not dead. Look with your own eyes."

"Aye. I'll come with you and see. Good night!"

"Good night," said the astronomer, and turned back to the side-tunnel as they went on. He carried no lamp or candle; they saw him one moment, darkness the next.

In the morning he was not there to meet them. He did not come.

Bran and Hanno sought him, idly at first, then for one whole day. They went as far down as they dared, and came at last to the entrance of the caves, and entered, calling sometimes, though in the great caverns even they, miners all their lives, dared not call aloud because of the terror of the endless echoes in the dark.

"He has gone down," Bran said. "Down farther. That's what he said. Go farther, you must go farther, to find the light."

"There is no light," Hanno whispered. "There was never light here. Not since the world's creation."

But Bran was an obstinate old man, with a literal and credulous mind; and Per listened to him. One day the two went to the place the astronomer had spoken of, where a great vein of hard light granite that cut down through the darker rock had been left untouched, fifty years ago, as barren stone. They re-timbered the roof of the old stope where the supports had weakened, and began to dig, not into the white rock but down, beside it; the astronomer had left a mark there, a kind of chart or symbol drawn with candleblack on the stone floor. They came on silver ore a foot down, beneath the shell of quartz; and under that— all eight of them working now—the striking picks laid bare the raw silver, the veins and branches and knots and nodes shining among broken crystals in the shattered rock, like stars and gatherings of stars, depth below depth without end, the light.

STRAW

Gene Wolfe

*The halcyon quiet of the upper air, wind, dogs barking
below; the stench and clamor of war; a hot-air balloon with
slogans painted on the side; a flight of snow geese;
straw. . . .*

*Nebula-winner Gene Wolfe—generally regarded as one of
the best SF writers of the decade—knits these disparate
elements together in a simple but eloquent story about a
boy's coming-of-age in an alternate Dark-Age Europe that
never was.*

○ YES, I REMEMBER killing my first man very well; I was just seventeen. A flock of snow geese flew under us that day about noon. I remember looking over the side of the basket, and seeing them; and thinking that they looked like a pike-head. That was an omen, of course, but I did not pay any attention.

It was clear, fall weather—a trifle chilly. I remember that. It must have been about the mid-part of October. Good weather for the balloon. Clow would reach up every quarter hour or so with a few double handsful of straw for the brazier, and that was all it required. We cruised, usually, at about twice the height of a steeple.

You have never been in one? Well, that shows how things have changed. Before the Fire-wights came, there was hardly any fighting at all, and free swords had to travel all over the continent looking for what there was. A balloon was better than walking, believe me. Miles—he was our captain in those days—said that where there were three soldiers to-gether, one was certain to put a shaft through a balloon; it was too big a target to resist, and that would show you where the armies were.

No, we would not have been killed. You would have had to slit the thing wide open before it would fall fast, and a little hole like the business end of a pike would make would just barely let you know it was there. The baskets do not swing, either, as people think. Why should they? They feel no wind—they are traveling with it. A man just seems to hang there, when he is up in one of them, and the world turns under him. He can hear everything—pigs and chick-ens, and the squeak the windlass makes drawing water from a well.

"Good flying weather," Clow said to me.

I nodded. Solemnly, I suppose.

"All the lift you want, in weather like this. The colder it is, the better she pulls. The heat from the fire doesn't like the chill, and tries to escape from it. That's what they say."

Blond Bracata spat over the side. "Nothing in our bellies," she said, "that's what makes it lift. If we don't eat today you won't have to light the fire tomorrow—I'll take us up myself."

She was taller than any of us except Miles, and the heaviest of us all; but Miles would not allow for size when the food was passed out, so I suppose she was the hungriest too.

Derek said: "We should have stretched one of that last bunch over the fire. That would have fetched a pot of stew, at the least."

Miles shook his head. "There were too many."

"They would have run like rabbits."

"And if they hadn't?"

"They had no armor."

Unexpectantly, Bracata came in for the captain. "They had twenty-two men, and fourteen women. I counted them."

"The women wouldn't fight."

"I used to be one of them. I would have fought."

Clow's soft voice added, "Nearly any woman will fight if she can get behind you."

Bracata stared at him, not sure whether he was supporting her or not. She had her mitts on—she was as good with them as anyone I have ever seen—and I remember that I thought for an instant that she would go for Clow right there in the basket. We were packed in like fledglings in the nest, and fighting, it would have taken at least three of us to throw her out—by which time she would have killed us all, I suppose. But she was afraid of Clow. I found out why later. She respected Miles, I think, for his judgment and courage, without being afraid of him. She did not care much for Derek either way, and of course I was hardly there at all as far as she was concerned. But she was just a little frightened by Clow.

Clow was the only one I was not frightened by—but that is another story too.

"Give it more straw," Miles said.

"We're nearly out."

"We can't land in this forest."

Clow shook his head and added straw to the fire in the brazier—about half as much as he usually did. We were sinking toward what looked like a red and gold carpet.

"We got straw out of them anyway," I said, just to let the others know I was there.

"You can always get straw," Clow told me. He had drawn a throwing spike, and was feigning to clean his nails with it. "Even from swineherds, who you'd think wouldn't have it. They'll get it to be rid of us."

"Bracata's right," Miles said. He gave the impression that he had not heard Clow and me. "We have to have food today."

Derek snorted. "What if there are twenty?"

"We stretch one over the fire. Isn't that what you suggested? And if it takes fighting, we fight. But we have to eat today." He looked at me. "What did I tell you when you joined us, Jerr? High pay or nothing? This is the nothing. Want to quit?"

I said, "Not if you don't want me to."

Clow was scraping the last of the straw from the bag. It was hardly a handful. As he threw it in the brazier Bracata asked, "Are we going to set down in the trees?"

Clow shook his head and pointed. Away in the distance I could see a speck of white on a hill. It looked too far, but the wind was taking us there, and it grew and grew until we could see that it was a big house, all built of white brick, with gardens and outbuildings, and a road that ran up to the door. There are none like that now, I suppose.

Landings are the most exciting part of traveling by balloon, and sometimes the most unpleasant. If you are lucky, the basket stays upright. We were not. Our basket snagged and tipped over and was dragged along by the envelope,

which fought the wind and did not want to go down, cold
though it was by then. If there had been a fire in the brazier
still, I suppose we would have set the meadow ablaze. As
it was, we were tumbled about like toys. Bracata fell on top
of me, as heavy as stone: and she had the claws of her mitts
out, trying to dig them into the turf to stop herself, so that
for a moment I thought I was going to be killed. Derek's
pike had been charged, and the ratchet released in the confusion; the head went flying across the field, just missing
a cow.

By the time I recovered my breath and got to my feet,
Clow had the envelope under control and was treading it
down. Miles was up too, straightening his hauberk and
sword-belt. "Look like a soldier," he called to me. "Where
are your weapons?"

A pincer-mace and my pike were all I had, and the
pincer-mace had fallen out of the basket. After five minutes
of looking, I found it in the tall grass, and went over to help
Clow fold the envelope.

When we were finished, we stuffed it in the basket and
put our pikes through the rings on each side so we could
carry it. By that time we could see men on horseback coming down from the big house. Derek said, "We won't be
able to stand against horsemen in this field."

For an instant I saw Miles smile. Then he looked very
serious. "We'll have one of those fellows over a fire in
half an hour."

Derek was counting, and so was I. Eight horsemen, with
a cart following them. Several of the horsemen had lances,
and I could see the sunlight winking on helmets and breast-
plates. Derek began pounding the butt of his pike on the
ground to charge it.

I suggested to Clow that it might look more friendly
if we picked up the balloon and went to meet the horsemen, but he shook his head. "Why bother?"

The first of them had reached the fence around the field.
He was sitting a roan stallion that took it at a clean jump

and came thundering up to us looking as big as a donjon on wheels.

"Greetings," Miles called. "If this be your land, lord, we give thanks for your hospitality. We'd not have intruded, but our conveyance has exhausted its fuel."

"You are welcome," the horseman called. He was as tall as Miles or taller, as well as I could judge, and as wide as Bracata. "Needs must, as they say, and no harm done." Three of the others had jumped their mounts over the fence behind him. The rest were taking down the rails so the cart could get through.

"Have you straw, lord?" Miles asked. I thought it would have been better if he had asked for food. "If we could have a few bundles of straw, we'd not trouble you more."

"None here," the horseman said, waving a mail-clad arm at the fields around us, "yet I feel sure my bailiff could find you some. Come up to the hall for a taste of meat and a glass of wine, and you can make your ascension from the terrace; the ladies would be delighted to see it, I'm certain. You're floating swords, I take it?"

"We are that," our captain affirmed, "but persons of good character nonetheless. We're called the Faithful Five—perhaps you've heard of us? High-hearted, fierce-fighting wind-warriors all, as it says on the balloon."

A younger man, who had reined up next to the one Miles called "lord," snorted. "If that boy is high-hearted, or a fierce fighter either, I'll eat his breeks."

Of course, I should not have done it. I have been too mettlesome all my life, and it has gotten me in more trouble than I could tell you of if I talked till sunset, though it has been good to me too—I would have spent my days following the plow, I suppose, if I had not knocked down Derek for what he called our goose. But you see how it was. Here I had been thinking of myself as a hard-bitten balloon soldier, and then to hear something like that. Anyway, I swung the pincer-mace overhand once I had a good grip on his stirrup. I had been afraid the extension spring

was a bit weak, never having used one before, but it worked
well; the pliers got him under the left arm and between the
ear and the right shoulder, and would have cracked his
neck for him properly if he had not been wearing a gorget.
As it was, I jerked him off his horse pretty handily and got
out the little aniace that screwed into the mace handle. A
couple of the other horsemen couched their lances, and
Derek had a finger on the dog-catch of his pike; so all in all
it looked as if there could be a proper fight, but "lord" (I
learned afterwards that he was the Baron Ascolot) yelled
at the young man I had pulled out of his saddle, and Miles
yelled at me and grabbed my left wrist, and thus it all blew
over.

When we had tripped the release and gotten the mace
open and retracted again, Miles said: "He will be punished,
lord. Leave him to me. It will be severe, I assure you."

"No, upon my oath," the baron declared. "It will teach
my son to be less free with his tongue in the company of
armed men. He has been raised at the hall, Captain, where
everyone bends the knee to him. He must learn not to expect
that of strangers."

The cart rolled up just then, drawn by two fine mules—
either of them would have been worth my father's holding,
I judged—and at the baron's urging we loaded our balloon
into it and climbed in after it ourselves, sitting on the fabric.
The horsemen galloped off, and the cart driver cracked his
lash over the mules' backs.

"Quite a place," Miles remarked. He was looking up at
the big house toward which we were making.

I whispered to Clow, "A palace, I should say," and Miles
overheard me, and said: "It's a villa, Jerr—the unfortified
country property of a gentleman. If there were a wall and
a tower, it would be a castle, or at least a castellett."

There were gardens in front, very beautiful as I remember, and a fountain. The road looped up before the door,

and we got out and trooped into the hall, while the baron's man—he was richer-dressed than anybody I had ever seen up till then, a fat man with white hair—set two of the hostlers to watch our balloon while it was taken back to the stableyard.

Venison and beef were on the table, and even a pheasant with all his feathers put back; and the baron and his sons sat with us and drank some wine and ate a bit of bread each for hospitality's sake. Then the baron said, "Surely you don't fly in the dark, captain?"

"Not unless we must, lord."

"Then with the day drawing to a close, it's just as well for you that we've no straw. You can pass the night with us, and in the morning I'll send my bailiff to the village with the cart. You'll be able to ascend at mid-morning, when the ladies can have a clear view of you as you go up."

"No straw?" our captain asked.

"None, I fear, here. But they'll have aplenty in the village, never doubt it. They lay it in the road to silence the horses' hoofs when a woman's with child, as I've seen many a time. You'll have a cartload as a gift from me, if you can use that much." The baron smiled as he said that; he had a friendly face, round and red as an apple. "Now tell me," (he went on) "how it is to be a floating sword. I always find other men's trades of interest, and it seems to me you follow one of the most fascinating of all. For example, how do you gauge the charge you will make your employer?"

"We have two scales, lord," Miles began. I had heard all of that before, so I stopped listening. Bracata was next to me at table, so I had all I could do to get something to eat for myself, and I doubt I ever got a taste of the pheasant. By good luck, a couple of lasses—the baron's daughters—had come in, and one of them started curling a lock of Derek's hair around her finger, so that distracted him while he was helping himself to the venison, and Bracata put an arm around the other and warned her of Men. If it had

not been for that I would not have had a thing; as it was,
I stuffed myself on deer's meat until I had to loose my waist-
band. Flesh of any sort had been a rarity where I came
from.

I had thought that the baron might give us beds in the
house, but when we had eaten and drunk all we could hold,
the white-haired fat man led us out a side door and over
to a wattle-walled building full of bunks—I suppose it was
kept for the extra laborers needed at harvest. It was not the
palace bedroom I had been dreaming of; but it was cleaner
than home, and there was a big fireplace down at one end
with logs stacked ready by, so it was probably more comfortable for me than a bed in the big house itself would have
been.

Clow took out a piece of cherry wood, and started carv-
ing a woman in it, and Bracata and Derek lay down to sleep.
I made shift to talk to Miles, but he was full of thoughts,
sitting on a bench near the hearth and chinking the purse
(just like this one, it was) he had gotten from the baron;
so I tried to sleep too. But I had had too much to eat to sleep
so soon, and since it was still light out, I decided to walk
around the villa and try to find somebody to chat with. The
front looked too grand for me; I went to the back, thinking
to make sure our balloon had suffered no hurt, and perhaps
have another look at those mules.

There were three barns behind the house, built of stone
up to the height of my waist, and wood above that, and
whitewashed. I walked into the nearest of them, not thinking about anything much besides my full belly until a big
war horse with a white star on his forehead reached his head
out of his stall and nuzzled at my cheek. I reached out and
stroked his neck for him the way they like. He nickered,
and I turned to have a better look at him. That was when
I saw what was in his stall. He was standing on a span or
more of the cleanest, yellowest straw I had ever seen. I

looked up over my head then, and there was a loft full of it up there.

In a minute or so, I suppose it was, I was back in the building where we were to sleep, shaking Miles by the shoulder and telling him I had found all the straw anyone could ask for.

He did not seem to understand, at first. "Wagon loads of straw, Captain," I told him. "Why every horse in the place has as much to lay him on as would carry us a hundred leagues."

"All right," Miles told me.

"Captain—"

"There's no straw here, Jerr. Not for us. Now be a sensible lad and get some rest."

"But there is, Captain. I saw it. I can bring you back a helmetful."

"Come here, Jerr," he said, and got up and led me outside. I thought he was going to ask me to show him the straw; but instead of going back to where the barns were, he took me away from the house to the top of a grassy knoll. "Look out there, Jerr. Far off. What do you see?"

"Trees," I said. "There might be a river at the bottom of the valley; then more trees on the other side."

"Beyond that."

I looked to the horizon, where he seemed to be pointing. There were little threads of black smoke rising there, looking as thin as spider web at that distance.

"What do you see?"

"Smoke."

"That's straw burning, Jerr. House-thatch. That's why there's no straw here. Gold, but no straw, because a soldier gets straw only where he isn't welcome. They'll reach the river there by sundown, and I'm told it can be forded at this season. Now do you understand?"

They came that night at moonrise.

ON THE GEM PLANET

Cordwainer Smith

The late Cordwainer Smith—in "real" life Dr. Paul M.A. Linebarger, scholar and statesman—created a science fiction cosmology unique in its scope and complexity: a millennia-spanning Future History, logically outlandish and elegantly strange, set against a vivid, richly-colored, mythically-intense universe where animals assume the shape of men, vast planoform ships whisper through multidimensional space, immortality can be bought, and the mysterious Lords of the Instrumentality rule a haunted Earth too old for history.

"On the Gem Planet" is a slice of that universe: an adventure on the strange planet Pontoppidan, an airless world made of rubies and emeralds and amethysts, where the really valuable things are flowers and earthworms (which cost eight carats of diamond per worm), and nothing is more precious than dirt except, perhaps, life itself.

I

⦿ WHEN Casher O'Neill came to Pontoppidan, he found that the capital city was appropriately called Andersen.

This was the second century of the Rediscovery of Man. People everywhere had taken up old names, old languages, old customs, as fast as the robots and the underpeople could retrieve the data from the rubbish of forgotten starlanes or the subsurface ruins of Manhome itself.

Casher knew this very well, to his bitter cost. Re-accultur- ation had brought him revolution and exile. He came from the dry, beautiful planet of Mizzer. He was himself the nephew of the ruined ex-ruler, Kuraf, whose collection of objectionable books had at one time been unmatched in the settled galaxy; he had stood aside, half-assenting, when the colonels Gibna and Wedder took over the planet in the name of reform; he had implored the Instrumentality, vainly, for help when Wedder became a tyrant; and now he traveled among the stars, looking for men or weapons who might destroy Wedder and make Kaheer again the luxur- ious, happy city which it once had been.

He felt that his cause was hopeless when he landed on Pontoppidan. The people were warm-hearted, friendly, in- telligent, but they had no motives to fight for, no weapons to fight with, no enemies to fight against. They had little public spirit, such as Casher O'Neill had seen back on his native planet of Mizzer. They were concerned about little things.

Indeed, at the time of his arrival, the Pontoppidans were wildly excited about a horse.

A horse! Who worries about one horse?

Casher O'Neill himself said so. "Why bother about a horse? We have lots of them on Mizzer. They are four- handed beings, eight times the weight of a man, with only one finger on each of the four hands. The fingernail is very heavy and permits them to run fast. That's why our people have them, for running."

"Why run?" said the Hereditary Dictator of Pontoppidan. "Why run, when you can fly? Don't you have ornithopters?"

"We don't run with them," said Casher indignantly. "We make them run against each other and then we pay prizes to the one which runs fastest."

"But then," said Philip Vincent, the Hereditary Dictator, "you get a very illogical situation. When you have tried out these four-fingered beings, you know how fast each one goes. So what? Why bother?"

His niece interrupted. She was a fragile little thing, smaller than Casher O'Neill liked women to be. She had clear gray eyes, well-marked eyebrows, a very artificial coiffure of silver-blonde hair and the most sensitive little mouth he had ever seen. She conformed to the local fashion by wearing some kind of powder or face cream which was flesh-pink in color but which had overtones of lilac. On a woman as old as twenty-two, such a coloration would have made the wearer look like an old hag, but on Genevieve it was pleasant, if rather startling. It gave the effect of a happy child playing grown-up and doing the job joyfully and well. Casher knew that it was hard to tell ages in these off-trail planets. Genevieve might be a grand dame in her third or fourth rejuvenation.

He doubted it, on second glance. What she said was sensible, young, and pert:

"But uncle, they're *animals!*"

"I know that," he rumbled.

"But uncle, don't you see it?"

"Stop saying 'but uncle' and tell me what you mean," growled the Dictator, very fondly.

"Animals are always *uncertain.*"

"Of course," said the uncle.

"That makes it a game, uncle," said Genevieve. "They're never sure that any one of them would do the same thing twice. Imagine the excitement—the beautiful big beings from earth running around and around on their four middle fingers, the big fingernails making the gems jump loose from the ground!"

"I'm not at all sure it's that way. Besides, Mizzer may be covered with something valuable, such as earth or sand, instead of gemstones like the ones we have here on Pontoppidan. You know your flowerpots with their rich, warm, wet, soft earth?"

"Of course I do, uncle. And I know what you paid for them. You were very generous. And still are," she added diplomatically, glancing quickly at Casher O'Neill to see how the familial piety went across with the visitor.

"We're not that rich on Mizzer. It's mostly sand, with farmland along the Twelve Niles, our big rivers."

"I've seen pictures of rivers," said Genevieve. "Imagine living on a whole world full of flowerpot stuff!"

"You're getting off the subject, darling. We were wondering why anyone would bring one horse, just one horse, to Pontoppidan. I suppose you could race a horse against himself, if you had a stopwatch. But would it be fun? Would you do that, young man?"

Casher O'Neill tried to be respectful. "In my home we used to have a lot of horses. I've seen my uncle time them one by one."

"Your uncle?" said the Dictator interestedly. "Who was your uncle that he had all these four-fingered 'horses' running around? They're all Earth animals and very expensive."

Casher felt the coming of the low, slow blow he had met so many times before, right from the whole outside world into the pit of his stomach. "My uncle"—he stammered—"my uncle—I thought you knew—was the old Dictator of Mizzer, Kuraf."

Philip Vincent jumped to his feet, very lightly for so well-fleshed a man. The young mistress, Genevieve, clutched at the throat of her dress.

"Kuraf!" cried the old Dictator. "Kuraf! We know about

him, even here. But you were supposed to be a Mizzer
patriot, not one of Kuraf's people."

"He doesn't have any children—" Casher began to explain.

"I should think not, not with those habits!" snapped the
old man.

"—so I'm his nephew and his heir. But I'm not trying to
put the Dictatorship back, even though I should be dictator.
I just want to get rid of Colonel Wedder. He has ruined my
people, and I am looking for money or weapons or help
to make my home-world free." This was the point, Casher
O'Neill knew, at which people either started believing him
or did not. If they did not, there was not much he could
do about it. If they did, he was sure to get some sympathy.
So far, no help. Just sympathy.

But the Instrumentality, while refusing to take action
against Colonel Wedder, had given young Casher O'Neill
an all-world travel pass—something which a hundred life-
times of savings could not have purchased for the ordinary
man. (His obscene old uncle had gone off to Sunvale, on
Ttiollé, the resort planet, to live out his years between the
casino and the beach.) Casher O'Neill held the conscience
of Mizzer in his hand. Only he, among the star travelers,
cared enough to fight for the freedom of the Twelve Niles.
Here, now, in this room, there was a turning point.

"I won't give you anything," said the Hereditary Dictator,
but he said it in a friendly voice. His niece started tugging
at his sleeve.

The older man went on. "Stop it, girl. I won't give you
anything, not if you're part of that rotten lot of Kuraf's,
not unless—"

"Anything, sir, anything, just so that I get help or
weapons to go home to the Twelve Niles!"

"All right, then. Unless you open your mind to me. I'm
a good telepath myself."

"Open my mind! Whatever for?" The incongruous indecency of it shocked Casher O'Neill. He'd had men and women and governments ask a lot of strange things from him, but no one before had had the cold impudence to ask him to open his mind. "And why you?" he went on, "What would you get out of it? There's nothing much in my mind."

"To make sure," said the Hereditary Dictator, "that you are not too honest and sharp in your beliefs. If you're positive that you know what to do, you might be another Colonel Wedder, putting your people through a dozen torments for a Utopia which never quite comes true. If you don't care at all, you might be like your uncle. He did no real harm. He just stole his planet blind and he had some extraordinary habits which got him talked about between the stars. He never killed a man in his life, did he?"

"No, sir," said Casher O'Neill, "he never did." It relieved him to tell the one little good thing about his uncle; there was so very, very little which could be said in Kuraf's favor.

"I don't like slobbering old libertines like your uncle," said Philip Vincent, "but I don't hate them either. They don't hurt other people much. As a matter of actual fact, they don't hurt anyone but themselves. They waste property, though. Like these horses you have on Mizzer. We'd never bring living beings to this world of Pontoppidan, just to play games with. And you know we're not poor. We're no Old North Australia, but we have a good income here."

That, thought Casher O'Neill, is the understatement of the year, but he was a careful young man with a great deal at stake, so he said nothing.

The Dictator looked at him shrewdly. He appreciated the value of Casher's tactful silence. Genevieve tugged at his sleeve, but he frowned her interruption away.

"If," said the Hereditary Dictator, *"if,"* he repeated, "you pass two tests, I will give you a green ruby as big as my head. If my Committee will allow me to do so. But I think I can talk them around. One test is that you let me peep

all over your mind, to make sure that I am not dealing with
one more honest fool. If you're too honest, you're a fool and
a danger to mankind. I'll give you a dinner and ship you
off-planet as fast as I can. And the other test is—solve the
puzzle of this horse. The one horse on Pontoppidan. Why is
the animal here? What should we do with it? If it's good
to eat, how should we cook it? Or can we trade to some
other world, like your planet Mizzer, which seems to set
a value on horses?"

"Thank you, sir—" said Casher O'Neill.

"But, uncle—" said Genevieve.

"Keep quite, my darling, and let the young man speak,"
said the Dictator.

"—all I was going to ask, is," said Casher O'Neill, "what's
a green ruby good for? I didn't even know they came green."

"That, young man, is a Pontoppidan specialty. We have
a geology based on ultra-heavy chemistry. This planet was
once a fragment from a giant planet which imploded. The
use is simple. With a green ruby you can make a laser beam
which will boil away your city of Kaheer in a single sweep.
We don't have weapons here and we don't believe in them,
so I won't give you a weapon. You'll have to travel further
to find a ship and to get the apparatus for mounting your
green ruby. *If* I give it to you. But you will be one more
step along in your fight with Colonel Wedder."

"Thank you, thank you, most honorable sir!" cried
Casher O'Neill.

"But uncle," said Genevieve, "you shouldn't have picked
those two things because I know the answers."

"You know all about *him,*" said the Hereditary Dictator,
"by some means of your own?"

Genevieve flushed under her lilac-hued foundation cream.
"I know enough for us to know."

"How do you know it, my darling?"

"I just know," said Genevieve.

Her uncle made no comment, but he smiled widely and

indulgently as if he had heard that particular phrase before.

She stamped her foot. "And I know about the horse, too. *All* about it."

"Have you seen it?"

"No."

"Have you talked to it?"

"Horses don't talk, uncle."

"Most underpeople do," he said.

"This isn't an underperson, uncle. It's a plain unmodified old Earth animal. It never did talk."

"Then what do you know, my honey?" The uncle was affectionate, but there was the crackle of impatience under his voice.

"I taped it. The whole thing. The story of the horse of Pontoppidan. And I've edited it, too. I was going to show it to you this morning, but your staff sent that young man in."

Casher O'Neill looked his apologies at Genevieve.

She did not notice him. Her eyes were on her uncle.

"Since you've done this much, we might as well see it." He turned to the attendants. "Bring chairs. And drinks. You know mine. The young lady will take tea with lemon. Real tea. Will you have coffee, young man?"

"You have coffee!" cried Casher O'Neill. As soon as he said it, he felt like a fool. Pontoppidan was a *rich* planet. On most worlds' exchanges, coffee came out to about two man-years per kilo. Here halftracks crunched their way through gems as they went to load up the frequent trading vessels.

The chairs were put in place. The drinks arrived. The Hereditary Dictator had been momentarily lost in a brown study, as though he were wondering about his promise to Casher O'Neill. He had even murmured to the young man, "Our bargain stands? Never mind what my niece says." Casher had nodded vigorously. The old man had gone back to frowning at the servants and did not relax until a tiger-man bounded into the room, carrying a tray with acrobatic precision. The chairs were already in place.

The uncle held his niece's chair for her as a command that she sit down. He nodded Casher O'Neill into a chair on the other side of himself.

He commanded, "Dim the lights . . ."

The room plunged into semi-darkness.

Without being told, the people took their places immediately behind the three main seats and the underpeople perched or sat on benches and tables behind them. Very little was spoken. Casher O'Neill could sense that Pontoppidan was a well-run place. He began to wonder if the Hereditary Dictator had much real work left to do, if he could fuss that much over a single horse. Perhaps all he did was boss his niece and watch the robots load truckloads of gems into sacks while the underpeople weighed them, listed them and wrote out the bills for the customers.

II

THERE was no screen; this was a good machine.

The planet Pontoppidan came into view, its airless brightness giving strong hints of the mineral riches which might be found.

Here and there enormous domes, such as the one in which this palace was located, came into view.

Genevieve's own voice, girlish, impulsive and yet didactic, rang out with the story of her planet. It was as though she had prepared the picture not only for her own uncle but for off-world visitors as well. *By Joan, that's it!* thought Casher O'Neill. *If they don't raise much food here, outside of the hydroponics, and don't have any real People Places, they have to trade: that does mean visitors and many, many of them.*

The story was interesting, but the girl herself was more interesting. Her face shone in the shifting light which the images—a meter, perhaps a little more, from the floor—

reflected across the room. Casher O'Neill thought that he had never before seen a woman who so peculiarly combined intelligence and charm. She was girl, girl, girl, all the way through; but she was also very smart and pleased with being smart. It betokened a happy life. He found himself glancing covertly at her. Once he caught her glancing, equally covertly, at him. The darkness of the scene enabled them both to pass it off as an accident without embarrassment.

Her viewtape had come to the story of the *dipsies,* enormous canyons which lay like deep gashes on the surface of the planet. Some of the color views were spectacular beyond belief. Casher O'Neill, as the "appointed one" of Mizzer, had had plenty of time to wander through the nonsalacious parts of his uncle's collections, and he had seen pictures of the most notable worlds.

Never had he seen anything like this. One view showed a sunset against a six-kilometer cliff of a material which looked like solid emerald. The peculiar bright sunshine of Pontoppidan's small, penetrating, lilac-hued sun ran like living water over the precipice of gems. Even the reduced image, one meter by one meter, was enough to make him catch his breath.

The bottom of the dipsy had vapor emerging in curious cylindrical columns which seemed to erode as they reached two or three times the height of a man. The recorded voice of Genevieve was explaining that the very thin atmosphere of Pontoppidan would not be breathable for another 2,520 years, since the settlers did not wish to squander their resources on a luxury like breathing when the whole planet only had 60,000 inhabitants; they would rather go on with masks and use their wealth in other ways. After all, it was not as though they did not have their domed cities, some of them many kilometers in radius. Besides the usual hydroponics, they had even imported 7.2 hectares of garden soil, 5.5 centimeters deep, together with enough water to make the gardens rich and fruitful. They had brought worms, too, at the price of eight carats of diamond per living worm, in order to keep the soil of the gardens loose and living.

Genevieve's transcribed voice rang out with pride as she listed these accomplishments of her people, but a note of sadness came in which she returned to the subject of the dipsies. ". . . and though we would like to live in them and develop their atmosphere, we dare not. There is too much escape of radioactivity. The geysers themselves may or may not be contaminated from one hour to the next. So we just look at them. Not one of them has ever been settled, except for the Hippy Dipsy, where the horse came from. Watch this next picture."

The camera sheered up, up, up from the surface of the planet. Where it had wandered among mountains of diamonds and valleys of tourmalines, it now took to the blue-black of near, inner space. One of the canyons showed (from high altitude) the grotesque pattern of a human woman's hips and legs, though what might have been the upper body was lost in a confusion of broken hills which ended in a bright almost-iridescent plain to the North.

"That," said the real Genevieve, overriding her own voice on the screen, "is the Hippy Dipsy. There, see the blue? That's the only lake on all of Pontoppidan. And here we drop to the hermit's house."

Casher O'Neill almost felt vertigo as the camera plummeted from off-planet into the depths of that immense canyon. The edges of the canyon almost seemed to move like lips with the plunge, opening and folding inward to swallow him up.

Suddenly they were beside a beautiful little lake.

A small hut stood beside the shore.

In the doorway there sat a man, dead.

His body had been there a long time; it was already mummified.

Genevieve's recorded voice explained the matter: ". . .

in Norstrilian law and custom, they told him that his time had come. They told him to go to the Dying House, since he was no longer fit to live. In Old North Australia, they are so rich that they let everyone live as long as he wants, unless the old person can't take rejuvenation any more, even with stroon, and unless he or she gets to be a real pest to the living. If that happens, they are invited to go to the Dying House, where they shriek and pant with delirious joy for weeks or days until they finally die of an overload of sheer happiness and excitement. . . ." There was a hesitation, even in the recording. "We never knew why this man refused. He stood off-planet and said that he had seen views of the Hippy Dipsy. He said it was the most beautiful place on all the worlds, and that he wanted to build a cabin there, to live alone, except for his non-human friend. We thought it was some small pet. When we told him that the Hippy Dipsy was very dangerous, he said that this did not matter in the least to him, since he was old and dying anyhow. Then he offered to pay us twelve times our planetary income if we would lease him twelve hectares on the condition of absolute privacy. No pictures, no scanners, no help, no visitors. Just solitude and scenery. His name was Perinö. My great-grandfather asked for nothing more, except the written transfer of credit. When he paid it, Perinö even asked that he be left alone after he was dead. Not even a vault rocket so that he could either orbit Pontoppidan forever or start a very slow journey to nowhere, the way so many people like it. So this is our first picture of him. We took it when the light went off in the People Room and one of the tiger-men told us that he was sure a human consciousness had come to an end in the Hippy Dipsy.

"And we never even thought of the pet. After all, we had never made a picture of him. This is the way he arrived from Perinö's shack."

A robot was shown in a control room, calling excitedly in the old Common Tongue.

"People, people! Judgment needed! Moving object coming out of the Hippy Dipsy. Object has improper shape. Not a correct object. Should not rise. Does so anyhow. People, tell me, people, tell me! Destroy or not destroy? This is an improper object. It should fall, not rise. Coming out of the Hippy Dipsy."

A firm click shut off the robot's chatter. A well-shaped woman took over. From the nature of her work and the lithe, smooth tread with which she walked, Casher O'Neill suspected that she was of cat origin, but there was nothing in her dress or in her manner to show that she was underpeople.

The woman in the picture lighted a screen.

She moved her hands in the air in front of her, like a blind person feeling his way through open day.

The picture on the inner screen came to resolution.

A face showed in it.

What a face! thought Casher O'Neill, and he heard the other people around him in the viewing room.

The horse!

Imagine a face like that of a newborn cat, thought Casher. Mizzer is full of cats. But imagine the face with a huge mouth, with big yellow teeth—a nose long beyond imagination. Imagine eyes which look friendly. In the picture they were rolling back and forth with exertion, but even there—when they did not feel observed—there was nothing hostile about the set of the eyes. They were tame, companionable eyes. Two ridiculous ears stood high, and a little tuft of golden hair showed on the crest of the head between the ears.

The viewed scene was comical, too. The cat-woman was as astonished as the viewers. It was lucky that she had touched the emergency switch, so that she not only saw the horse, but had recorded herself and her own actions while bringing him into view.

Genevieve whispered across the chest of the Hereditary Dictator: "Later we found he was a palomino pony. That's a very special kind of horse. And Perinö had made him immortal, or almost immortal."

"Sh-h!" said her uncle.

The screen-within-the-screen showed the cat-woman waving her hands in the air some more. The view broadened.

The horse had four hands and no legs, or four legs and no hands, whichever way you want to count them.

The horse was fighting his way up a narrow cleft of rubies which led out of the Hippy Dipsy. He panted heavily. The oxygen bottles on his sides swung wildly as he clambered. He must have seen something, perhaps the image of the cat-woman, because he said a word:

Whay-yay-yay-yay-whay-yay!

The cat-woman in the nearer picture spoke very distinctly:

"Give your name, age, species and authority for being on the planet." She spoke clearly and with the utmost possible authority.

The horse obviously heard her. His ears tipped forward. But his reply was the same as before:

Whay-yay-yay!

Casher O'Neill realized that he had followed the mood of the picture and had seen the horse the way that the people on Pontoppidan would have seen him. On second thought, the horse was nothing special, by the standards of the Twelve Niles or the Little Horse Market in the city of Kaheer. It was an old pony stallion, no longer fit for breeding and probably not for riding either. The hair had whitened among the gold; the teeth were worn. The animal showed many injuries and burns. Its only use was to be killed, cut up and fed to the racing dogs. But he said nothing to the people around him. They were still spellbound by the picture.

The cat-woman repeated:

"Your name isn't Whayayay. Identify yourself properly; name first."

The horse answered her with the same word in a higher key.

Apparently forgetting that she had recorded herself as well as the emergency screen, the cat-woman said, "I'll call real people if you don't answer! They'll be annoyed at being bothered."

The horse rolled his eyes at her and said nothing.

The cat-woman pressed an emergency button on the side of the room. One could not see the other communication screen which lighted up, but her end of the conversation was plain.

"I want an ornithopter. Big one. Emergency."

A mumble from the side screen.

"To go to the Hippy Dipsy. There's an underperson there, and he's in so much trouble that he won't talk." From the screen beside her, the horse seemed to have understood the sense of the message, if not the words, because he repeated:

Whay-yay-whay-yay-yay!

"See," said the cat-woman to the person in the other screen, "that's what he's doing. It's obviously an emergency."

The voice from the other screen came through, tinny and remote by double recording:

"Fool, yourself, cat-woman! Nobody can fly an ornithopter into a dipsy. Tell your silly friend to go back to the floor of the dipsy and we'll pick him up by space rocket."

Whay-yay-yay! said the horse impatiently.

"He's not my *friend*," said the cat-woman with brisk annoyance. "I just discovered him a couple of minutes ago. He's asking for help. Any idiot can see that, even if we don't know his language."

The picture snapped off.

The next scene showed tiny human figures working with

searchlights at the top of an immeasurably high cliff. Here and there, the beam of the searchlight caught the cliff face; the translucent faceted material of the cliff looked almost like rows of eerie windows, their lights snapping on and off, as the searchlight moved.

Far down there was a red glow. Fire came from inside the mountain.

Even with telescopic lenses the cameraman could not get the close-up of the glow. On one side there was the figure of the horse, his four arms stretched at impossible angles as he held himself firm in the crevasse; on the other side of the fire there were the even tinier figures of men, laboring to fit some sort of sling to reach the horse.

For some odd reason having to do with the techniques of recording, the voices came through very plainly, even the heavy, tired breathing of the old horse. Now and then he uttered one of the special horse-words which seemed to be the limit of his vocabulary. He was obviously watching the men, and was firmly persuaded of their friendliness to him. His large, tame, yellow eyes rolled wildly in the light of the searchlight and every time the horse looked down, he seemed to shudder.

Casher O'Neill found this entirely understandable. The bottom of the Hippy Dipsy was nowhere in sight; the horse, even with nothing more than the enlarged fingernails of his middle fingers to help him climb, had managed to get about four of the six kilometers' height of the cliff face behind him.

The voice of a tiger-man sounded clearly from among the shift of men, underpeople and robots who were struggling on the face of the cliff.

"It's a gamble, but not much of a gamble. I weigh six hundred kilos myself, and, do you know, I don't think I've ever had to use my full strength since I was a kitten. I *know* that I can jump across the fire and help that thing be more comfortable. I can even tie a rope around him so that he won't slip and fall after all the work we've done.

And the work he's done, too," added the tiger-man grimly. *"Perhaps* I can just take him in my arms and jump back with him. It will be perfectly safe if you have a safety rope around each of us. After all, I never saw a less prehensile creature in my life. You can't call those fingers of his 'fingers.' They look like little boxes of bone, designed for running around and not much good for anything else."

There was a murmur of other voices and then the command of the supervisor. "Go ahead."

No one was prepared for what happened next.

The cameraman got the tiger-man right in the middle of his frame, showing the attachment of one rope around the tiger-man's broad waist. The tiger-man was a modified type whom the authorities had not bothered to put into human cosmetic form. He still had his ears on top of his head, yellow and black fur over his face, huge incisors overlapping his lower jaw and enormous antenna-like whiskers sticking out from his moustache. He must have been thoroughly modified inside, however, because his temperament was calm, friendly and even a little humorous; he must have had a carefully re-done mouth, because the utterance of human speech came to him clearly and without distortion.

He jumped—a mighty jump, right through the top edges of the flame.

The horse saw him.

The horse jumped too, almost in the same moment, also through the top of the flame, going the other way.

The horse had feared the tiger-man more than he did the cliff.

The horse landed right in the group of workers. He tried not to hurt them with his flailing limbs, but he did knock one man—a true man, at that—off the cliff. The man's scream faded as he crashed into the impenetrable darkness below.

The robots were quick. Having no emotions except *on,* *off,* and *high,* they did not get excited. They had the horse

trussed and, before the true man and underpeople had en-
sured their footing, they had signaled the crane operator
at the top of the cliff. The horse, his four arms swinging
limply, disappeared upward.

The tiger-man jumped back through the flames to the
nearer ledge. The picture went off.

In the viewing room, the Hereditary Dictator Philip Vincent stood up. He stretched, looking around.

Genevieve looked at Casher O'Neill expectantly.

"That's the story," said the Dictator mildly. "Now you
solve it."

"Where is the horse now?" said Casher O'Neill.

"In the hospital, of course. My niece can take you to
see him."

III

AFTER A short, painful and very thorough peeping of his
own mind by the Hereditary Dictator, Casher O'Neill and
Genevieve set off for the hospital in which the horse was
being kept in bed. The people of Pontoppidan had not
known what else to do with him, so they had placed him
under strong sedation and were trying to feed him with
sugar-water compounds going directly into his veins. Genevieve told Casher that the horse was wasting away.

They walked to the hospital over amethyst pebbles.

Instead of wearing his spacesuit, Casher wore a surface
helmet which enriched his oxygen. His hosts had not counted
on his getting spells of uncontrollable itching from the
sharply reduced atmospheric pressure. He did not dare
mention the matter, because he was still hoping to get the
green ruby as a weapon in his private war for the liberation
of the Twelve Niles from the rule of Colonel Wedder. Whenever the itching became less than excruciating, he enjoyed
the walk and the company of the slight, beautiful girl who
accompanied him across the fields of jewels to the hospital.
(In later years, he sometimes wondered what might have

happened. Was the itching a part of his destiny, which
saved him for the freedom of the city of Kaheer and the
planet Mizzer? Might not the innocent brilliant loveliness of
the girl have otherwise tempted him to forswear his duty
and stay forever on Pontoppidan?)

The girl wore a new kind of cosmetic for outdoor walking—a warm peachhued powder which let the natural pink
of her cheeks show through. Her eyes, he saw, were a living,
deep gray; her eyelashes, long; her smile, innocently pro-
vocative beyond all ordinary belief. It was a wonder that
the Hereditary Dictator had not had to stop duels and
murders between young men vying for her favor.

They finally reached the hospital, just as Casher O'Neill
thought he could stand it no longer and would have to ask
Genevieve for some kind of help or carriage to get indoors
and away from the frightful itching.

The building was underground.

The entrance was sumptuous. Diamonds and rubies,
the size of building-bricks on Mizzer, had been set to frame
the doorway, which was apparently enameled steel. Kuraf
at his most lavish had never wasted money on anything
like this door-frame. Genevieve saw his glance.

"It did cost a lot of credits. We had to bring a blind
artist all the way from Olympia to paint that enamel-work.
The poor man. He spent most of his time trying to steal
extra gemstones when he should have known that we pay
justly and never allowed anyone to get away with stealing."

"What do you do?" asked Casher O'Neill.

"We cut thieves up in space, just at the edge of the atmosphere. We have more manned boats in orbit than any
other planet I know of. Maybe Old North Australia has
more, but, then, nobody ever gets close enough to Old North
Australia to come back alive and tell."

They went on into the hospital.

A respectful chief surgeon insisted on keeping them in

the office and entertaining them with tea and confectionery, when they both wanted to go see the horse; common politeness prohibited their pushing through. Finally they got past the ceremony and into the room in which the horse was kept.

Close up, they could see how much he' had suffered. There were cuts and abrasures over almost all of his body. One of his *hooves*—the doctor told them that was the correct name, *hoof,* for the big middle fingernail on which he walked—was split; the doctor had put a cadmium-silver bar through it. The horse lifted his head when they entered, but he saw that they were just more people, not horsey people, so he put his head down, very patiently.

"What's the prospect, doctor?" asked Casher O'Neill, turning away from the animal.

"Could I ask you, sir, a foolish question first?"

Surprised, Casher could only say yes.

"You're an O'Neill. Your uncle is Kuraf. How do you happen to be called 'Casher'?"

"That's simple," laughed Casher. "This is my young-man-name. On Mizzer, everybody gets a baby name, which nobody uses. Then he gets a nickname. Then he gets a young-man-name, based on some characteristic or some friendly joke, until he picks out his career. When he enters his profession, he picks out his own career name. If I liberate Mizzer and overthrow Colonel Wedder, I'll have to think up a suitable career name for myself."

"But why 'Casher,' sir?" persisted the doctor.

"When I was a little boy and people asked me what I wanted, I always asked for cash. I guess that contrasted with my uncle's wastefulness, so they called me Casher."

"But what is cash? One of your crops?"

It was Casher's time to look amazed. "Cash is money. Paper credits. People pass them back and forth when they buy things."

"Here on Pontoppidan, all the money belongs to me.

All of it," said Genevieve. "My uncle is trustee for me. But I have never been allowed to touch it or to spend it. It's all just planet business."

The doctor blinked respectfully. "Now this horse, sir, if you will pardon my asking about your name, is a very strange case. Physiologically he is a pure earth type. He is suited only for a vegetable diet, but otherwise he is a very close relative of man. He has a single stomach and a very large cone-shaped heart. That's where the trouble is. The heart is in bad condition. He is dying."

"Dying?" cried Genevieve.

"That's the sad, horrible part," said the doctor. "He is dying but he cannot die. He could go on like this for many years. Perinö wasted enough stroon on this animal to make a planet immortal. Now the animal is worn out but cannot die."

Casher O'Neill let out a long, low, ululating whistle. Everybody in the room jumped. He disregarded them. It was the whistle he had used near the stables, back among the Twelve Niles, when he wanted to call a horse.

The horse knew it. The large head lifted. The eyes rolled at him so imploringly that he expected tears to fall from them, even though he was pretty sure that horses could not lachrymate.

He squatted on the floor, close to the horse's head, with a hand on its mane.

"Quick," he murmured to the surgeon. "Get me a piece of sugar and an underperson-telepath. The underperson-telepath must not be of carnivorous origin."

The doctor looked stupid. He snapped "Sugar" at an assistant, but he squatted down next to Casher O'Neill and said, "You will have to repeat that about an underperson. This is not an underperson hospital at all. We have very few of them here. The horse is here only by command of His Excellency Philip Vincent, who said that the horse of Perinö should be given the best of all possible care. He even told me," said the doctor, "that if anything wrong happened to this horse, I would ride patrol for it for the next eighty years. So I'll do what I can. Do you find me too talkative? Some people do. What kind of an underperson do you want?"

"I need," said Casher, very calmly, "a telepathic underperson, both to find out what this horse wants and to tell the horse that I am here to help him. Horses are vegetarians and they do not like meat-eaters. Do you have a vegetarian underperson around the hospital?"

"We used to have some squirrel-men," said the chief surgeon, "but when we changed the air circulating system the squirrel-men went away with the old equipment. I think they went to a mine. We have tiger-men, cat-men, and my secretary is a wolf."

"Oh, no!" said Casher O'Neill. "Can you imagine a sick horse confiding in a wolf?"

"It's no more than you are doing," said the surgeon, very softly, glancing up to see if Genevieve were in hearing range, and apparently judging that she was not. "The Hereditary Dictators here sometimes cut suspicious guests to pieces on their way off the planet. That is, unless the guests are licensed, regular traders. You are not. You might be a spy, planning to rob us. How do I know? I wouldn't give a diamond chip for your chances of being alive next week. What do you want to do about the horse? That might please the Dictator. And *you* might live."

Casher O'Neill was so staggered by the confidence of the surgeon that he squatted there thinking about himself, not about the patient. The horse licked him, seemingly sensing that he needed solace.

The surgeon had an idea. "Horses and dogs used to go together, didn't they, back in the old days of Manhome, when all the people lived on planet Earth?"

"Of course," said Casher. "We still run them together in hunts on Mizzer, but under these new laws of the Instrumentality we've run out of underpeople-criminals to hunt."

"I have a good dog," said the chief surgeon. "She talks pretty well, but she is so sympathetic that she upsets the patients by loving them too much. I have her down in the second underbasement tending the dish-sterilizing machinery."

"Bring her up," said Casher in a whisper.

He remembered that he did not need to whisper about this, so he stood up and spoke to Genevieve:

"They have found a good dog-telepath who may reach through to the mind of the horse. It may give us the answer."

She put her hand on his forearm gently, with the approbatory gesture of a princess. Her fingers dug into his flesh. Was she wishing him well against her uncle's habitual treachery, or was this merely the impulse of a kind young girl who knew nothing of the way the world was run?

IV

THE interview went extremely well.

The dog-woman was almost perfectly humaniform. She looked like a tired, cheerful, worn-out old woman, not valuable enough to be given the life-prolonging santaclara drug called *stroon*. Work had been her life and she had had plenty of it. Casher O'Neill felt a twinge of envy when he realized that happiness goes by the petty chances of life and not by the large destiny. This dog-woman, with her haggard face and her stringy gray hair, had more love, happiness and sympathy than Kuraf had found with his pleasures, Colonel Wedder with his powers, or himself with his crusade. Why did life do that? Was there no justice, ever? Why should a worn-out worthless old underwoman be happy when he was not?

"Never mind," she said, "you'll get over it and then you will be happy."

"Over what?" he said. "I didn't say anything."

"I'm not going to say it," she retorted, meaning that she

was telepathic. "You're a prisoner of yourself. Some day you will escape to unimportance and happiness. You're a good man. You're trying to save yourself, but you really *like* this horse."

"Of course I do," said Casher O'Neill. "He's a brave old horse, climbing out of that hell to get back to people."

When he said the word *hell* her eyes widened, but she said nothing. In his mind, he saw the sign of a fish scrawled on a dark wall and he felt her think at him, *So you too know something of the "dark wonderful knowledge" which is not yet to be revealed to all mankind?*

He thought a *cross* back at her and then turned his thinking to the horse, lest their telepathy be monitored and strange punishments await them both.

She spoke in words, "Shall we link?"

"Link," he said.

Genevieve stepped up. Her clear-cut, pretty, sensitive face was alight with excitement. "Could I—could I be cut in?"

"Why not?" said the dog-woman, glancing at him. He nodded. The three of them linked hands and then the dog-woman put her left hand on the forehead of the old horse.

The sand splashed beneath their feet as they ran toward Kaheer. The delicious pressure of a man's body was on their backs. The red sky of Mizzer gleamed over them. There came the shout:

"I'm a horse, I'm a horse, I'm a horse!"

"You're from Mizzer," thought Casher O'Neill, "from Kaheer itself!"

"I don't know names," thought the horse, "but you're from my land. The land, the good land."

"What are you doing here?"

"Dying," thought the horse. "Dying for hundreds and thousands of sundowns. The old one brought me. No riding, no running, no people. Just the old one and the small ground. I have been dying since I came here."

Casher O'Neill got a glimpse of Perinö sitting and watching the horse, unconscious of the cruelty and loneliness which he had inflicted on his large pet by making it immortal and then giving it no work to do.

"Do you know what dying is?"

Thought the horse promptly: "Certainly. No-horse."

"Do you know what life is?"

"Yes. Being a horse."

"I'm not a horse," thought Casher O'Neill, "but I am alive."

"Don't complicate things," thought the horse at him, though Casher realized it was his own mind and not the horse's which supplied the words.

"Do you want to die?"

"To no-horse? Yes, if this room, forever, is the end of things."

"What would you like better?" thought Genevieve, and her thoughts were like a cascade of newly-minted silver coins falling into all their minds: brilliant, clean, bright, innocent.

The answer was quick: "Dirt beneath my hooves, and wet air again, and a man on my back."

The dog-woman interrupted: "Dear horse, you know me?"

"You're a dog," thought the horse. "Goo-oo-oo-ood dog!"

"Right," thought the happy old slattern, "and I can tell these people how to take care of you. Sleep now, and when you waken you will be on the way to happiness."

She thought the command *sleep* so powerfully at the old horse that Casher O'Neill and Genevieve both started to fall unconscious and had to be caught by the hospital attendants.

As they re-gathered their wits, she was finishing her commands to the surgeon. "—put about 40% supplementary oxygen into the air. He'll have to have a real person to ride him, but some of your orbiting sentries would rather ride a horse up there than do nothing. You can't

repair the heart. Don't try it. Hypnosis will take care of the
sand of Mizzer. Just load his mind with one or two of the
drama-cubes packed full of desert adventure. Now, don't
you worry about me. I'm not going to give you any more
suggestions. People-man, you!" She laughed. "You can for-
give us dogs anything, except for being right. It makes you
feel inferior for a few minutes. Never mind. I'm going back
downstairs to my dishes. I love them, I really do. Good-bye,
you pretty thing," she said to Genevieve. "And good-bye,
wanderer! Good luck to you," she said to Casher O'Neill.
"You will remain miserable as long as you seek justice,
but when you give up, righteousness will come to you and
you will be happy. Don't worry. You're young and it won't
hurt you to suffer a few more years. Youth is an extremely
curable disease, isn't it?"

She gave them a full curtsy, like one Lady of the Instrumentality saying good-bye to another. Her wrinkled old
face was lit up with smiles, in which happiness was mixed
with a tiniest bit of playful mockery.

"Don't mind me, boss," she said to the surgeon. "Dishes,
here I come." She swept out of the room.

"See what I mean?" said the surgeon. "She's so horribly
happy! How can anyone run a hospital if a dishwasher gets
all over the place, making people happy? We'd be out of
jobs. Her ideas were good, though."

They were. They worked. Down to the last letter of the
dog-woman's instructions.

There was argument from the council. Casher O'Neill
went along to see them in session.

One councillor, Bashnack, was particularly vociferous in
objecting to any action concerning the horse. "Sire," he
cried, "sire! We don't even know the name of the animal!
I must protest this action, when we don't know—"

"That we don't," assented Philip Vincent. "But what does
a name have to do with it?"

"The horse has no identity, not even the identity of an animal. It is just a pile of meat left over from the estate of Perinö. We should kill the horse and eat the meat ourselves. Or, if we do not want to eat the meat, then we should sell it off-planet. There are plenty of peoples around here who would pay a pretty price for genuine earth meat. Pay no attention to me, sire! You are the Hereditary Dictator and I am nothing. I have no power, no property, nothing. I am at your mercy. All I can tell you is to follow your own best interests. I have only a voice. You cannot reproach me for using my voice when I am trying to help you, sire, can you? That's all I am doing, helping you. If you spend any credits at all on this animal you will be doing wrong, wrong, wrong. We are not a rich planet. We have to pay for expensive defenses just in order to stay alive. We cannot even afford to pay for air that our children can go out and play. And you want to spend money on a horse which cannot even talk! I tell you, sire, this council is going to vote against you, just to protect your own interests and the interests of the Honorable Genevieve as Eventual Title-holder of all Pontoppidan. You are not going to get away with this, sire! We are helpless before your power, but we will insist on advising you—"

"Hear! Hear!" cried several of the councillors, not the least dismayed by the slight frown of the Hereditary Dictator.

"I will take the word," said Philip Vincent himself.

Several had had their hands raised, asking for the floor. One obstinate man kept his hand up even when the Dictator announced his intention to speak. Philip Vincent took note of him, too:

"You can talk when I am through, if you want to."

He looked calmly around the room, smiled imperceptibly at his niece, gave Casher O'Neill the briefest of nods, and then announced:

"Gentlemen, it's not the horse which is on trial. It's Pontoppidan. It's we who are trying ourselves. And before whom are we trying ourselves, gentlemen? Each of us is before that most awful of courts, his own conscience.

"If we kill that horse, gentlemen, we will not be doing the horse a great wrong. He is an old animal, and I do not think that he will mind dying very much, now that he is away from the ordeal of loneliness which he feared more than death. After all, he has already had his great triumph— the climb up the cliff of gems, the jump across the volcanic vent, the rescue by people whom he wanted to find. The horse has done so well that he is really beyond us. We can help him, a little, or we can hurt him, a little; beside the immensity of his accomplishment, we cannot really do very much either way.

"No, gentlemen, we are not judging the case of the horse. We are judging space. What happens to a man when he moves out into the Big Nothing? Do we leave Old Earth behind? Why did civilization fall? Will it fall again? Is civilization a gun or a blaster or a laser or a rocket? Is it even a planoforming ship or a pinlighter at his work? You know as well as I do, gentlemen, that civilization is not what we can do. If it had been, there would have been no fall of Ancient Man. Even in the Dark Ages they had a few fusion bombs, they could make some small guided missiles and they even had weapons like the Kaskaskis Effect, which we have never been able to rediscover. The Dark Ages weren't dark because people lost techniques or science. They were dark *because people lost people*. It's a lot of work to be human and it's work which must be kept up, or it begins to fade. Gentlemen, the horse judges us.

"Take the word, gentlemen. 'Civilization' is itself a lady's word. There were female writers in a country called France who made that word popular in the third century before space travel. To be 'civilized' meant for people to be tame, to be kind, to be polished. If we kill this horse, we are wild. If we treat the horse gently, we are tame. Gentlemen, I have only one witness and that witness will utter only one word. Then you shall vote and vote freely."

There was a murmur around the table at this announcement. Philip Vincent obviously enjoyed the excitement he had created. He let them murmur on for a full minute or two before he slapped the table gently and said, "Gentlemen, the witness. Are you ready?"

There was a murmur of assent. Bashnack tried to say, "It's still a question of public funds!" but his neighbors shushed him. The table became quiet. All faces turned toward the Hereditary Dictator.

"Gentlemen, the testimony. Genevieve, is that what you yourself told me to say? Is civilization always a woman's choice first, and only later a man's?"

"Yes," said Genevieve, with a happy, open smile.

The meeting broke up amid laughter and applause.

V

A MONTH later Casher O'Neill sat in a room in a medium-size planoforming liner. They were out of reach of Pontoppidan. The Hereditary Dictator had not changed his mind and cut him down with green beams. Casher had strange memories, not bad ones for a young man.

He remembered Genevieve weeping in the garden.

"I'm romantic," she cried, and wiped her eyes on the sleeve of his cape. "Legally I'm the owner of this planet, rich, powerful, free. But I can't leave here. I'm too important. I can't marry whom I want to marry. I'm too important. My uncle can't do what *he* wants to do—he's Hereditary Dictator and he always must do what the Council decides after weeks of chatter. I can't love you. You're a prince and a wanderer, with travels and battles and justice and strange things ahead of you. I can't go. I'm too important. I'm too sweet! I'm too nice; I hate, hate, hate myself sometimes. Please, Casher, could you take a flier and run away with me into space?"

"Your uncle's lasers could cut us to pieces before we got out."

He held her hands and looked gently down into her face. At this moment he did not feel the fierce, aggressive, happy glow which an able young man feels in the presence of a beautiful and tender young woman. He felt something much stranger, softer, quieter—an emotion very sweet to the mind and restful to the nerves. It was the simple, clear compassion of one person for another. He took a chance for her sake, because the "dark knowledge" was wonderful but very dangerous in the wrong hands.

He took both her beautiful little hands in his, so that she looked up at him and realized that he was not going to kiss her. Something about his stance made her realize that she was being offered a more precious gift than a sky-lit romantic kiss in a garden. Besides, it was just touching helmets.

He said to her, with passion and kindness in his voice:

"You remember that dog-woman, the one who works with the dishes in the hospital?"

"Of course. She was good and bright and happy, and helped us all."

"Go work with her, now and then. Ask her nothing. Tell her nothing. Just work with her at her machines. Tell her I said so. Happiness is catching. You might catch it. I think I did myself, a little."

"I think I understand you," said Genevieve softly. "Casher, good-bye and good, good luck to you. My uncle expects us."

Together they went back into the palace.

Another memory was the farewell to Philip Vincent, the Hereditary Dictator of Pontoppidan. The calm, clean-shaven, ruddy, well-fleshed face looked at him with benign

regard. Casher O'Neill felt more respect for this man when
he realized that ruthlessness is often the price of peace, and
vigilance the price of wealth.

"You're a clever young man. A very clever young man.
You may win back the power of your Uncle Kuraf."

"I don't want *that* power!" cried Casher O'Neill.

"I have advice for you," said the Hereditary Dictator,
"and it is good advice or I would not be here to give it.
I have learned the political arts well: otherwise I would
not be alive. Do not refuse power. Just take it and use it
wisely. Do not hide from your wicked uncle's name. Obliter-
ate it. Take the name yourself and rule so well that, in a
few decades, no one will remember your uncle. Just you.
You are young. You can't win now. But it is in your fate
to grow and to triumph. I know it. I am good at these
things. I have given you your weapon. I am not tricking
you. It is packed safely and you may leave with it."

Casher O'Neill was breathing softly, believing it all, and
trying to think of words to thank the stout, powerful older
man when the dictator added, with a little laugh in his
voice:

"Thank you, too, for saving me money. You've lived
up to your name, Casher."

"Saved you money?"

"The alfalfa. The horse wanted alfalfa."

"Oh, that idea!" said Casher O'Neill. "It was obvious.
I don't deserve much credit for that."

"*I* didn't think of it," said the Hereditary Dictator, "and
my staff didn't either. We're not stupid. That shows you
are bright. You realized that Perinö must have had a food
converter to keep the horse alive in the Hippy Dipsy. All
we did was set it to alfalfa and we saved ourselves the cost
of a shipload of horse food. twice a year. We're glad to
save that credit. We're well off here, but we don't like to
waste things. You may bow to me now, and leave."

Casher O'Neill had done so, with one last glance at the

lovely Genevieve, standing fragile and beautiful beside her uncle's chair.

His last memory was very recent.

He had paid two hundred thousand credits for it, right on this liner. He had found the Stop-Captain, bored now that the ship was in flight and the Go-Captain had taken over.

"Can you get me a telepathic fix on a horse?"

"What's a horse?" said the Go-Captain. "Where is it? Do you want to pay for it?"

"A horse," said Casher O'Neill patiently, "is an unmodified earth animal. Not underpeople. A big one, but quite intelligent. This one is in orbit right around Pontoppidan. And I will pay the usual price."

"A million Earth credits," said the Stop-Captain.

"Ridiculous!" cried Casher O'Neill.

They settled on two hundred thousand credits for a good fix and ten thousand for the use of the ship's equipment even if there were failure. It was not a failure. The technician was a snake-man: he was deft, cool, and superb at his job. In only a few minutes he passed the headset to Casher O'Neill, saying politely, "This is it, I think."

It was. He had reached right into the horse's mind.

The endless sands of Mizzer swam before Casher O'Neill. The long lines of the Twelve Niles converged in the distance. He galloped steadily and powerfully. There were other horses nearby, other riders, other things, but he himself was conscious only of the beat of the hooves against the strong moist sand, the firmness of the appreciative rider upon his back. Dimly, as in a hallucination, Casher O'Neill could also see the little orbital ship in which the old horse cantered in mid-air, with an amused cadet sitting on his back. Up there, with no weight, the old worn-out heart would be good for many, many years. Then he saw the horse's paradise again. The flash of hooves threatened to overtake him, but he outran them all. There was the expectation of a stable at the end, a rubdown, good succulent green food, and the glimpse of a filly in the morning.

The horse of Pontoppidan felt extremely wise. He had trusted *people*—people, the source of all kindness, all cruelty, all power among the stars. And the people had been good. The horse felt very much horse again. Casher felt the old body course along the river's edge like a dream of power, like a completion of service, like an ultimate fulfillment of companionship.

BEAM US HOME

James Tiptree, Jr.

There are many different battlefields and many kinds of war—some are as external as a bullet in flesh, others as deep and secret as the soul.

Hugo- and-Nebula-winner James Tiptree, Jr., considered by many to be one of the two or three best short story writers in the genre, is represented here at the very top of his form with this brilliant, sharp-etched study of isolation, war, and love—of the wounds that burn like fire, of the wounds that burn like ice.

◦ HOBIE'S PARENTS might have seen the first signs if they
had been watching about 8:30 on Friday nights. But Hobie
was the youngest of five active bright-normal kids. Who was
to notice one more uproar around the TV?

A couple of years later Hobie's Friday night battles
shifted to 10 P.M. and then his sisters got their own set.
Hobie was growing fast then. In public he featured chiefly
as a tanned streak on the tennis courts and a ninety-ninth
percentile series of math grades. To his parents, Hobie
featured as the one without problems. This was hard to
avoid in a family that included a diabetic, a girl with an IQ
of 185 and another with controllable petit mal, and a
would-be ski star who spent most of his time in a cast.
Hobie's own IQ was in the fortunate one-forties, the range
where you're superior enough to lead, but not too superior
to be followed. He seemed perfectly satisfied with his com-
munications with his parents, but he didn't use them much.

Not that he was in any way neglected when the need
arose. The time he got staph in a corneal scratch, for instance, his parents did a great job of supporting him through
the pain bit and the hospital bit and so on. But they couldn't
know all the little incidents. Like the night when Hobie
called so fiercely for Dr. McCoy that a young intern named
McCoy went in and joked for half an hour with the feverish
boy in his dark room.

To the end, his parents probably never understood that
there was anything to understand about Hobie. And what
was to see? His tennis and his model rocket collection made
him look almost too normal for the small honors school
he went to first.

Then his family moved to an executive bedroom suburb
where the school system had a bigger budget than Monaco
and a soccer team loaded with National Merit Science
finalists. Here Hobie blended right in with the scenery. One
more healthy, friendly, polite kid with bright gray eyes

under a blond bowl-cut and very fast with any sort of ball game.

The brightest eyes around him were reading *The Double Helix* to find out how to make it in research, or marking up the Dun & Bradstreet flyers. If Hobie stood out at all, it was only that he didn't seem to be worried about making it in research or any other way, particularly. But that fitted in, too. Those days a lot of boys were standing around looking as if they couldn't believe what went on, as if they were waiting for—who knows?—a better world, their glands, something. Hobie's faintly aghast expression was not unique. Events like the installation of an armed patrol around the school enclave were bound to have a disturbing effect on the more sensitive kids.

People got the idea that Hobie *was* sensitive in some indefinite way. His usual manner was open but quiet, tolerant of a put-on that didn't end.

His advisor did fret over his failure to settle on a major field in time for the oncoming threat of college. First his math interest seemed to evaporate after the special calculus course, although he never blew an exam. Then he switched to the pre-college anthropology panel the school was trying. Here he made good grades and acted very motivated, until the semester when the visiting research team began pounding on sampling techniques and statistical significance. Hobie had no trouble with things like Chi square, of course. But after making his A in the final he gave them his sweet, unbelieving smile and faded. His advisor found him spending a lot of hours polishing a six-inch telescope lens in the school shop.

So Hobie was tagged as some kind of an under-achiever, but nobody knew what kind because of those grades. And something about that smile bothered them; it seemed to stop sound.

The girls liked him, though, and he went through the

usual phases rather fast. There was the week he and various birds went to thirty-five drive-in movies. And the month he went around humming *Mrs. Robinson* in a meaningful way. And the warm, comfortable summer when he and his then girl and two other couples went up to Stratford, Ontario with sleeping bags to see the Czech multimedia thing.

Girls regarded him as "different" although he never knew why. "You look at me like it's always good-bye," one of them told him. Actually he treated girls with an odd detached gentleness, as though he knew a secret that might make them all disappear. Some of them hung around because of his quick brown hands or his really great looks, some because they hoped to share the secret. In this they were disappointed. Hobie talked, and he listened carefully, but it never was mutual talk-talk-talk of total catharsis that most couples went through. But how could Hobie know that?

Like most of his peer group, Hobie stayed away from heavies and agreed that pot was preferable to getting juiced. His friends never crowded him too much after the beach party where he spooked everybody by talking excitedly for hours to people who weren't there. They decided he might have a vulnerable ego-structure.

The official high school view was that Hobie had no real problems. In this they were supported by a test battery profile that could have qualified him as the ideal normal control. Certainly there was nothing to get hold of in his routine interviews with the high-school psychologist.

Hobie came in after lunch, a time when Dr. Morehouse knew he was not at his most intuitive. They went through the usual openers, Hobie sitting easily, patient and interested, with an air of listening to some sound back of the acoustical ceiling tiles.

"I meet a number of young people involved in discovering who they really are. Searching for their own identities,"

Morehouse offered. He was idly trueing up a stack of typing headed *Sex differences in the adolescent identity crisis.*

"Do you?" Hobie asked politely.

Morehouse frowned at himself and belched disarmingly. .

"Sometimes I wonder who *I* am," he smiled.

"Do you?" inquired Hobie.

"Don't you?"

"No," said Hobie.

Morehouse reached for the hostility that should have been there, found it wasn't. Not passive aggression. What? His intuition awoke briefly. He looked into Hobie's light hazel eyes and suddenly found himself slipping toward some very large uninhabited dimension. A real pubescent preschiz, he wondered hopefully? No again, he decided, and found himself thinking, what if a person is sure of his identity but it isn't his identity? He often wondered that; perhaps it could be worked up into a creative insight.

"Maybe it's the other way around," Hobie was saying before the pause grew awkward.

"How do you mean?"

"Well, maybe you're all wondering who you are," Hobie's lips quirked; it was clear he was just making conversation.

"I asked for that," Morehouse chuckled. They chatted about sibling rivalry and psychological statistics and wound up in plenty of time for Morehouse's next boy, who turned out to be a satisfying High Anx. Morehouse forgot about the empty place he had slid into. He often did that, too.

It was a girl who got part of it out of Hobie, at three in the morning. "Dog," she was called then, although her name was Jane. A tender, bouncy little bird who cocked her head to listen up at him in a way Hobie liked. Dog would listen with the same soft intensity to the supermarket clerk and the pediatrician later on, but neither of them knew that.

They had been talking about the state of the world,
which was then quite prosperous and peaceful. That is to
say, about seventy million people were starving to death, a
number of advanced nations were maintaining themselves on
police terror tactics, four or five borders were being fought
over, Hobie's family's maid had just been cut up by the
suburban peacekeeper squad, and the school had added
a charged wire and two dogs to its patrol. But none of the
big nations were waving fissionables, and the U.S.-Sino-
Soviet détente was a twenty-year reality.

Dog was holding Hobie's head over the side of her car
because he had been the one who found the maid crawling
on her handbones among the azaleas.

"If you feel like that, why don't you do something?"
Dog asked him between spasms. "Do you want some
Slurp? It's all we've got."

"Do what?" Hobie quavered.

"Politics?" guessed Dog. She really didn't know. The
Protest Decade was long over, along with the New Politics
and Ralph Nader. There was a school legend about a senior
who had come back from Miami with a busted collarbone.
Some time after that the kids had discovered that flowers
weren't really very powerful, and that movement organizers
had their own bag. Why go on the street when you could
really do more in one of the good jobs available Inside?
So Dog could offer only a vague image of Hobie running
for something, a sincere face on TV.

"You could join the Young Statesmen."

"Not to interfere," gasped Hobie. He wiped his mouth.
Then he pulled himself together and tried some of the
Slurp. In the dashlight his seventeen-year-old sideburns
struck Dog as tremendously mature and beautiful.

"Oh, it's not so bad," said Hobie. "I mean, it's not *unu-
sually* bad. It's just a stage. This world is going through a
primitive stage. There's a lot of stages. It takes a long time.
They're just very very backward, that's all."

"They," said Dog, listening to every word.

"I mean," he said.

"You're alienated," she told him. "Rinse your mouth out with that. You don't relate to people."

"I think you're people," he said, rinsing. He'd heard this before. "I relate to you," he said. He leaned out to spit. Then he twisted his head to look up at the sky and stayed that way awhile, like an animal's head sticking out of a crate. Dog could feel him trembling the car.

"Are you going to barf again?" she asked.

"No."

But then suddenly he did, roaringly. She clutched at his shoulders while he heaved. After awhile he sagged down, his head lolling limply out on one arm.

"It's such a mess," she heard him whispering. "It's such a shitting miserable mess mess mess MESS MESS—"

He was pounding his hand on the car side.

"I'll hose it," said Dog, but then she saw he didn't mean the car.

"Why does it have to go on and on?" he croaked. "Why don't they just *stop* it? I can't bear it much longer, please, please, I can't—"

Dog was scared now.

"Honey, it's not that bad, Hobie honey, it's not that bad," she told him, patting at him, pressing her soft front against his back.

Suddenly he came back into the car on top of her, spent.

"It's unbearable," he muttered.

"What's unbearable?" she snapped, mad at him for scaring her. "What's unbearable for you and not for me? I mean, I know it's a mess, but why is it so bad for *you?* I have to live here too."

"It's your world," he told her absently, lost in some private desolation.

Dog yawned.

"I better drive you home now," she said.

He had nothing more to say and sat quietly. When Dog glanced at his profile she decided he looked calm. Almost stupid, in fact; his mouth hung open a little. She didn't recognize the expression, because she had never seen people looking out of cattle cars.

Hobie's class graduated that June. His grades were well up, and everybody understood that he was acting a little unrelated because of the traumatic business with the maid. He got a lot of sympathy.

It was after the graduation exercises that Hobie surprised his parents for the first and last time. They had been congratulating themselves in having steered their fifth offspring safely through the college crisis and into a high-status Eastern. Hobie announced that he had applied for the United States Air Force Academy.

This was a bomb, because Hobie had never shown the slightest interest in things military. Just the opposite, really. Hobie's parents took it for granted that the educated classes viewed the military with tolerant distaste. Why did their son want this? Was it another of his unstable motivational orientations?

But Hobie persisted. He didn't have any reasons, he had just thought carefully and felt that this was for him. Finally they recalled that early model rocket collection; his father decided he was serious, and began sorting out the generals his research firm did business with. In September Hobie disappeared into Colorado Springs. He reappeared for Christmas in the form of an exotically hairless, erect and polite stranger in uniform.

During the next four years Hobie the person became effectively invisible behind a growing pile of excellent evaluation reports. There seemed to be no doubt that he was working very hard, and his motivation gave no sign of flagging. Like any cadet, he bitched about many of the Academy's little ways and told some funny stories. But he never seemed discouraged. When he elected to spend his summers in special aviation skills training, his parents realized that Hobie had found himself.

Enlightenment—of a sort—came in his senior year when he told them he had applied for and been accepted into the new astronaut training program. The U.S. space program was just then starting up again after the revulsion caused by the wreck of the first manned satellite lab ten years before.

"I bet that's what he had in mind all along," Hobie's father chuckled. "He didn't want to say so before he made it." They were all relieved. A son in the space program was a lot easier to live with, status-wise.

When she heard the news, Dog, who was now married and called herself Jane, sent him a card with a picture of the Man in the Moon. Another girl, more percipient, sent him a card showing some stars.

But Hobie never made it to the space program.

It was the summer when several not-very-serious events happened all together. The British devalued their wobbly pound again, just when it was found that far too many dollars were going out of the States. North and South Korea moved a step closer to reunion, which generated a call for strengthening the U.S. contribution to the remains of SEATO. Next there was an expensive, though luckily nonlethal fire at Kennedy, and the Egyptians announced a new Soviet aid pact. And in August it was discovered that the Guévarrista rebels in Venezuela were getting some very unpleasant-looking hardware from their U.A.R. allies.

Contrary to the old saying that nations never learn from history, the U. S. showed that it had learned from its long agony in Viet Nam. What it had learned was not to waste time messing around with popular elections and military advisory and training programs, but to ball right in. Hard.

When the dust cleared, the space program and astronaut training were dead on the pad and a third of Hobie's graduating class was staging through Caracas. Technically, he had volunteered.

He found this out from the task force medico.

"Look at it this way, lieutenant. By entering the Academy, you volunteered for the Air Force, right?"

"Yes. But I opted for the astronaut program. The Air Force is the only way you can get in. And I've been accepted."

"But the astronaut program has been suspended. Temporarily, of course. Meanwhile the Air Force—for which you volunteered—has an active requirement for your training. You can't expect them to just let you sit around until the program resumes, can you? Moreover you have been given the very best option available. Good God, man, the Volunteer Airpeace Corps is considered a super elite. You should see the fugal depressions we have to cope with among men who have been rejected for the VAC."

"Mercenaries," said Hobie. "Regressive."

"Try 'professional,' it's a better word. Now—about those headaches."

The headaches eased up some when Hobie was assigned to long-range sensor recon support. He enjoyed the work of flying, and the long, calm, lonely sensor missions were soothing. They were also quite safe. The Guévarristas had no air strength to waste on recon planes and the Chicom SAM sites were not yet operational. Hobie flew the pattern, and waited zombie-like for the weather, and flew again. Mostly he waited, because the fighting was developing in a steamy jungle province where clear sensing was a sometime thing. It was poorly mapped. The ground troops could never be sure about the little brown square men who gave them so much trouble; on one side of an unknown line they were Guévarristas who should be obliterated, and on the other side they were legitimate national troops warning the blancos away. Hobie's recon tapes were urgently needed, and for several weeks he was left alone.

Then he began to get pulled up to a forward strip for one-day chopper duty when their tactical duty roster was disrupted by geegee. But this was relatively peaceful too, being mostly defoliant spray missions. Hobie in fact put in several months without seeing, hearing, smelling or feeling the war at all. He would have been grateful for this if he had realized it. As it was he seemed to be trying not to realize anything much. He spoke very little, did his work and moved like a man whose head might fall off if he jostled anything.

Naturally he was one of the last to hear the rumors about geegee when they filtered back to the coastal base, where Hobie was quartered with the long-range stuff. Geegee's proper name was Guairas Grippe. It was developing into a severe problem in the combat zone. More and more replacements and relief crews were being called forward for temporary tactical duty. On Hobie's next trip in, he couldn't help but notice that people were acting pretty haggard, and the roster was all scrawled up with changes. When they were on course he asked about it.

"Are you kidding?" his gunner grunted.

"No. What is it?"

"B.W."

"What?"

"Bacteriological weapon, skyhead. They keep promising us vaccines. Stuck in their zippers—look out, there's a ground burst."

They held Hobie up front for another mission, and another after that, and then they told him that a sector quarantine was now in force.

The official notice said that movement of personnel between sectors would be reduced to a minimum as a temporary measure to control the spread of respiratory ailments. Translation: you could go from the support zone to the front, but you couldn't go back.

Hobie was moved into a crowded billet and assigned to

Casualty and Supply. Shortly he discovered that there was a translation for respiratory ailments too. Geegee turned out to be a multiform misery of groin rash, sore throat, fever and unending trots. It didn't seem to become really acute, it just cycled along. Hobie was one of those who were only lightly affected, which was lucky because the hospital beds were full. So were the hospital aisles. Evacuation of all casualties had been temporarily suspended until a controlled corridor could be arranged.

The Gués did not, it seemed, get geegee. The ground troops were definitely sure of that. Nobody knew how it was spread. Rumor said it was bats one week, and then the next week they were putting stuff in the water. Poisoned arrows, roaches, women, disintegrating cannisters, all had their advocates. However it was done, it was clear that the U.A.R. technological aid had included more than hardware. The official notice about a forthcoming vaccine yellowed on the board.

Ground fighting was veering closer to Hobie's strip. He heard mortars now and then, and one night the Gués ran in a rocket launcher and nearly got the fuel dump before they were chased back.

"All they got to do is wait," said the gunner. "We're dead."

"Geegee doesn't kill you," said C/S control. "You just wish it did."

"They say."

The strip was extended, and three attack bombers came in. Hobie looked them over. He had trained on AX92's all one summer; he could fly them in his sleep. It would be nice to be alone.

He was pushing the C/S chopper most of the daylight hours now. He had got used to being shot at and to being sick. Everybody was sick, except a couple of replacement crews who were sent in two weeks apart, looking startlingly healthy. They said they had been immunized with a new antitoxin. Their big news was that geegee could be cured outside the zone.

"We're getting reinfected," the gunner said. "That figures. They want us out of here."

That week there was a big drive on bats, but it didn't help. The next week the first batch of replacements were running fevers. Their shots hadn't worked and neither did the stuff they gave the second batch.

After that, no more men came in except a couple of volunteer medicos. The billets and the planes and the mess were beginning to stink. That dysentery couldn't be controlled after you got weak.

What they did get was supplies. Every day or so another ton of stuff would drift down. Most of it was dragged to one side and left to rot. They were swimming in food. The staggering cooks pushed steak and lobster at men who shivered and went out to retch. The hospital even had ample space now, because it turned out that geegee really did kill you in the end. By that time you were glad to go. A cemetery developed at the far side of the strip, among the skeletons of the defoliated trees.

On the last morning Hobie was sent out to pick up a forward scout team. He was one of the few left with enough stamina for long missions. The three-man team was far into Gué territory, but Hobie didn't care. All he was thinking about was his bowels. So far he had not fouled himself or his plane. When he was down by their signal he bolted out to squat under the chopper's tail. The grunts climbed in, yelling at him.

They had a prisoner with them. The Gué was naked and astonishingly broad. He walked springily; his arms were lashed with wire and a shirt was tied over his head. This was the first Gué Hobie had been close to. As he got in he saw how the Gué's firm brown flesh glistened and bulged around the wire. He wished he could see his face. The gunner said the Gué was a Sirionó, and this was important

because the Sirionós were not known to be with the Gués.
They were a very primitive nomadic tribe.

When Hobie began to fly home he realized he was getting sicker. It became a fight to hold onto consciousness
and keep on course. Luckily nobody shot at them. At one
point he became aware of a lot of screaming going on behind him, but couldn't pay attention. Finally he came over
the strip and horsed the chopper down. He let his head
down on his arms.

"You O.K.?" asked the gunner.

"Yeah," said Hobie, hearing them getting out. They
were moving something heavy. Finally he got up and followed them. The floor was wet. That wasn't unusual. He
got down and stood staring in, the floor a foot under his
nose. The wet stuff was blood. It was sprayed around, with
one big puddle. In the puddle was something soft and fleshy-
looking.

Hobie turned his head. The ladder was wet, too. He
held up one hand and looked at the red. The other one,
too. Holding them out stiffly he turned and began to walk
away across the strip.

Control, who still hoped to get an evening flight out of
him, saw him fall and called the hospital. The two replacement parameds were still in pretty good shape. They came
out and picked him up.

When Hobie came to, one of the parameds was tying
his hands down to the bed so he couldn't tear the IV out
again.

"We're going to die here," Hobie told him.

The paramed looked noncommittal. He was a thin dark
boy with a big Adam's apple.

"But I shall dine at journey's end with Landor and with
Donne," said Hobie. His voice was light and facile.

"Yeats," said the paramed. "Want some water?"

Hobie's eyes flickered. The paramed gave him some
water.

"I really believed it, you know," Hobie said chattily. "I had it all figured out." He smiled, something he hadn't done for a long time.

"Landor and Donne?" asked the medic. He unhooked the empty IV bottle and hung up a new one.

"Oh, it was pathetic, I guess," Hobie said. "It started ou . . . I believed they were real, you know? Kirk, Spock, McCoy, all of them. And the ship. To this day, I swear . . . one of them talked to me once, I mean, he really did. . . . I had it all figured out, they had left me behind as an observer." Hobie giggled.

"They were coming back for me. It was secret. All I had to do was sort of fit in and observe. Like a report. One day they would come back and haul me up in that beam thing; maybe you know about that? And there I'd be back in real time where human beings were, where they were human. I wasn't really stuck here in the past. On a backward planet."

The paramed nodded.

"Oh, I mean, I didn't really *believe* it, I knew it was just a show. But I did believe it, too. It was like *there,* in the background, underneath, no matter what was going on. They were coming for me. All I had to do was observe. And not to interfere. You know? Prime directive . . . Of course after I grew up, I realized they weren't, I mean I realized consciously. So I was going to go to them. Somehow, somewhere. Out there . . . Now I know. It really isn't so. None of it. Never. There's nothing. . . . Now I know I'll die here."

"Oh now," said the paramed. He got up and started to take things away. His fingers were shaky.

"It's clean there," said Hobie in a petulant voice. "None of this shit. Clean and friendly. They don't torture people," he explained, thrashing his head. "They don't kill—" He slept. The paramed went away.

Somebody started to yell monotonously.

Hobie opened his eyes. He was burning up.

The yelling went on, became screaming. It was dusk. Footsteps went by, headed for the screaming. Hobie saw they had put him in a bed by the door.

Without his doing much about it the screaming seemed to be lifting him out of the bed, propelling him through the door. Air. He kept getting close-ups of his hands clutching things. Bushes, shadows. Something scratched him.

After a while the screaming was a long way behind him. Maybe it was only in his ears. He shook his head, felt himself go down onto boards. He thought he was in the cemetery.

"No," he said. "Please. Please no." He got himself up, balanced, blundered on, seeking coolness.

The side of the plane felt cool. He plastered his hot body against it, patting it affectionately. It seemed to be quite dark now. Why was he inside with no lights? He tried the panel, the lights worked perfectly. Vaguely he noticed some yelling starting outside again. It ignited the screaming in his head. The screaming got very loud—loud —LOUD—and appeared to be moving him, which was good.

He came to above the overcast and climbing. The oxy-support tube was hitting him in the nose. He grabbed for the mask, but it wasn't there. Automatically, he had leveled off. Now he rolled and looked around.

Below him was a great lilac sea of cloud, with two mountains sticking through it, their western tips on fire. As he looked, they dimmed. He shivered, found he was wearing only sodden shorts. How had he got here? Somebody had screamed intolerably and he had run.

He flew along calmly, checking his board. No trouble except the fuel. Nobody serviced the AX92's any more. Without thinking about it, he began to climb again. His hands were a yard away and he was shivering but he felt clear. He reached up and found his headphones were in place; he must have put them on along with the rest of the drill. He clicked on. Voices rattled and roared at him. He switched off. Then he took off the headpiece and dropped it on the floor.

He looked around. 18,000, heading 88-05. He was over the Atlantic. In front of him the sky was darkening fast. A pinpoint glimmer 10 o'clock high. Sirius, probably.

He thought about Sirius, trying to recall his charts. Then he thought about turning and going back down. Without paying much attention, he noticed he was crying with his mouth open.

Carefully he began feeding his torches and swinging the nose of his pod around and up. He brought it neatly to a point on Sirius. Up. Up. Behind him a great pale swing of contrail fell away above the lilac shadow, growing, towering to the tiny plane that climbed at its tip. Up. Up. The contrail cut off as the plane burst into the high cold dry.

As it did so Hobie's ears skewered and he screamed wildly. The pain quit; his drums had burst. Up! Now he was gasping for air, strangling. The great torches drove him on, up, above the curve of the world. He was hanging on the star. Up! The fuel gauges were knocking. Any second they would quit and he and the bird would be a falling stone. "Beam us up, Scotty!" he howled at Sirius, laughing, coughing—coughing to death, as the torches faltered—

—And was still coughing as he sprawled on the shining resiliency under the arcing grids. He gagged, rolled, finally focused on a personage leaning toward him out of a complex chair. The personage had round eyes, a slitted nose and the start of a quizzical smile.

Hobie's head swiveled slowly. It was not the bridge of the *Enterprise*. There were no view-screens, only a View. And Lieutenant Uhura would have had trouble with the

freeform flashing objects suspended in front of what appeared to be a girl wearing spots. The spots, Hobie made
out, were fur.

Somebody who was not Bones McCoy was doing something to Hobie's stomach. Hobie got up a hand and touched
the man's gleaming back. Under the mesh it was firm and
warm. The man looked up, grinned; Hobie looked back
at the captain.

"Do not have fear," a voice was saying. It seemed to be
coming out of a globe by the captain's console. "We will
tell you where you are."

"I know where I am," Hobie whispered. He drew a
deep, sobbing breath.

"I'm HOME!" he yelled. Then he passed out.

THE BARBARIAN

Joanna Russ

Sophistication and superiority are relative terms, shifting like sand with each change in cultural context, sometimes defining themselves in unexpected and unsettling ways.

In "The Barbarian" Nebula-winner Joanna Russ, novelist and critic, gives us the sleek and darkly elegant story of a deadly battle of wits between a barbarian adventuress and a seemingly omnipotent time-traveler, some reflections on cultural relativism, and a word of caution for those in danger of confusing the weapon and the arm.

○ ALYX, the gray-eyed, the silent woman. Wit, arm, kill-quick for hire, she watched the strange man thread his way through the tables and the smoke toward her. This was in Ourdh, where all things are possible. He stopped at the table where she sat alone and with a certain indefinable gallantry, not pleasant but perhaps its exact opposite, he said:

"A woman—here?"

"You're looking at one," said Alyx dryly, for she did not like his tone. It occurred to her that she had seen him before—though he was not so fat then, no, not quite so fat—and then it occurred to her that the time of their last meeting had almost certainly been in the hills when she was four or five years old. That was thirty years ago. So she watched him very narrowly as he eased himself into the seat opposite, watched him as he drummed his fingers in a lively tune on the tabletop, and paid him close attention when he tapped one of the marine decorations that hung from the ceiling (a stuffed blowfish, all spikes and parchment, that moved lazily to and fro in a wandering current of air) and made it bob. He smiled, the flesh around his eyes straining into folds.

"I know you," he said. "A raw country girl fresh from the hills who betrayed an entire religious delegation to the police some ten years ago. You settled down as a picklock. You made a good thing of it. You expanded your profession to include a few more difficult items and you did a few things that turned heads hereabouts. You were not unknown, even then. Then you vanished for a season and reappeared as a fairly rich woman. But that didn't last, unfortunately."

"Didn't have to," said Alyx.

"Didn't last," repeated the fat man imperturbably, with a lazy shake of the head. "No, no, it didn't last. And now," (he pronounced the "now" with peculiar relish) "you are getting old."

"Old enough," said Alyx, amused.

"Old," said he, "old. Still neat, still tough, still small. But old. You're thinking of settling down."

"Not exactly."

"Children?"

She shrugged, retiring a little into the shadow. The fat man did not appear to notice.

"It's been done," she said.

"You may die in childbirth," said he, "at your age."

"That, too, has been done."

She stirred a little, and in a moment a short-handled Southern dagger, the kind carried unobtrusively in sleeves or shoes, appeared with its point buried in the tabletop, vibrating ever so gently.

"It is true," said she, "that I am growing old. My hair is threaded with white. I am developing a chunky look around the waist that does not exactly please me, though I was never a ballet-girl." She grinned at him in the semi-darkness. "Another thing," she said softly, "that I develop with age is a certain lack of patience. If you do not stop making personal remarks and taking up my time—which is valuable—I shall throw you across the room."

"I would not, if I were you," he said.

"You could not."

The fat man began to heave with laughter. He heaved until he choked. Then he said, gasping, "I beg your pardon." Tears ran down his face.

"Go on," said Alyx. He leaned across the table, smiling, his fingers mated tip to tip, his eyes little pits of shadow in his face.

"I come to make you rich," he said.

"You can do more than that," said she steadily. A quarrel broke out across the room between a soldier and a girl he had picked up for the night; the fat man talked through it, or rather under it, never taking his eyes off her face.

"Ah!" he said, "you remember when you saw me last

and you assume that a man who can live thirty years
without growing older must have more to give—if he
wishes—than a handful of gold coins. You are right. I
can make you live long. I can insure your happiness. I
can determine the sex of your children. I can cure all dis-
eases. I can even" (and here he lowered his voice) "turn
this table, or this building, or this whole city to pure gold,
if I wish it.

"Can anyone do that?" said Alyx, with the faintest
whisper of mockery.

"I can," he said. "Come outside and let us talk. Let me
show you a few of the things I can do. I have some business
here in the city that I must attend to myself and I need a
guide and an assistant. That will be you."

"If you can turn the city into gold," said Alyx just as
softly, "can you turn gold into a city?"

"Anyone can do that," he said, laughing; "come along,"
so they rose and made their way into the cold outside air—
it was a clear night in early spring—and at a corner of the
street where the moon shone down on the walls and the
pits in the road, they stopped.

"Watch," said he.

On his outstretched palm was a small black box. He
shook it, turning it this way and that, but it remained wholly
featureless. Then he held it out to her and, as she took it
in her hand, it began to glow until it became like a piece of
glass lit up from the inside. There in the middle of it was
her man, with his tough, friendly, young-old face and his
hair a little gray, like hers. He smiled at her, his lips moving
soundlessly. She threw the cube into the air a few times,
held it to the side of her face, shook it, and then dropped
it on the ground, grinding it under her heel. It remained
unhurt.

She picked it up and held it out to him, thinking:
Not metal, very light. And warm. A toy? Wouldn't

*break, though. Must be some sort of small machine, though
God knows who made it and of what. It follows thoughts!
Marvelous. But magic? Bah! Never believed in it before;
why now? Besides, this thing too sensible; magic is elabor-
ate, undependable, useless. I'll tell him*—but then it occurred to her that someone had gone to a good deal of
trouble to impress her when a little bit of credit might
have done just as well. And this man walked with an al-
mighty confidence through the streets for someone who
was unarmed. And those thirty years—so she said very
politely:

"It's magic!"

He chuckled and pocketed the cube.

"You're a little savage," he said, "but your examination of it was most logical. I like you. Look! I am an old
magician. There is a spirit in that box and there are more
spirits under my control than you can possibly imagine. I
am like a man living among monkeys. There are things
spirits cannot do—or things I choose to do myself, take it
any way you will. So I pick one of the monkeys who seems
brighter than the rest and train it. I pick you. What do you
say?"

"All right," said Alyx.

"Calm enough!" he chuckled. "Calm enough! Good.
What's your motive?"

"Curiosity," said Alyx. "It's a monkeylike trait." He
chuckled again; his flesh choked it and the noise came out
in a high, muffled scream.

"And what if I bite you," said Alyx, "like a monkey?"

"No, little one," he answered gaily, "you won't. You may
be sure of that." He held out his hand, still shaking with
mirth. In the palm lay a kind of blunt knife which he
pointed at one of the whitewashed walls that lined the
street. The edges of the wall burst into silent smoke, the
whole section trembled and slid, and in an instant it had

vanished, vanished as completely as if it had never existed, except for a sullen glow at the raw edges of brick and a pervasive smell of burning. Alyx swallowed.

"It's quiet, for magic," she said softly. "Have you ever used it on men?"

"On armies, little one."

So the monkey went to work for him. There seemed as yet to be no harm in it. The little streets admired his generosity and the big ones his good humor; while those too high for money or flattery he won by a catholic ability that was—so the little picklock thought—remarkable in one so stupid. For about his stupidity there could be no doubt. She smelled it. It offended her. It made her twitch in her sleep, like a ferret. There was in this woman—well hidden away—an anomalous streak of quiet humanity that abhorred him, that set her teeth on edge at the thought of him, though she could not have put into words just what was the matter. *For stupidity,* she thought, *is hardly—is not exactly—*

Four months later they broke into the governor's villa. She thought she might at last find out what this man was after besides pleasure jaunts around the town. Moreover, breaking and entering always gave her the keenest pleasure; and doing so "for nothing" (as he said) tickled her fancy immensely. The power in gold and silver that attracts thieves was banal, in this thief's opinion, but to stand in the shadows of a sleeping house, absolutely silent, with no object at all in view and with the knowledge that if you are found you will probably have your throat cut—! She began to think better of him. This dilettante passion for the craft, this reckless silliness seemed to her as worthy as the love of a piece of magnetite for the North and South poles—the "faithful stone" they call it in Ourdh.

"Who'll come with us?" she asked, wondering for the fiftieth time where the devil he went when he was not with her, whom he knew, where he lived, and what that persistently bland expression on his face could possibly mean.

"No one," he said calmly.

"What are we looking for?"

"Nothing."

"Do you ever do anything for a reason?"

"Never." And he chuckled.

And then, "Why are you so fat?" demanded Alyx, halfway out of her own door, half into the shadows. She had recently settled in a poor quarter of the town, partly out of laziness, partly out of necessity. The shadows playing in the hollows of her face, the expression of her eyes veiled, she said it again, "Why are you so goddamned fat?" He laughed until he wheezed.

"The barbarian mind!" he cried, lumbering after her in high good humor, "Oh—oh, my dear!—oh, what freshness!" She thought:

That's it! and then

The fool doesn't even know I hate him.

But neither had she known, until that very moment.

They scaled the northeast garden wall of the villa and crept along the top of it without descending, for the governor kept dogs. Alyx, who could walk a taut rope like a circus performer, went quietly. The fat man giggled. She swung herself up to the nearest window and hung there by one arm and a toehold for fifteen mortal minutes while she sawed through the metal hinge of the shutter with a file. Once inside the building (he had to be pulled through the window) she took him by the collar with uncanny accuracy, considering that the inside of the villa was stone dark. "Shut up!" she said, with considerable emphasis.

"Oh?" he whispered.

"I'm in charge here," she said, releasing him with a jerk, and melted into the blackness not two feet away,

moving swiftly along the corridor wall. Her fingers brushed
lightly alongside her, like a creeping animal: stone, stone,
a gap, warm air rising . . . In the dark she felt wolfish,
her lips skinned back over her teeth; like another species
she made her way with hands and ears. Through them the
villa sighed and rustled in its sleep. She put the tips of
the fingers of her free hand on the back of the fat man's
neck, guiding him with the faintest of touches through the
turns of the corridor. They crossed an empty space where
two halls met; they retreated noiselessly into a room where
a sleeper laȳ breathing against a dimly lit window, while
someone passed in the corridor outside. When the steps
faltered for a moment, the fat man gasped and Alyx wrung
his wrist, hard. There was a cough from the corridor, the
sleeper in the room stirred and murmured, and the steps
passed on. They crept back to the hall. Then he told
her where he wanted to go.

"What!" She had pulled away, astonished, with a reckless hiss of indrawn breath. Methodically he began poking
her in the side and giving her little pushes with his other
hand—she moving away, outraged—but all in silence. In
the distant reaches of the building something fell—or
someone spoke—and without thinking, they waited silently
until the sounds had faded away. He resumed his continual
prodding. Alyx, her teeth on edge, began to creep forward,
passing a cat that sat outlined in the vague light from a
window, perfectly unconcerned with them and rubbing its
paws against its face, past a door whose cracks shone yellow,
past ghostly staircases that opened up in vast wells of darkness, breathing a faint, far updraft, their steps rustling and
creaking. They were approaching the governor's nursery.
The fat man watched without any visible horror—or any
interest, for that matter—while Alyx disarmed the first
guard, stalking him as if he were a sparrow, then the one
strong pressure on the blood vessel at the back of the neck
(all with no noise except the man's own breathing; she was

quiet as a shadow). Now he was trussed up, conscious and glaring, quite unable to move. The second guard was asleep in his chair. The third Alyx decoyed out the anteroom by a thrown pebble (she had picked up several in the street). She was three motionless feet away from him as he stooped to examine it; he never straightened up. The fourth guard (he was in the anteroom, in a feeble glow that stole through the hangings of the nursery beyond) turned to greet his friend—or so he thought—and then Alyx judged she could risk a little speech. She said thoughtfully, in a low voice, "That's dangerous, on the back of the head."

"Don't let it bother you," said the fat man. Through the parting of the hangings they could see the nurse, asleep on her couch with her arms bare and their golden circlets gleaming in the lamplight, the black slave in a profound huddle of darkness at the farther door, and a shining tented basket—the royal baby's royal house. The baby was asleep. Alyx stepped inside—motioning the fat man away from the lamp—and picked the governor's daughter out of her gilt cradle. She went round the apartment with the baby in one arm, bolting both doors and closing the hangings, draping the fat man in a guard's cloak and turning down the lamp so that a bare glimmer of light reached the farthest walls.

"Now you've seen it," she said, "shall we go?"

He shook his head. He was watching her curiously, his head tilted to one side. He smiled at her. The baby woke up and began to chuckle at finding herself carried about; she grabbed at Alyx's mouth and jumped up and down, bending in the middle like a sort of pocket-compass or enthusiastic spring. The woman lifted her head to avoid the baby's fingers and began to soothe her, rocking her in her arms. "Good Lord, she's cross-eyed," said Alyx. The nurse and her slave slept on, wrapped in the profoundest unconsciousness. Humming a little, soft tune to the governor's daughter, Alyx walked her about the room, humming and rocking, rocking and humming, until the baby yawned.

"Better go," said Alyx.

"No," said the fat man.

"Better," said Alyx again. "One cry and the nurse—"

"Kill the nurse," said the fat man.

"The slave—"

"He's dead." Alyx started, rousing the baby. The slave still slept by the door, blacker than the blackness, but under him oozed something darker still in the twilight flame of the lamp. "You did that?" whispered Alyx, hushed. She had not seen him move. He took something dark and hollow, like the shell of a nut, from the palm of his hand and laid it next the baby's cradle; with a shiver half of awe and half of distaste Alyx put that richest and most fortunate daughter of Ourdh back into her gilt cradle. Then she said:

"Now we'll go."

"But I have not what I came for," said the fat man.

"And what is that?"

"The baby."

"Do you mean to steal her?" said Alyx curiously.

"No," said he, "I mean for you to kill her."

The woman stared. In sleep the governor's daughter's nurse stirred; then she sat bolt upright, said something incomprehensible in a loud voice, and fell back to her couch, still deep in sleep. So astonished was the picklock that she did not move. She only looked at the fat man. Then she sat by the cradle and rocked it mechanically with one hand while she looked at him.

"What on earth for?" she said at length. He smiled. He seemed as easy as if he were discussing her wages or the price of pigs; he sat down opposite her and he too rocked the cradle, looking on the burden it contained with a benevolent, amused interest. If the nurse had woken up at that moment, she might have thought she saw the governor and his wife, two loving parents who had come to visit their child by lamplight. The fat man said:

"Must you know?"

"I must," said Alyx.

"Then I will tell you," said the fat man, "not because you must, but because I choose. This little six-months morsel is going to grow up."

"Most of us do," said Alyx, still astonished.

"She will become a queen," the fat man went on, "and a surprisingly wicked woman for one who now looks so innocent. She will be the death of more than one child and more than one slave. In plain fact, she will be a horror to the world. This I know."

"I believe you," said Alyx, shaken.

"Then kill her," said the fat man. But still the picklock did not stir. The baby in her cradle snored, as infants sometimes do, as if to prove the fat man's opinion of her by showing a surprising precocity; still the picklock did not move, but stared at the man across the cradle as if he were a novel work of nature.

"I ask you to kill her," said he again.

"In twenty years," said she, "when she has become so very wicked."

"Woman, are you deaf? I told you—"

"In twenty years!" In the feeble light from the lamp she appeared pale, as if with rage or terror. He leaned deliberately across the cradle, closing his hand around the shell or round-shot or unidentifiable object he had dropped there a moment before; he said very deliberately:

"In twenty years you will be dead."

"Then do it yourself," said Alyx softly, pointing at the object in his hand, "unless you had only one?"

"I had only one."

"Ah, well then," she said, "here!" and she held out to him across the sleeping baby the handle of her dagger, for

she had divined something about this man in the months
they had known each other; and when he made no move
to take the blade, she nudged his hand with the handle.

"You don't like things like this, do you?" she said.

"Do as I say, woman!" he whispered. She pushed the
handle into his palm. She stood up and poked him deliberately with it, watching him tremble and sweat; she
had never seen him so much at a loss. She moved round
the cradle, smiling and stretching out her arm seductively.
"Do as I say!" he cried.

"Softly, softly."

"You're a sentimental fool!"

"Am I?" she said. "Whatever I do, I must feel; I can't
just twiddle my fingers like you, can I?"

"Ape!"

"You chose me for it."

"Do as I say!"

"Sh! You will wake the nurse." For a moment both
stood silent, listening to the baby's all-but-soundless breathing and the rustling of the nurse's sheets. Then he said,
"Woman, your life is in my hands."

"Is it?" said she.

"I want your obedience!"

"Oh no," she said softly, "I know what you want. You
want importance because you have none; you want to
swallow up another soul. You want to make me fear you
and I think you can succeed, but I think also that I can
teach you the difference between fear and respect. Shall
I?"

"Take care!" he gasped.

"Why?" she said. "Lest you kill me?"

"There are other ways," he said, and he drew himself
up, but here the picklock spat in his face. He let out a
strangled wheeze and lurched backwards, stumbling against
the curtains. Behind her Alyx heard a faint cry; she whirled

about to see the governor's nurse sitting up in bed, her eyes
wide open.

"Madam, quietly, quietly," said Alyx, "for God's sake!"

The governor's nurse opened her mouth.

"I have done no harm," said Alyx passionately, "I
swear it!" but the governor's nurse took a breath with the
clear intention to scream, a hearty, healthy, full-bodied
scream like the sort picklocks hear in nightmares. In the
second of the governor's nurse's shuddering inhalation—
in that split second that would mean unmentionably unpleasant things for Alyx, as Ourdh was not a kind city—
Alyx considered launching herself at the woman, but the
cradle was between. It would be too late. The house would
be roused in twenty seconds. She could never make it to
a door—or a window—not even to the garden, where the
governor's hounds could drag down a stranger in two steps.
All these thoughts flashed through the picklock's mind as
she saw the governor's nurse inhale with that familiar,
hideous violence; her knife was still in her hand; with the
smooth simplicity of habit it slid through her fingers and
sped across the room to bury itself in the governor's nurse's
neck, just above the collarbone in that tender hollow Ourdh-
ian poets love to sing of. The woman's open-mouthed expression froze on her face; with an "uh!" of surprise she
fell forward, her arms hanging limp over the edge of the
couch. A noise came from her throat. The knife had opened
a major pulse, and in the blood's slow, powerful, rhythmic
tides across sheet and slippers and floor Alyx could discern
a horrid similarity to the posture and appearance of the
black slave. One was hers, one was the fat man's. She
turned and hurried through the curtains into the anteroom,
only noting that the soldier blindfolded and bound in the
corner had managed patiently to work loose the thongs
around two of his fingers with his teeth. He must have been at
it all this time. Outside in the hall the darkness of the house

was as undisturbed as if the nursery were that very Well of Peace whence the gods first drew (as the saying is) the dawn and the color—but nothing else—for the eyes of women. On the wall someone had written in faintly shining stuff, like snail-slime, the single word *Fever*.

But the fat man was gone.

Her man was raving and laughing on the floor when she got home. She could not control him—she could only sit with her hands over her face and shudder—so at length she locked him in and gave the key to the old woman who owned the house, saying, "My husband drinks too much. He was perfectly sober when I left earlier this evening and now look at him. Don't let him out."

Then she stood stock-still for a moment, trembling and thinking: of the fat man's distaste for walking, of his wheezing, his breathlessness, of his vanity that surely would have led him to show her any magic vehicle he had that took him to whatever he called home. He must have walked. She had seen him go out the north gate a hundred times.

She began to run.

To the south Ourdh is built above marshes that will engulf anyone or anything unwary enough to try to cross them, but to the north the city peters out into sand dunes fringing the seacoast and a fine monotony of rocky hills that rise to a countryside of sandy scrub, stunted trees and what must surely be the poorest farms in the world. Ourdh believes that these farmers dream incessantly of robbing travelers, so nobody goes there, all the fashionable world frequenting the great north road that loops a good fifty miles to avoid this region. Even without its stories the world would have no reason to go here; there is nothing to see but dunes and weeds and now and then a shack (or more properly speaking, a hut) resting on an outcropping of rock or nesting right on the sand like a toy boat in a basin. There is only one landmark in the whole place—

an old tower hardly even fit for a wizard—and that was abandoned nobody knows how long ago, though it is only twenty minutes' walk from the city gates. Thus it was natural that Alyx (as she ran, her heart pounding in her side) did not notice the stars, or the warm night-wind that stirred the leaves of the trees, or indeed the very path under her feet; though she knew all the paths for twenty-five miles around. Her whole mind was on that tower. She felt its stones stick in her throat. On her right and left the country flew by, but she seemed not to move; at last, panting and trembling, she crept through a nest of tree-trunks no thicker than her wrist (they were very old and very tough) and sure enough, there it was. There was a light shining halfway between bottom and top. Then someone looked out, like a cautious householder out of an attic, and the light went out.

Ah! thought she, and moved into the cover of the trees. The light—which had vanished—now reappeared a story higher and so on, higher and higher, until it reached the top. It wobbled a little, as if held in the hand. So this was his country seat! Silently and with great care, she made her way from one pool of shadow to another. One hundred feet from the tower she circled it and approached it from the northern side. A finger of the sea cut in very close to the base of the building (it had been slowly falling into the water for many years) and in this she first waded and then swam, disturbing the faint, cold radiance of the starlight in the placid ripples. There was no moon. Under the very walls of the tower she stopped and listened; in the darkness under the sea she felt along the rocks; then, expelling her breath and kicking upwards, she rushed head-down; the water closed round, the stone rushed past and she struggled up into the air. She was inside the walls.

And so is he, she thought. For somebody had cleaned the place up. What she remembered as choked with stone rubbish (she had used the place for purposes of her own a few years back) was bare and neat and clean; all was square, all was orderly, and someone had cut stone steps from the level of the water to the most beautifully precise archway in the world. But of course she should not have been able to see any of this at all. The place should have been in absolute darkness. Instead, on either side of the arch was a dim glow, with a narrow beam of light going between them; she could see dancing in it the dust-motes that are never absent from this earth, not even from air that has lain quiet within the rock of a wizard's mansion for unaccountable years. Up to her neck in the ocean, this barbarian woman then stood very quietly and thoughtfully for several minutes. Then she dove down into the sea again, and when she came up her knotted cloak was full of the tiny crabs that cling to the rocks along the seacoast of Ourdh. One she killed and the others she suspended captive in the sea; bits of the blood and flesh of the first she smeared carefully below the two sources of that narrow beam of light; then she crept back into the sea and loosed the others at the very bottom step, diving underwater as the first of the hurrying little creatures reached the arch. There was a brilliant flash of light, then another, and then darkness. Alyx waited. Hoisting herself out of the water, she walked through the arch—not quickly, but not without nervousness. The crabs were pushing and quarreling over their dead cousin. Several climbed over the sources of the beam, *pulling,* she thought, *the crabs over his eyes.* However he saw, he had seen nothing. The first alarm had been sprung.

Wizards' castles—and their country residences—have every right to be infested with all manner of horrors, but Alyx saw nothing. The passage wound on, going fairly constantly upward, and as it rose it grew lighter until every now and then she could see a kind of lighter shape against the blackness and a few stars. These were windows. There was no sound but her own breathing and once in a while the complaining rustle of one or two little creatures she had inadvertently carried with her in a corner of her cloak. When she stopped she heard nothing. The fat man was either very quiet or very far away. She hoped it was quietness. She slung the cloak over her shoulder and began the climb again.

Then she ran into a wall.

This shocked her, but she gathered herself together and tried the experiment again. She stepped back, than walked forward and again she ran into a wall, not rock but something at once elastic and unyielding, and at the very same moment someone said (as it seemed to her, inside her head) *You cannot get through.*

Alyx swore, religiously. She fell back and nearly lost her balance. She put out one hand and again she touched something impalpable, tingling and elastic; again the voice sounded close behind her ear, with an uncomfortable, frightening intimacy as if she were speaking to herself: *You cannot get through.* "Can't I!" she shouted, quite losing her nerve, and drew her sword; it plunged forward without the slightest resistance, but something again stopped her bare hand and the voice repeated with idiot softness, over and over *You cannot get through. You cannot get through—*

"Who are you!" said she, but there was no answer. She backed down the stairs, sword drawn, and waited. Nothing happened. Round her the stone walls glimmered, barely visible, for the moon was rising outside; patiently she waited, pressing the corner of her cloak with her foot, for as it lay on the floor one of the crabs had chewed his way to freedom and had given her ankle a tremendous nip on the way out. The light increased.

There was nothing there. The crab, who had scuttled busily ahead on the landing of the stair, seemed to come to the place himself and stood there, fiddling. There was absolutely nothing there. Then Alyx, who had been watching the little animal with something close to hopeless calm, gave an exclamation and threw herself flat on the stairs— for the crab had begun to climb upward between floor and ceiling and what it was climbing on was nothing. Tears forced themselves to her eyes. Swimming behind her lids she could see her husband's face, appearing first in one place, then in another, as if frozen on the black box the fat man had showed her the first day they met. She laid herself on the stone and cried. Then she got up, for the face seemed to settle on the other side of the landing and it occurred to her that she must go through. She was still crying. She took off one of her sandals and pushed it through the something-nothing (the crab still climbed in the air with perfect comfort). It went through easily. She grew nauseated at the thought of touching the crab and the thing it climbed on, but she put one hand involuntarily over her face and made a grab with the other *(You cannot* said the voice). When she had got the struggling animal thoroughly in her grasp, she dashed it against the rocky side wall of the tunnel and flung it forward with all her strength. It fell clattering twenty feet further on.

The distinction then, she thought, *is between life and death,* and she sat down hopelessly on the steps to figure this out, for the problem of dying so as to get through and yet getting through without dying, struck her as insoluble. Twenty feet down the tunnel (the spot was in darkness and she could not see what it was) something rustled. It sounded remarkably like a crab that had been stunned and was now recovering, for these animals think of nothing but food and disappointments only seem to give them fresh strength for the search. Alyx gaped into the dark. She felt the hairs rise on the back of her neck. She would have given a great deal to see into that spot, for it seemed to her that she now guessed at the principle of the fat man's demon, which kept out any conscious mind—as it had spoken in hers—but perhaps would let through . . . She pondered. This cynical woman had been a religious enthusiast before circumstances forced her into a drier way of thinking; thus it was that she now slung

her cloak ahead of her on the ground to break her fall
and leaned deliberately, from head to feet, into the horrid,
springy net she could not see. Closing her eyes and pressing
the fingers of both hands over an artery in the back of her
neck, she began to repeat to herself a formula that she
had learned in those prehistoric years, one that has to be
altered slightly each time it is repeated—almost as effective
a self-hypnotic device as counting backward. And the voice,
too, whispering over and over *You cannot get through, you
cannot get through—cannot—cannot—*

Something gave her a terrific shock through teeth, bones
and flesh, and she woke to find the floor of the landing
tilted two inches from her eyes. One knee was twisted
under her and the left side of her face ached dizzily, warm
and wet under a cushion of numbness. She guessed that
her face had been laid open in the fall and her knee
sprained, if not broken.

But she was through.

She found the fat man in a room at the very top of the
tower, sitting in a pair of shorts in a square of light at the
end of a corridor; and, as she made her way limping towards
him, he grew (unconscious and busy) to the size of a
human being, until at last she stood inside the room,
vaguely aware of blood along her arm and a stinging on
her face where she had tried to wipe her wound with her
cloak. The room was full of machinery. The fat man (he
had been jiggling some little arrangement of wires and
blocks on his lap) looked up, saw her, registered surprise
and then broke into a great grin.

"So it's you," he said.

She said nothing. She put one arm along the wall to
steady herself.

"You are amazing," he said, "perfectly amazing. Come
here," and he rose and sent his stool spinning away with
a touch. He came up to where she stood, wet and shivering,

staining the floor and wall, and for a long minute he studied her. Then he said softly:

"Poor animal. Poor little wretch."

Her breathing was ragged. She glanced rapidly about her, taking in the size of the room (it broadened to encompass the whole width of the tower) and the four great windows that opened to the four winds, and the strange things in the shadows: multitudes of little tables, boards hung on the walls, knobs and switches and winking lights innumerable. But she did not move or speak.

"Poor animal," he said again. He walked back and surveyed her contemptuously, both arms akimbo, and then he said, "Do you believe the world was once a lump of rock?"

"Yes," she said.

"Many years ago," he said, "many more years than your mind can comprehend, before there were trees—or cities—or women—I came to this lump of rock. Do you believe that?"

She nodded.

"I came here," said he gently, "in the satisfaction of a certain hobby, and I made all that you see in this room— all the little things you were looking at a moment ago— and I made the tower, too. Sometimes I make it new inside and sometimes I make it look old. Do you understand that, little one?"

She said nothing.

"And when the whim hits me," he said, "I make it new and comfortable and I settle into it, and once I have settled into it I begin to practice my hobby. Do you know what my hobby is?" He chuckled.

"My hobby, little one," he said, "came from this tower and this machinery, for this machinery can reach all over the world and then things happen exactly as I choose. Now do you know what my hobby is? My hobby is world-making. I make worlds, little one."

She took a quick breath, like a sigh, but she did not speak. He smiled at her.

"Poor beast," he said, "you are dreadfully cut about the face and I believe you have sprained one of your limbs. Hunting animals are always doing that. But it won't last. Look," he said, "look again," and he moved one fat hand in a slow circle around him. "It is I, little one," he said, "who made everything that your eyes have ever rested on. Apes and peacocks, tides and times" (he laughed) "and the fire and the rain. I made you. I made your husband. Come," and he ambled off into the shadows. The circle of light that had rested on him when Alyx first entered the room now followed him, continually keeping him at its center, and although her hair rose to see it, she forced herself to follow, limping in pain past the tables, through stacks of tubing and wire and between square shapes the size of stoves. The light fled always before her. Then he stopped, and as she came up to the light, he said:

"You know, I am not angry at you."

Alyx winced as her foot struck something, and grabbed her knee.

"No, I am not," he said. "It has been delightful—except for tonight, which demonstrates, between ourselves, that the whole thing was something of a mistake and shouldn't be indulged in again—but you must understand that I cannot allow a creation of mine, a paring of my fingernail, if you take my meaning, to rebel in this silly fashion." He grinned. "No, no," he said, "that I cannot do. And so" (here he picked up a glass cube from the table in back of him) "I have decided" (here he joggled the cube a little) "that tonight—why, my dear, what is the matter with you? You are standing there with the veins in your fists knotted as if you would like to strike me, even though your knee is giving you a great deal of trouble just at present and you would be better employed in supporting some of your weight with your hands or I am very much

mistaken." And he held out to her—though not far enough
for her to reach it—the glass cube, which contained an
image of her husband in little, unnaturally sharp, like a
picture let into crystal. "See?" he said. "When I turn the
lever to the right, the little beasties rioting in his bones
grow ever more calm and that does him good. A great
deal of good. But when I turn the lever to the left—"

"Devil!" said she.

"Ah, I've gotten something out of you at last!" he said,
coming closer. "At last you know! Ah, little one, many
and many a time I have seen you wondering whether the
world might not be better off if you stabbed me in the
back, eh? But you can't, you know. Why don't you try it?"
He patted her on the shoulder. "Here I am, you see, quite
close enough to you, peering, in fact, into those tragic,
blazing eyes—wouldn't it be natural to try and put an
end to me? But you can't, you know. You'd be puzzled if
you tried. I wear an armor plate, little beast, that any
beast might envy, and you could throw me from a ten-
thousand-foot mountain, or fry me in a furnace, or do a
hundred and one other deadly things to me without the
least effect. My armor plate has *in-er-tial dis-crim-in-a-tion*,
little savage, which means that it lets nothing too fast and
nothing too heavy get through. So you cannot hurt me
at all. To murder me, you would have to strike me, but that
is too fast and too heavy and so is the ground that hits
me when I fall and so is fire. Come here."

She did not move.

"Come here, monkey," he said. "I'm going to kill your
man and then I will send you away; though since you
operate so well in the dark, I think I'll bless you and
make that your permanent condition. What do you think
you're doing?" for she had put her fingers to her sleeve;
and while he stood, smiling a little with the cube in his
hand, she drew her dagger and fell upon him, stabbing
him again and again.

"There," he said complacently, "do you see?"

"I see," she said hoarsely, finding her tongue.

"Do you understand?"

"I understand," she said.

"Then move off," he said, "I have got to finish," and he brought the cube up to the level of his eyes. She saw her man, behind the glass as in a refracting prism, break into a multiplicity of images; she saw him reach out grotesquely to the surface; she saw his fingertips strike at the surface as if to erupt into the air; and while the fat man took the lever between thumb and forefinger and—prissily and precisely, his lips pursed into wrinkles, prepared to move it all the way to the left—

She put her fingers in his eyes and then, taking advantage of his pain and blindness, took the cube from him and bent him over the edge of a table in such a way as to break his back. This all took place inside the body. His face worked spasmodically, one eye closed and unclosed in a hideous parody of a wink, his fingers paddled feebly on the tabletop and he fell to the floor.

"My dear!" he gasped.

She looked at him expressionlessly.

"Help me," he whispered, "eh?" His fingers fluttered. "Over there," he said eagerly, "medicines. Make me well, eh? Good and fast. I'll give you half."

"All," she said.

"Yes, yes, all," he said breathlessly, "all—explain all—fascinating hobby—spend most of my time in this room—get the medicine—"

"First show me," she said, "how to turn it off."

"Off?" he said. He watched her, bright-eyed.

"First," she said patiently, "I will turn it all off. And then I will cure you."

"No," he said, "no, no! Never!" She knelt down beside him.

"Come," she said softly, "do you think I want to destroy

it? I am as fascinated by it as you are. I only want to make
sure you can't do anything to me, that's all. You must
explain it all first until I am master of it, too, and then
we will turn it on."

"No, no," he repeated suspiciously.

"You must," she said, "or you'll die. What do you think
I plan to do? I have to cure you, because otherwise how
can I learn to work all this? But I must be safe, too. Show
me how to turn it off."

He pointed, doubtfully.

"Is that it?" she said.

"Yes," he said, "but—"

"Is that it?"

"Yes, but—no—wait!" for Alyx sprang to her feet and
fetched from his stool the pillow on which he had been sitting, the purpose of which he did not at first seem to comprehend, but then his eyes went wide with horror, for she
had got the pillow in order to smother him, and that is just
what she did.

When she got to her feet, her legs were trembling.
Stumbling and pressing both hands together as if in
prayer to subdue their shaking, she took the cube that
held her husband's picture and carefully—oh, how carefully!—turned the lever to the right. Then she began to
sob. It was not the weeping of grief, but a kind of reaction and triumph, all mixed; in the middle of that eerie
room she stood, and threw her head back and yelled. The
light burned steadily on. In the shadows she found the fat
man's master switch, and leaning against the wall, put
one finger—only one—on it and caught her breath. Would
the world end? She did not know. After a few minutes'
search she found a candle and flint hidden away in a cupboard and with this she made herself a light; then, with
eyes closed, with a long shudder, she leaned—no, sagged
—against the switch, and stood for a long moment, expecting and believing nothing.

But the world did not end. From outside came the wind

and the sound of the sea-wash (though louder now, as if some indistinct and not quite audible humming had just ended) and inside fantastic shadows leapt about the candle—the lights had gone out. Alyx began to laugh, catching her breath. She set the candle down and searched until she found a length of metal tubing that stood against the wall, and then she went from machine to machine, smashing, prying, tearing, toppling tables and breaking controls. Then she took the candle in her unsteady hand and stood over the body of the fat man, a phantasmagoric lump on the floor, badly lit at last. Her shadow loomed on the wall. She leaned over him and studied his face, that face that had made out of agony and death the most appalling trivialities. She thought:

Make the world? You hadn't the imagination. You didn't even make these machines; that shiny finish is for customers, not craftsmen, and controls that work by little pictures are for children. You are a child yourself, a child and a horror, and I would ten times rather be subject to your machinery than master of it.

Aloud she said:

"Never confuse the weapon and the arm," and taking the candle, she went away and left him in the dark.

She got home at dawn and, as her man lay asleep in bed, it seemed to her that he was made out of the light of the dawn that streamed through his fingers and his hair, irradiating him with gold. She kissed him and he opened his eyes..

"You've come home," he said.

"So I have," said she.

"I fought all night," she added, "with the Old Man of the Mountain," for you must know that this demon is a legend in Ourdh; he is the god of this world who dwells in a cave containing the whole world in little, and from his cave he rules the fates of men.

"Who won?" said her husband, laughing, for in the

sunrise when everything is suffused with light it is difficult to see the seriousness of injuries.

"I did!" said she. "The man is dead." She smiled, splitting open the wound on her cheek, which began to bleed afresh. "He died," she said, "for two reasons only: because he was a fool. And because we are not."

And all the birds in the courtyard broke out shouting at once.

AMONG THE HAIRY EARTHMEN

R. A. Lafferty

Ever since Chariots of the Gods *galloped to the top of the best-seller list a few years ago, we have been deluged by books purporting to reveal evidence that Earth at the dawn of history, was visited by a race of highly advanced aliens, hailed as "gods" by our ignorant and credulous forebears. Supposedly, these godlike aliens were then obliging enough to act as mentors to the infant civilizations of Earth—if indeed they weren't the founders of those civilizations in the first place—and the saucerfolk have subsequently been credited with every major human accomplishment from Stonehenge to Chichén Itzá, not forgetting the Great Pyramid of Cheops and the Easter Island statues.*

But there's more to civilization than earthworks and monuments and giant statues, and there are more types of cultural influence than just the ham-handed obvious kind. Here Hugo-winner R.A. Lafferty—a writer possessed of SF's wildest and most incisive imagination—depicts a variety of alien meddling with human civilization more bizarre, more droll, more far-reaching, and, frighteningly, more plausible than anything in Von Daniken.

○ THERE IS ONE PERIOD of our World History that has aspects so different from anything that went before and after that we can only gaze back on those several hundred years and ask:

"Was that *ourselves* who behaved so?"

Well, no, as a matter of fact, it wasn't. It was beings of another sort who visited us briefly and who acted so gloriously and abominably.

This is the way it was:

The Children had a Long Afternoon free. They could go to any of a dozen wonderful places, but they were already in one.

Seven of them—full to the craw of wonderful places—decided to go to Eretz.

"Children are attracted to the oddest and most shambling things," said the Mothers. "Why should they want to go to Eretz?"

"Let them go," said the Fathers. "Let them see—before they be gone—one of the few simple peoples left. We ourselves have become a contrived and compromised people. Let the Children be children for half a day."

Eretz was the Planet of the Offense, and therefore it was to be (perhaps it recently had been) the Planet of the Restitution also. But in no other way was it distinguished. The Children had received the tradition of Eretz as children receive all traditions—like lightning.

Hobble, Michael Goodgrind, Ralpha, Lonnie, Laurie, Bea and Joan they called themselves as they came down on Eretz—for these were their idea of Eretzi names. But they could have as many names as they wished in their games.

An anomalous intrusion of great heat and force! The rocks ran like water where they came down, and there was formed a scarp-pebble enclave.

It was all shanty country and shanty towns on Eretz—

clumsy hills, badly done plains and piedmonts, ragged fields, uncleansed rivers, whole weedpatches of provinces—not at all like Home. And the Towns! Firenze, Praha, Venezia, Londra, Colonia, Gant, Roma—why, they were nothing but towns made out of stone and wood! And these were the greatest of the towns of Eretz, not the meanest.

The Children exploded into action. Like children of the less transcendent races running wild on an ocean beach for an afternoon, they ran wild over continents. They scattered. And they took whatever forms first came into their minds.

Hobble—dark and smoldering like crippled Vulcan.

Michael Goodgrind—a broken-nosed bull of a man. How they all howled when he invented that first form!

Ralpha—like young Mercury.

And Lonnie—a tall giant with a golden beard.

Laurie was fire, Bea was light, Joan was moon-darkness.

But in these, or in any other forms they took, you'd always know that they were cousins or brethren.

Lonnie went pure Gothic. He had come onto it at the tail end of the thing and he fell in love with it.

"I am the Emperor!" he told the people like giant thunder. He pushed the Emperor Wenceslas off the throne and became Emperor.

"I am the true son of Charles, and you had thought me dead," he told the people. "I am Sigismund." Sigismund was really dead, but Lonnie became Sigismund and reigned, taking the wife and all the castles of Wenceslas. He grabbed off gangling old forts and mountain-rooks and raised howling Eretzi armies to make war. He made new castles. He loved the tall sweeping things and raised them to a new height. Have you never wondered that the last of those castles—in the late afternoon of the Gothic—were the tallest and oddest?

One day the deposed Wenceslas came back, and he was possessed of a new power.

"Now we will see who is the real Emperor!" the new Wenceslas cried like a rising storm.

They clashed their two forces and broke down each other's bridges and towns and stole the high ladies from each other's strongholds. They wrestled like boys. But they wrestled with a continent.

Lonnie (who was Sigismund) learned that the Wenceslas he battled was Michael Goodgrind wearing a contrived Emperor body. So they fought harder.

There came a new man out of an old royal line.

"I am Jobst," the new man cried. "I will show you two princelings who is the real Emperor!"

He fought the two of them with overwhelming verve. He raised fast-striking Eretzi armies, and used tricks that only a young Mercury would know. He was Ralpha, entering the game as the third Emperor. But the two combined against him and broke him at Constance.

They smashed Germany and France and Italy like a clutch of eggs. Never had there been such spirited conflict. The Eretzi were amazed by it all, but they were swept into it; it was the Eretzi who made up the armies.

Even today the Eretzi or Earthers haven't the details of it right in their histories. When the King of Aragon, for an example, mixed into it, they treated him as a separate person. They did not know that Michael Goodgrind was often the King of Aragon, just as Lonnie was often the Duke of Flanders. But, played for itself, the Emperor game would be quite a limited one. Too limited for the children.

The girls played their own roles. Laurie claimed to be thirteen different queens. She was consort of all three Emperors in every one of their guises, and she also dabbled with the Eretzi. She was the wanton of the group.

Bea liked the Grande Dame part and the Lady Bountiful bit. She was very good on Great Renunciations. In her different characters, she beat paths from thrones to nunneries and back again; and she is now known as five different saints. Every time you turn to the Common of the Mass of Holy Women who are Neither Virgins nor Martyrs, you are likely to meet her.

And Joan was the dreamer who may have enjoyed the Afternoon more than any of them.

Laurie made up a melodrama—Lucrezia Borgia and the Poison Ring. There is an advantage in doing these little melodramas on Eretzi. You can have as many characters as you wish—they come free. You can have them act as extravagantly as you desire—who is there to object to it? Lucrezia was very well done, as children's burlesques go, and the bodies were strewn from Napoli to Vienne. The Eretzi play with great eagerness any convincing part offered them, and they go to their deaths quite willingly if the part calls for it.

Lonnie made one up called The Pawn-Broker and the Pope. It was in the grand manner, all about the Medici family, and had some very funny episodes in the fourth act. Lonnie, who was vain of his acting ability, played Medici parts in five succeeding generations. The drama left more corpses than did the Lucrezia piece, but the killings weren't so sudden or showy; the girls had a better touch at the bloody stuff.

Ralpha did a Think Piece called One, Two, Three—Infinity. In its presentation he put all the rest of the Children to roast grandly in Hell; he filled up Purgatory with Eretzi-type people—the dullards; and for the Paradise he did a burlesque of Home. The Eretzi use a cropped version of Ralpha's piece and call it the Divine Comedy, leaving out a lot of fun.

Bea did a poetic one named the Witches' Bonfire. All the Children spent many a happy evening with that one, and they burnt twenty thousand witches. There was something satisfying about those Eretzi autumnal twilights with the scarlet sky and the frosty fields and the kine lowing in the meadows and the evening smell of witches burning. Bea's was really a pastoral piece.

All the Children ranged far except Hobble. Hobble (who was Vulcan) played with his sick toys. He played at Ateliers and Smithies, at Furnaces and Carousels. And often the other Children came and watched his work, and joined in for a while.

They played with the glass from the furnaces. They made goldtoned goblets, iridescent glass poems, figured spheres, goblin pitchers, glass music boxes, gargoyle heads, dragon chargers, princess salieras, figurines of lovers. So many things to make of glass! To make, and to smash when made!

But some of the things they exchanged as gifts instead of smashing them—glass birds and horses, fortune-telling globes that showed changing people and scenes within, tuned chiming balls that rang like bells, glass cats that sparkled when stroked, wolves and bears, witches that flew.

The Eretzi found some of these things that the Children discarded. They studied them and imitated them.

And again, in the interludes of their other games, the Children came back to Hobble's shops where he sometimes worked with looms. They made costumes of wool and linen and silk. They made trains and cloaks and mantles, all the things for their grand masquerades. They fabricated tapestries and rugs and wove in all sorts of scenes: vistas of Home and of Eretz, people and peacocks, fish and cranes, dingles and dromedaries, larks and lovers. They set their creations in the strange ragged scenery of Eretz and in the rich contrived gardens of Home. A spark went from the Children to their weaving so that none could tell where they left off and their creations began.

Then they left poor Hobble and went on to their more vital games.

There were seven of them (six, not counting the backward Hobble), but they seemed a thousand. They built themselves Castles in Spain and Gardes in Languedoc. The girls played always at Intrigue, for the high pleasure of it, and to give a causus for the wars. And the wars were the things that the boys seldom tired of. It is fun to play at armies with live warriors; and the Eretzi were live . . . in a sense.

The Eretzi had had wars and armies and sieges long before this, but they had been aimless things. Oh, this was one field where the Eretzi needed the Children. Consider the battles that the Children engineered that afternoon:

Gallipoli—how they managed the ships in that one! The Fathers could not have maneuvered more intricately in their four-dimension chess at Home.

Adrianople, Kunovitza, Dibra, Varna, Hexamilion! It's fun just to call out the bloody names of battles.

Constantinople! That was the one where they first used the big cannon. But who cast the big cannon for the Turks there? In their histories the Eretzi say that it was a man named Orban or Urban, and that he was Dacian, or he was Hungarian, or he was Danish. How many places did you tell them that you came from, Michael Goodgrind?

Belgrad, Trebizond, Morat, Blackheath, Napoli, Dornach!

Cupua and Taranto—Ralpha's armies beat Michael's at both of those.

Carignola—Lonnie foxed both Michael and Ralpha there, and nearly foxed himself. (You didn't intend it all that way, Lonnie. It was seven-cornered luck and you know it!)

Garigliano where the sea was red with blood and the ships were like broken twigs on the water!

Brescia! Ravenna! Who would have believed that such things could be done with a device known as Spanish infantry?

Villalar, Milan, Pavia! Best of all, the sack of Rome!

There were a dozen different games blended into that one.
The Eretzi discovered new emotions in themselves there—a
deeper depravity and a higher heroism.

Siege of Florence! That one called out the Children's
every trick. A wonderfully well played game!

Turin, San Quentin, Moncontour, Mookerhide!

Lepanto! The great sea-siege where the castled ships
broke asunder and the tall Turk Ochiali Pasha perished
with all his fleet and was drowned forever. But it wasn't
so forever as you might suppose, for he was Michael Goodgrind who had more bodies than one. The fish still remember Lepanto. Never had there been such feastings.

Alcazar-Quivar! That was the last of the excellent ones—
the end of the litany. The Children left off the game. They
remembered (but conveniently, and after they had worn out
the fun of it) that they were forbidden to play Warfare
with live soldiers. The Eretzi, left to themselves again, once
more conducted their battles as dull and uninspired affairs.

You can put it to a test, now, tonight. Study the conflicts
of the earlier times, of this high period, and of the time
that followed. You will see the difference. For a short two
or three centuries you will find really well contrived battles.
And before and after there is only ineptitude.

Often the Children played at Jealousies and raised up all
the black passions in themselves. They played at Immoralities, for there is an abiding evil in all children.

Maskings and water-carnivals and balls, and forever the
emotional intrigue!

Ralpha walked down a valley, playing a lute and wearing
the body of somebody else. He luted the birds out of the
trees and worked a charm on the whole countryside.

An old crone followed him and called, "Love me when
I'm old."

"Sempremai, tuttavia," sang Ralpha in Eretzi or Earthian.
"For Ever, For Always."

A small girl followed and called, "Love me when I'm young."

"Forever, for always," sang Ralpha.

The weirdest witch in the world followed him and called, "Love me when I'm ugly."

"For always, forever," sang Ralpha, and pulled her down on the grass. He knew that all the creatures had been Laurie playing Bodies.

But a peculiar thing happened: the prelude became more important than the play. Ralpha fell in love with his own song, and forgot Laurie who had inspired it. He made all manner of music and poem—aubade, madrigal, chanson; and he topped it off with one hundred sonnets. He made them in Eretzi words, Italy words, Languedoc words, and they were excellent. And the Eretzi still copy them.

Ralpha discovered there that poetry and songs are Passion Deferred. But Laurie would rather have deferred the song. She was long gone away and taking up with others before Ralpha finished singing his love for her, but he never noticed that she had left him. After Hobble, Ralpha was the most peculiar of them all.

In the meanwhile, Michael Goodgrind invented another game of Bodies. He made them of marble—an Eretzi limestone that cuts easily without faulting. And he painted them on canvas. He made the People of Home, and the Eretzi. He said that he would make angels.

"But you cannot make angels," said Joan.

"We know that," said Michael, "but do the Eretzi know that I cannot? I will make angels for the Eretzi."

He made them grotesque, like chicken men, like bird men, with an impossible duplication of humeral function. And the Children laughed at the carven jokes.

But Michael had sudden inspiration. He touched his creations up and added an element of nobility. So an iconography was born.

All the Children did it then, and they carried it into other mediums. They made the Eretzi, and they made themselves. You can still see their deep features on some of those statues, that family look that was on them no matter what faces they wore or copied.

Bronze is fun! Bronze horses are the best. Big bronze doors can be an orgy of delight, or bronze bells whose shape is their tone.

The Children went to larger things. They played at Realms and Constitutions, and Banks and Ships and Provinces. Then they came down to smaller things again and played at Books, for Hobble had just invented the printing thing.

Of them all, Hobble had the least imagination. He didn't range wide like the others. He didn't outrage the Eretzi. He spent all his time with his sick toys as though he were a child of much younger years.

The only new body he acquired was another one just like his own. Even this he didn't acquire as did the other Children theirs. He made it laboriously in his shop, and animated it. Hobble and the Hobble Creature worked together thereafter, and you could not tell them apart. One was as dull and laboring as the other.

The Eretzi had no effect whatsoever on the Children, but the Children had great effect on the Eretzi. The Children had the faculty of making whatever little things they needed or wanted, and the Eretzi began to copy them. In this manner the Eretzi came onto many tools, processes, devices and arts that they had never known before. Out of ten thousand, there were these:

The Astrolabe, Equatorium, Quadrant, Lathes and Traversing Tools, Ball-Bearings, Gudgeons, Gig-Mills, Barometers, Range-Finders, Cantilever Construction, Machine-Saws, Screw-Jacks, Hammer-Forges and Drop-Forges, Printing, Steel that was more than puddled Iron, Logarithms,

Hydraulic Rams, Screw-Dies, Spanner-Wrenches, Flux-Solder, Telescopes, Microscopes, Mortising Machines, Wire-Drawing, Stanches (Navigation-Locks), Gear Trains, Paper Making, Magnetic Compass and Wind-Rhumb, Portulan Charts and Projection Maps, Pinnule-Sights, Spirit-Levels, Fine Micrometers, Porcelain, Fire-Lock Guns, Music Notation and Music Printing, Complex Pulleys and Snatch-Blocks, the Seed-Drill, Playing Cards (the Children's masquerade faces may still be seen on them), Tobacco, the Violin, Whiskey, the Mechanical Clock.

They were forbidden, of course, to display any second-aspect powers or machines, as these would disrupt things. But they disrupted accidently in building, in tooling, in armies and navies, in harbors and canals, in towns and bridges, in ways of thinking and recording. They started a thing that couldn't be reversed. It was only the One Afternoon they were here, only two or three Eretzi Centuries, but they set a trend. They overwhelmed by the very number of their new devices, and it could never be simple on Eretz again.

There were many thousands of Eretz days and nights in that Long Afternoon. The Children had begun to tire of it, and the hour was growing late. For the last time they wandered off, this time all Seven of them together.

In the bodies of Kings and their Ladies, they strode down a High Road in the Levant. They were wondering what last thing they could contrive, when they found their way blocked by a Pilgrim with a staff.

"Let's tumble the hairy Eretzi," shouted Ralpha. "Let him not stand in the way of Kings!" For Ralpha was King of Bulgaria that day.

But they did *not* tumble the Pilgrim. That man knew how to handle his staff, and he laid the bunch of them low. It was nothing to him that they were the high people of the World who ordered Nations. He flogged them flat.

"Bleak Children!" that Pilgrim cried out as he beat them
into the ground. "Unfledged little oafs! Is it so that you
waste your Afternoon on Earth! I'll give you what your
Fathers forgot."

Seven-colored thunder, how he could use that staff! He
smashed the gaudy bodies of the Children and broke many
of their damnable bones. Did he know that it didn't matter?
Did he understand that the bodies they wore were only for
an antic?

"Lay off, old Father!" begged Michael Goodgrind, bleeding and half beaten into the earth. "Stay your bloody
bludgeon. You do not know who we are."

"I know you," maintained the Pilgrim mountainously.
"You are ignorant Children who have abused the Afternoon
given to you on Earth. You have marred and ruined and
warped everything you have touched."

"No, no," Ralpha protested—as he set in new bones for
his old damaged ones—"You do not understand. We have
advanced you a thousand of your years in one of our after-
noons. Consider the Centuries we have saved you! It's as
though we had increased your life by that thousand years."

"We have all the time there is," said the Pilgrim solidly.
"We were well and seriously along our road, and it was not
so crooked as the one you have brought us over. You have
broken our sequence with your meddling. You've set us
back more ways than you've advanced us. You've shattered
our Unity."

"Pigs have unity!" Joan shouted. "We've brought you
diversity. Think deep. Consider all the machines we have
showed you, the building and the technique. I can name
you a thousand things we've given you. You will never
be the same again."

"True. We will never be the same," said the Pilgrim.
"You may not be an unmixed curse. I'm a plain man and
I don't know. Surety is one of the things you've lost us.

But you befouled us. You played the game of Immoralities and taught it to us earthlings."

"You had it already," Laurie insisted. "We only brought elegance instead of piggishness to its practice." Immoralities was Laurie's own game, and she didn't like to hear it slighted.

"You have killed many thousands of us in your battles," said the Pilgrim. "You're a bitter fruit—sweet at the first taste only."

"You would yourselves have killed the same numbers in battles, and the battles wouldn't have been so good," said Michael. "Do you not realize that we are the higher race? We have roots of great antiquity."

"We have roots older than antiquity," averred the Pilgrim. "You are wicked Children without compassion."

"Compassion? For the Eretzi?" shouted Lonnie in disbelief.

"Do you have compassion for mice?" demanded Ralpha.

"Yes. I have compassion for mice," the Pilgrim said softly.

"I make a guess," Ralpha shot in shrewdly after they had all repaired their damaged bodies. "You travel as a Pilgrim, and Pilgrims sometimes come from very far away. You are not Eretzi. You are one of the Fathers from Home going in the guise of an Eretzi Pilgrim. You have this routine so that sometimes one of you comes to this world—and to every world—to see how it goes. You may have come to investigate an event said to have happened on Eretz a day ago."

Ralpha did not mean an Eretzi day ago, but a day ago at Home. The High Road they were on was in Coele-Syria not far from where the Event was thought to have happened, and Ralpha pursued his point:

"You are no Eretzi, or you would not dare to confront us, knowing what we are."

"You guess wrong in this and in everything," said the

Pilgrim. "I am of this Earth, earthly. And I will not be in-
timidated by a gangle of children of whatever species!
You're a weaker flesh than ourselves. You hide in other
bodies, and you get earthlings to do your slaughter. And
you cannot stand up to my staff!"

"Go home, you witless weanlings!" and he raised his
terrible staff again.

"Our time is nearly up. We will be gone soon," said Joan
softly.

The last game they played? They played Saints—for the
Evil they had done in playing Bodies wrongly, and in playing Wars with live soldiers. But they repented of the things
only after they had enjoyed them for the Long Afternoon.
They played Saints in hairshirt and ashes, and revived that
affair among the Eretzi.

And finally they all assembled and took off from the
high hill between Prato and Firenze in Italy. The rocks
flowed like water where they left, and now there would
be a double scarp formation.

They were gone, and that was the end of them here.

There is a theory, however, that one of the Hobbles remained and is with us yet. Hobble and his creature could
not be told apart and could not finally tell themselves apart.
They flipped an Eretzi coin, Emperors or Shields, to see
which one would go and which one would stay. One went
and one stayed. One is still here.

But, after all, Hobble was only concerned with the sick
toys, the mechanical things, the material inventions. Would
it have been better if Ralpha or Joan stayed with us? They'd
have burned us crisp by now! They were damnable and
irresponsible children.

This short Historical Monograph was not assembled
for a distraction or an amusement. We consider the evidence that Children have spent their short vacations here

more than once and in both hemispheres. We set out the theses in ordered parallels and we discover that we have begun to tremble unaccountably.

When last came such visitors here? What thing has beset us during the last long Eretzi lifetime?

We consider a new period—and it impinges on the Present—with aspects so different from anything that went before that we can only gasp aghast and gasp in sick wonder:

"Is it *ourselves* who behave so?

"Is it beings of another sort, or have we become those beings?

"Are we ourselves? Are these our deeds?"

There are great deep faces looking over our shoulder, there are cold voices of ancient Children jeering "Compassion? For Earthlings?", there is nasty frozen laughter that does not belong to our species.

MAN IN THE JAR

Damon Knight

Damon Knight is so well-known these days as a critic, editor, and anthologist—author of the Hugo-winning book of criticism, In Search of Wonder; *editor of the award-winning* Orbit *series and a score of other excellent anthologies—that it is sometimes forgotten that he is also one of the very finest short-story writers ever to work in the genre.*

Proof of that is the following sly and deceptively simple tale of intrigue and controntation on a far world; of a young alien boy who must somehow deal with that most dangerous of all dangerous creatures—the man who knows he is right.

○ THE HOTEL ROOM on the planet Meng was small and crowded. Blue-tinged sunlight from the window fell on a soiled gray carpet, a massive sandbox dotted with cigarette butts, a clutter of bottles. One corner of the room was piled high with baggage and curios. The occupant, a Mr. R. C. Vane of Earth, was sitting near the door: a man about fifty, clean shaven, with bristling iron-gray hair. He was quietly, murderously drunk.

There was a tap on the door and the bellhop slipped in— a native, tall and brown, with greenish black hair cut too long in the back. He looked about nineteen. He had one green eye and one blue.

"Set it there," said Vane.

The bellhop put his tray down. "Yes, sir." He took the unopened bottle of Ten Star off the tray, and the ice bucket, and the seltzer bottle, crowding them in carefully among the things already on the table. Then he put the empty bottles and ice bucket back on the tray. His hands were big and knob-jointed; he seemed too long and wide-shouldered for his tight green uniform.

"So this is Meng City," said Vane, watching the bellhop. Vane was sitting erect and unrumpled in his chair, with his striped moth-wing jacket on and his string tie tied. He might have been sober, except for the deliberate way he spoke, and the redness of his eyes.

"Yes, sir," said the bellhop, straightening up with the tray in his hands. "This your first time here, sir?"

"I came through two weeks ago," Vane told him. "I did not like it then, and I do not like it now. Also, I do not like this room."

"Management is sorry if you don't like the room, sir. Very good view from this room."

"It's dirty and small," said Vane, "but it doesn't matter. I'm checking out this afternoon. Leaving on the afternoon rocket. I wasted two weeks upcountry, investigating Marack

stories. Nothing to it—just native talk. Miserable little
planet." He sniffed, eyed the bellhop. "What's your name,
boy?"

"Jimmy Rocksha, sir."

"Well, Jimmy Rocks in the Head, look at that pile of
stuff." Tourist goods, scarves and tapestries, rugs, blankets
and other things were mounded over the piled suitcases. It
looked like an explosion in a curio shop. "There's about
forty pounds of it I have no room for, not counting that
knocked-down jar. Any suggestions?"

The bellhop thought about it slowly. "Sir, if I might sug-
gest, you might put the scarves and things inside the jar."

Vane said grudgingly, "That might work. You know how
to put those things together?"

"I don't know, sir."

"Well, let us see you try. Go on, don't stand there."

The bellhop set his tray down again and crossed the room.
A big bundle of gray pottery pieces, tied together with
twine, had been stowed on top of Vane's wardrobe trunk, a
little above the bellhop's head. Rocksha carefully removed
his shoes and climbed on a chair. His brown feet were bare
and clean. He lifted the bundle without effort, got down, set
the bundle on the floor, and put his shoes back on.

Vane took a long swallow of his lukewarm highball,
finishing it. He closed his eyes while he drank, and nodded
over the glass for a moment afterward, as if listening to
something inside him. "All right," he said, getting up, "let
us see."

The bellhop loosened the twine. There were six long,
thick, curving pieces, shaped a little like giant shoehorns.
Then there were two round ones. One was bigger; that was
the bottom. The other had a handle; that was the lid. The
bellhop began to separate the pieces carefully, laying them
out on the carpet.

"Watch out how you touch those together," Vane grunted,

coming up behind him. "I wouldn't know how to get them apart again."

"Yes, sir."

"That's an antique which I got upcountry. They used to be used for storing grain and oil. The natives claim the Maracks had the secret of making them stick the way they do. Ever heard that?"

"Upcountry boys tell a lot of fine stories, sir," said the bellhop. He had the six long pieces arranged, well separated, in a kind of petal pattern around the big flat piece. They took up most of the free space; the jar would be chest-high when it was assembled.

Standing up, the bellhop took two of the long curved pieces and carefully brought the sides closer together. They seemed to jump the last fraction of an inch, like magnets, and merged into one smooth piece. Peering, Vane could barely make out the join.

In the same way, the bellhop added another piece to the first two. Now he had half the jar assembled. Carefully he lowered this half jar toward the edge of the big flat piece. The pieces clicked together. The bellhop stooped for another side piece.

"Hold on a minute," said Vane suddenly. "Got an idea. Instead of putting that thing all together, then trying to stuff things into it, use your brain. Put the things in, *then* put the rest of the side on."

"Yes, sir," said the bellhop. He laid the piece of crockery down again and picked up some light blankets, which he dropped on the bottom of the jar.

"Not that way, dummy," said Vane impatiently. "Get *in* there—pack them down tight."

The bellhop hesitated. "Yes, sir." He stepped delicately over the remaining unassembled pieces and knelt on the bottom of the jar, rolling the blankets and pressing them snugly in.

Behind him, Vane moved on tiptoe like a dancer, putting two long pieces quietly together—*tic!*—then a third—*tic!*—and then as he lifted them, *tic, clack!* the sides merged into the bottom and the top. The jar was complete.

The bellhop was inside.

Vane breathed hard through flared nostrils. He took a cigar out of a green-lizard pocket case, cut it with a lapel knife, and lit it. Breathing smoke, he leaned over and looked down into the jar.

Except for a moan of surprise when the jar closed, the bellhop had not made a sound. Looking down, Vane saw his brown face looking up. "Let me out of this jar, please, sir," said the bellhop.

"Can't do that," said Vane. "They didn't tell me how, upcountry."

The bellhop moistened his lips. "Upcountry, they use a kind of tree grease," he said. "It creeps between the pieces, and they fall apart."

"They didn't give me anything like that," said Vane indifferently.

"Then please, sir, you break this jar and let me come out."

Vane picked a bit of tobacco off his tongue. He looked at it curiously and then flicked it away. "I spotted you," he said, "in the lobby the minute I came in this morning. Tall and thin. Too strong for a native. One green eye, one blue. Two weeks I spent, upcountry, looking; and there you were in the lobby."

"Sir—?"

"You're a Marack," said Vane flatly.

The bellhop did not answer for a moment. "But sir," he said incredulously, "Maracks are *legends,* sir. Nobody believes that anymore. There are no Maracks."

"You lifted that jar down like nothing," said Vane. "Two boys put it up there. You've got the hollow temples. You've got the long jaw and the hunched shoulders." Frowning, he took a billfold out of his pocket and took out a yellowed card. He showed it to the bellhop. "Look at that."

It was a faded photograph of a skeleton in a glass case. There was something disturbing about the skeleton. It was too long and thin; the shoulders seemed hunched, the skull was narrow and hollow-templed. Under it, the printing said, ABORIGINE OF NEW CLEVELAND, MENG (SIGMA LYRAE II) and in smaller letters, *Newbold Anthropological Museum, Ten Eyck, Queensland, N. T.*

"Found it between the pages of a book two hundred years old," said Vane, carefully putting it back. "It was mailed as a postcard to an ancestor of mine. A year later, I happened to be on Nova Terra. Now get this. The museum is still there, but that skeleton is not. They deny it ever was there. Curator seemed to think it was a fake. None of the native races on Meng have skeletons like that, he said."

"Must be a fake, sir," the bellhop agreed.

"I will tell you what I did next," Vane went on. "I read all the contemporary accounts I could find of frontier days on this planet. A couple of centuries ago, nobody on Meng thought the Maracks were legends. They looked enough like the natives to pass, but they had certain special powers. They could turn one thing into another. They could influence your mind by telepathy, if you weren't on your guard against them. I found this interesting. I next read all the export records back to a couple of centuries ago. Also, the geological charts in *Planetary Survey*. I discovered something. It just happens, there is no known source of natural diamonds anywhere on Meng."

"No, sir?" said the bellhop nervously.

"Not one. No diamonds, and no place where they ever could have been mined. But until two hundred years ago, Meng exported one billion stellors' worth of flawless diamonds every year. I ask, where did they come from? And why did they stop?"

"I don't know, sir."

"The Maracks made them," said Vane. "For a trader named Soong and his family. They died. After that, no more diamonds from Meng." He opened a suitcase, rummaged inside it a moment, and took out two objects. One was a narrow oval bundle of something wrapped in stiff yellow plant fibers; the other was a shiny gray-black lump half the size of his first.

"Do you know what this is?" Vane asked, holding up the oval bundle.

"No, sir."

"Air weed, they call it upcountry. One of the old men had this one buried under his hut, along with the jar. *And* this." He held up the black lump. "Nothing special about it, would you say? Just a piece of graphite, probably from the old mine at Badlong. But graphite is pure carbon. And so is a diamond."

He put both objects carefully down on the nearby table, and wiped his hands. The graphite had left black smudges on them. "Think about it," he said. "You've got exactly one hour, till three o'clock." Delicately he tapped his cigar over the mouth of the jar. A few flakes of powdery ash floated down on the bellhop's upturned face.

Vane went back to his chair. He moved deliberately and a little stiffly, but did not stagger. He peeled the foil off the bottle of Ten Star. He poured himself a substantial drink, added ice, splashed a little seltzer in. He took a long, slow swallow.

"Sir," said the bellhop finally, "you know I can't make any diamonds out of black rock. What's going to happen, when it comes three o'clock, and that rock is still just a piece of rock?"

"I think," said Vane, "I will just take the wrappings off that air weed and drop it in the jar with you. Air weed, I am told, will expand to hundreds of time its volume in air. When it fills the jar to the brim, I will put the lid on. And when we're crossing that causeway to the spaceport, I think you may get tipped off the packrat into the bay. The bottom is deep silt, they tell me." He took another long, unhurried swallow.

"Think about it," he said, staring at the jar with red eyes.

Inside the jar, it was cool and dim. The bellhop had enough room to sit fairly comfortably with his legs crossed, or else he could kneel, but then his face came right up to the mouth of the jar. The opening was too small for his head. He could not straighten up any farther, or put his legs out. The bellhop was sweating in his tight uniform. He was afraid. He was only nineteen, and nothing like this had ever happened to him before.

The clink of ice came from across the room. The bellhop said, "Sir?"

The chair springs whined, and after a moment the Earthman's face appeared over the mouth of the jar. His chin was dimpled. There were gray hairs in his nostrils, and a few gray and black bristles in the creases of loose skin around his jaw. His red eyes were hooded and small. He looked down into the bellhop's face without speaking.

"Sir," the bellhop said earnestly, "do you know how much they pay me here at this hotel?"

"No."

"Twelve stellors a week, sir, and my meals. If I could make diamonds, sir, why would I be working here?"

Vane's expression did not change. "I will tell you that," he said. "Soong must have been sweating you Maracks to get a billion stellors a year. There used to be thousands of you on this continent alone, but now there are so few that you can disappear among the natives. I would guess the diamonds took too much out of you. You're close to extinction now. And you're all scared. You've gone underground. You've still got your powers, but you don't dare use them— unless there's no other way to keep your secret. You were lords of this planet once, but you'd rather stay alive. Of course, all this is merely guesswork."

"Yes, sir," said the bellhop despairingly.

The house phone rang. Vane crossed the room and thumbed the key down, watching the bellhop from the corner of his eye. "Yes?"

"Mr. Vane," said the voice of the desk clerk, "if I may ask, did the refreshments you ordered arrive?"

"The bottle came," Vane answered. "Why?"

The bellhop was listening, balling his fists on his knees. Sweat stood out on his brown forehead.

"Oh nothing really, Mr. Vane," said the clerk's voice, "only the boy did not come back. He is usually very reliable, Mr. Vane. But excuse me for troubling you."

"All right," said Vane stonily, and turned the phone off. He came back to the jar. He swayed a little, rocking back and forth from heels to toes. In one hand he had the highball glass; with the other he was playing with the little osmiridium knife that hung by an expanding chain from his lapel. After a while he said, "Why didn't you call for help?"

The bellhop did not answer. Vane went on softly, "Those hotel phones will pick up a voice across the room, I know. So why were you so quiet?"

The bellhop said unhappily, "If I did yell, sir, they would find me in this jar."

"And so?"

The bellhop grimaced. "There's some other people that still believe in Maracks, sir. I have to be careful, with my eyes. They would know there could only be the one reason why you would treat me like this."

Vane studied him for a moment. "And you'd take a chance on the air weed, and the bay, just to keep anyone from finding out?"

"It's a long time since we had any Marack hunts on this planet, sir."

Vane snorted softly. He glanced up at the wall clock. "Forty minutes," he said, and went back to his chair by the door.

The bellhop said nothing. The room was silent except for the faint whir of the clock. After a while Vane moved to the writing desk. He put a printed customs declaration form in the machine and began tapping keys slowly, muttering over the complicated Interstellar symbols.

"Sir," said the bellhop quietly, "you know you can't kill a biped person and just get away. This is not like the bad old times."

Vane grunted, tapping keys. "Think not?" He took a sip from his highball and set it down again with a clink of ice.

"Even if they find out you have mistreated the headman upcountry, sir, they will be very severe."

"They won't find out," Vane said. "Not from him."

"Sir, even if I could make you your diamond, it would only be worth a few thousand stellors. That is nothing to a man like you."

Vane paused and half turned. "Flawless, that weight, it would be worth a hundred thousand. But I'm not going to sell it." He turned back to the machine, finished a line, and started another.

"No, sir?"

"No. I'm going to keep it." Vane's eyes half closed; his fingers poised motionless on the keys. He seemed to come to himself with a start, hit another key, and rolled the paper out of the machine. He picked up an envelope and rose, looking over the paper in his hand.

"Just to keep it, sir, and look at it now and then?" the bellhop asked softly. Sweat was running down into his eyes, but he kept his fists motionless on his knees.

"That's it," said Vane with the same faraway look. He folded the paper slowly and put it into the envelope as he walked toward the message chute near the door. At the last moment he checked himself, snapped the paper open again and stared at it. A slow flush came to his cheeks. Crumpling the paper slowly in his hands, he said, "That almost worked." He tore the paper across deliberately, and then again, and again, before he threw the pieces away.

"Just one symbol in the wrong box," he said, "but it was the right wrong symbol. I'll tell you where you made your mistake though, boy." He came closer.

"I don't understand," said the bellhop.

"You thought if you could get me to thinking about that diamond, my mind would wander. It did—but I knew what was happening. Here's where you made your mistake. I don't give a damn about that diamond."

"Sir?" said the bellhop in bewilderment.

"A stellor to you is a new pair of pants. A stellor to me, or a thousand stellors is just a poker chip. It's the game that counts. The excitement."

"Sir, I don't know what you mean."

Vane snorted. "You know, all right. You're getting a little dangerous now, aren't you? You're cornered, and the time's running out. So you took a little risk." He stooped, picked up one of the scraps of paper, unfolded it and smoothed it out. "Right here, in the box where the loyalty oath to the Archon is supposed to go, I wrote the symbol for 'pig.' If I sent that down, the thought police would be up here in fifteen minutes." He balled up the paper again, into an even smaller wad, and dropped it on the carpet. "Think you can make me forget to pick that up again and burn it, before I leave?" he said amiably. "Try."

The bellhop swallowed hard. "Sir, you did that *yourself.* You made a slip of the finger."

Vane smiled at him for the first time, and walked away.

The bellhop put his back against the wall of the jar and pushed with all his strength against the opposite side. He pushed until the muscles of his back stood out in knotted ropes. The pottery walls were as solid as rock.

He was sweating more than ever. He relaxed, breathing

hard; he rested his head on his knees and tried to think. The bellhop had heard of bad Earthmen before, but he had never seen one like this.

He straightened up. "Sir, are you still there?"

The chair creaked and Vane came over, glass in hand.

"Sir," said the bellhop earnestly, "if I can prove to you that I'm really not a Marack, will you let me go? I mean, you'll have to let me go then, won't you?"

"Why, certainly," said Vane agreeably. "Go ahead and prove it."

"Well, sir, haven't you heard other things about the Marack—some other test?"

Vane looked thoughtful; he put his chin down on his chest and his eyes filmed over.

"About what they can or can't do?" the bellhop suggested. "If I tell you, sir, you might think I made it up."

"Wait a minute," said Vane. He was swaying slightly, back and forth, his eyes half closed. His string tie was still perfectly tied, his striped moth-wing jacket immaculate. He said, "I remember something. The Marack hunters used this a good deal, I understand. Maracks can't stand liquor. It makes them sick."

"You're positive about that, sir?" the bellhop said eagerly.

"Of course I'm positive. It's like poison to a Marack."

"All right then, sir!"

Vane nodded, and went to the table to get the bottle of Ten Star. It was still two-thirds full. He came back with it and said, "Open your mouth."

The bellhop opened his mouth wide and shut his eyes. He did not like Earth liquor, especially brandy, but he thought he could drink it if it would get him out of this jar.

The liquor hit his teeth and the back of his mouth in one solid splash; it poured down both cheeks and some of it ran up his nose. The bellhop choked and strangled. The liquor burned all the way down his throat and windpipe; tears blinded him; he couldn't breathe. When the paroxysm was over, he gasped, "Sir—sir—that wasn't a fair test. You shouldn't have poured it on me like that. Give me a little bit, in a glass."

"Now, I want to be fair," said Vane. "We'll try it again." He found an empty glass, poured two fingers of brandy into it, and came back. "Easy does it," he said, and trickled a little into the bellhop's mouth.

The bellhop swallowed, his head swimming in brandy fumes. "Once more," said Vane, and poured again. The bellhop swallowed. The liquor was gathering in a ball of heat inside him. "Again." He swallowed.

Vane stood back. The bellhop opened his eyes and looked blissfully up at him. "You see, sir? No sickness. I drank it, and I'm not sick!"

"Hmm," said Vane with an interested expression. "Well, imagine that. Maracks *can* drink liquor."

The bellhop's victorious smile slowly faded. He looked incredulous. "Sir, don't joke with me," he said.

Vane sniffed. "If you think it's a joke—" he said with heavy humor.

"Sir, you *promised*."

"Oh, no. By no means," said Vane. "I said if you could prove to me that you are not a Marack. Go ahead, prove it. Here's another little test for you, incidentally. An anatomist I know looked at that skeleton and told me it was constricted at the shoulders. A Marack can't lift his hand higher than his head. So begin by telling me why you stood on a chair to get my bundle down—or better yet, just put your arm out the neck of that jar."

There was a silence. Vane took another cigar out of the green-lizard case, cut it with the little osmiridium knife, and lit it without taking his eyes off the bellhop. "Now you're getting dangerous again," he said. "You're thinking it over, down there. This begins to get interesting. You're wondering how you can kill me from inside that jar, without using your Marack powers. Go ahead. Think about it."

He breathed smoke, leaning toward the jar. "You've got fifteen minutes."

Working without haste, Vane rolled up all the blankets and other souvenirs and strapped them into bundles. He removed some toilet articles from the dresser and packed them away in his grip. He took a last look around the room, saw the paper scraps on the floor and picked up the tiny pellet he had made of one of them. He showed it to the bell-hop with a grin, then dropped it into the ash-receiver and burned it. He sat down comfortably in the chair near the door. "Five minutes," he said.

"Four minutes," he said.

"Three minutes.

"Two minutes."

"All right," said the bellhop.

"Yes?" Vane got up and stood over the jar.

"I'll do it—I'll make the diamond."

"Ahh?" said Vane, half questioningly. He picked up the lump of graphite and held it out.

"I don't need to touch it," the bellhop said listlessly. "Just put it down on the table. This will take about a minute."

"Umm," said Vane, watching him keenly. The bellhop was crouched in the jar, eyes closed; all Vane could see of him was the glossy green-black top of his head.

His voice was muffled. "If you just hadn't had that air weed," he said sullenly.

Vane snorted. "I didn't need the air weed. I could have taken care of you in a dozen ways. This knife"—he held it up—"has a molar steel blade. Cut through anything, like cheese. I could have minced you up and floated you down the drain."

The bellhop's face turned up, pale and wide-eyed.

"No time for that now, though," Vane said. "It would have to be the air weed."

"Is that how you're going to get me loose, afterward?" the bellhop asked. "Cut the jar, with that knife?"

"Mm? Oh, certainly," said Vane, watching the graphite lump. Was there a change in its appearance, or not?

"I'm disappointed, in a way," he said. "I thought you'd give me a fight. You Maracks are overrated, I suppose."

"It's all done," said the bellhop. "Take it, please, and let me out."

Vane's eyes narrowed. "It doesn't look done to me," he said.

"It just looks black on the outside, sir. Just rub it off."

Vane did not move.

"Go ahead, sir," said the bellhop urgently. "Pick it up and see."

"You're a little too eager," Vane said. He took a fountain pen out of his pocket and used it to prod the graphite gingerly. Nothing happened; the lump moved freely across the tabletop. Vane touched it briefly with one finger, then picked it up in his hand. "No tricks?" he said quizzically. He felt the lump, weighed it, put it down again. There were black graphite smears in his palm.

Vane opened his lapel knife and cut the graphite lump down the middle. It fell into two shiny black pieces. "Graphite," said Vane, and with an angry gesture he struck the knife blade into the table.

He turned to the bellhop, dusting off his hands. "I don't get you," he said, prodding the oval bundle of the air weed experimentally. He picked it up. "All you did was stall. You won't fight like a Marack, you won't give in like a Marack. All you'll do is die like a Meng-boy, right?" He shook his head. "Disappointing." The dry wrappings came apart in his hands. Between the fibers a dirty-white bulge began to show.

Vane lifted the package to drop it into the jar, and saw that the bellhop's scared face filled the opening. While he hesitated briefly, the gray-white floss of the air weed foamed slowly out over the back of his hand. Vane felt a constriction, and instinctively tried to drop the bundle. He couldn't. The growing, billowing floss was sticky—it stuck to his hand. Then his sleeve. It grew, slowly but with a horrifying steadiness.

Gray-faced, Vane whipped his arm around, trying to shake off the weed. Like thick lather, the floss spattered downward but did not separate. A glob of it hit his trouser leg and clung. Another, swelling, dripped down to the carpet. His whole right arm and side were covered deep under a mound of white. The floss had now stopped growing and seemed to be stiffening.

The bellhop began to rock himself back and forth inside the jar. The jar tipped, then fell back. The bellhop rocked harder. The jar was inching its way across the carpet.

After a few moments the bellhop paused to put his face up and see which way he was going. Vane, held fast by the weed, was leaning toward the table, straining hard, reaching with his one free hand toward the knife he had put there. The carpet bulged after him in a low mound, but too much furniture was holding it.

The bellhop lowered his head and rocked the jar again, harder. When he looked up, Vane's eyes were closed tight, his face red with effort. He was extended as far as he could reach across the table, but his fingers were still clawing air an inch short of the knife. The bellhop rocked hard. The jar inched forward, came to rest solidly against the table, pinning Vane's arm against it by the flaring sleeve.

The bellhop relaxed and looked up. Feeling himself caught, the Earthman had stopped struggling and was looking down. He tugged, but could not pull the sleeve free.

Neither spoke for a moment.

"Stalemate," said Vane heavily. He showed his teeth to the bellhop. "Close, but no prize. I can't get at you, and you can't hurt me."

The bellhop's head bowed as if in assent. After a moment his long arm came snaking up out of the jar. His fingers closed around the deadly little knife.

"A Marack *can* lift his arm higher than his head, sir," he said.

OLD HUNDREDTH

Brian W. Aldiss

"Old Hundredth" depicts a muted, autumnal future, full of echoes and old ghosts: an ancient and ruinous Earth from which humankind has forever departed, inherited now by dolphins and sloths and mutated baluchitheriums; a strange world of Involutes and Impures and musicolumns, with Venus for a moon, and hogs as big as hippos; a world of stately, living music under dusty umbrella trees.

Hugo- and Nebula-winner Brian W. Aldiss has gained an international reputation as a novelist, editor, and critic, and "Old Hundredth" is Aldiss at his most vivid and evocative.

○ THE ROAD climbed dustily down between trees as sym-
metrical as umbrellas. Its length was punctuated at one
point by a musicolumn standing on the sandy verge.
From a distance, the column was only a faint stain in the
air. As sentient creatures neared it, their psyches activated it, it drew on their vitalities, and then it could be
heard as well as seen. Their presence made it flower into
pleasant noise, instrumental or chant.

All this region was called Ghinomon, for nobody lived
here any more, not even the odd hermit Impure. It was
given over to grass and the weight of time. Only a few
wild goats activated the musicolumn nowadays, or a scamp-
ering vole wrung a brief chord from it in passing.

When old Dandi Lashadusa came riding down that dusty
road on her baluchitherium, the column began to intone. It
was just an indigo trace on the air, hardly visible, for it
represented only a bonded pattern of music locked into the
fabric of that particular area of space. It was also a transub-
stantio-spatial shrine, the eternal part of a being that had
dematerialized itself into music.

The baluchitherium whinnied, lowered its head, and
sneezed onto the gritty road.

"Gently, Lass," Dandi told her mare, savouring the
growth of the chords that increased in volume as she approached. Her long nose twitched with pleasure as if she
could feel the melody along her olfactory nerves.

Obediently, the baluchitherium slowed, turning aside
to crop fern, although it kept an eye on the indigo stain. It
liked things to have being or not to have being; these half-
and-half objects disturbed it, though they could not impair
its immense appetite.

Dandi climbed down her ladder onto the ground, glad
to feel the ancient dust under her feet. She smoothed her
hair and stretched as she listened to the music.

She spoke aloud to her mentor, half the world away,
but he was not listening. His mind closed to her thoughts,

he muttered an obscure exposition that darkened what it sought to clarify.

". . . useless to deny that it is well-nigh impossible to improve anything, however faulty, that has so much tradition behind it. And the origins of your bit of metricism are indeed embedded in such a fearful antiquity that we must needs—"

"Tush, Mentor, come out of your black box and forget your hatred of my 'metricism' a moment," Dandi Lashadusa said, cutting her thought into his. "Listen to the bit of 'metricism' I've found here, look at where I have come to, let your argument rest."

She turned her eyes about, scanning the tawny rocks near at hand, the brown line of the road, the distant black and white magnificence of ancient Oldorajo's town, doing this all for him, tiresome old fellow. Her mentor was blind, never left his cell in Peterbroe to go farther than the sandy courtyard, hadn't physically left that green cathedral pile for over a century. Womanlike, she thought he needed change. Soul, how he rambled on! Even now, he was managing to ignore her and refute her.

". . . for consider, Lashadusa woman, nobody can be found to father it. Nobody wrought or thought it, phrases of it merely *came* together. Even the old nations of men could not own it. None of them knew who composed it. An element here from a Spanish pavan, an influence there of a French psalm tune, a flavour here of early English carol, a savour there of later German chorals. Nor are the faults of your bit of metricism confined to bastardy. . . ."

"Stay in your black box then, if you won't see or listen," Dandi said. She could not get into his mind; it was the Mentor's privilege to lodge in her mind, and in the minds of those few other wards he had, scattered round Earth. Only the mentors had the power of being in another's mind—which made them rather tiring on occasions like this, they would not get out of it. For over seventy years,

Dandi's mentor had been persuading her to die into a dirge of his choosing (and composing). Let her die, yes, let her transubstantio-spatialize herself a thousand times! His quarrel was not with her decision but her taste, which he considered execrable.

Leaving the baluchitherium to crop, Dandi walked away from the musicolumn towards a hillock. Still fed by her steed's psyche, the column continued to play. Its music was of a simplicity, with a dominant-tonic recurrent bass part suggesting pessimism. To Dandi, a savant in musicolumnology, it yielded other data. She could tell to within a few years when its founder had died and also what kind of creature, generally speaking, he had been.

Climbing the hillock, Dandi looked about. To the south where the road led were low hills, lilac in the poor light. There lay her home. At last she was returning, after wanderings covering half a century and most of the globe.

Apart from the blind beauty of Oldorajo's town lying to the west, there was only one landmark she recognized. That was the Involute. It seemed to hang iridal above the ground a few leagues on; just to look on it made her feel she must at once get nearer.

Before summoning the baluchitherium, Dandi listened once more to the sounds of the musicolumn, making sure she had them fixed in her head. The pity was her old fool wise man would not share it. She could still feel his sulks floating like sediment through his mind.

"Are you listening now, Mentor?"

"Eh? An interesting point is that back in 1556 by the old pre-Involutary calendar your same little tune may be discovered lurking in Knox's Anglo-Genevan Psalter, where it espoused the cause of the third psalm—"

"You dreary old fish! Wake yourself! How can you criticize my intended way of dying when you have such a fustian way of living?"

This time he heard her words. So close did he seem

that his peevish pinching at the bridge of his snuffy old
nose tickled hers too.

"What are you doing *now,* Dandi?" he inquired.

"If you had been listening, you'd know. Here's where
I am, on the last Ghinomon plain before Crotheria and
home." She swept the landscape again and he took it in,
drank it almost greedily. Many mentors went blind early
in life shut in their monastic underwater dens; their most
effective visions were conducted through the eyes of their
wards.

His view of what she saw enriched hers. He knew the
history, the myth behind this forsaken land. He could
stock the tired old landscape with pageantry, delighting
her and surprising her. Back and forward he went, flicking
her pictures; the Youdicans, the Lombards, the Ex-Europa
Emissary, the Grites, the Risorgimento, the Involuters—and
catch-words, costumes, customs, courtesans, pelted briefly
through Dandi Lashadusa's mind. Ah, she thought admir-
ingly, who could truly live without these priestly, beastly,
erudite, erratic mentors?

"Erratic?" he inquired, snatching at her lick of thought.
"A thousand years I live, for all that time to absent myself
from the world, to eat mashed fish here with my brothers,
learning history, studying *rapport,* sleeping with my bones
on stones—a humble being, a being in a million, a mentor
in a myriad, and your standards of judgment are so mun-
dane you find no stronger label for me than erratic? Fie,
Lashadusa, bother me no more for fifty years!"

The words nattered and squeaked in her head as if she
spoke herself. She felt his old chops work phantom-like
in hers, and half in anger half in laughter called aloud, "I'll
be dead by then!"

He snicked back hot and holy to reply, "And another
thing about your footloose swan song—in Marot and Beza's
Genevan Psalter of 1551, Old Time, it was musical mid-

wife to the one hundred and thirty-fourth psalm. Like you,
it never seemed to settle!" Then he was gone.

"Pooh!" Dandi said. She whistled Lass.

Obediently the great rhino-like creature, eighteen feet
high at the shoulder, ambled over. The musicolumn died
as the mare left it, faded, sank to a whisper, silenced: only
the purple stain remained, noiseless, in the lonely air. Lass
reached Dandi. Lowering its great Oligocene head, it nuzzled its mistress's hand. She climbed the ladder on to that
ridged plateau of back.

They made contentedly towards the Involute, lulled by
the simple and intricate feeling of being alive.

Night was settling in now, steady as snow. Hidden behind banks of mist, the sun prepared to set. But Venus was
high, a gallant half-crescent four times as big as the Moon
had been before the Moon, spiralling farther and farther
from Earth, had shaken off its parent's clutch to go dance
round the sun, a second Mercury. Even by that time Venus
had been moved by gravito-traction into Earth's orbit, so
that the two sister worlds circled each other as they circled
the sun.

The stamp of that great event still lay everywhere, its
tokens not only in the crescent in the sky. For Venus put
a strange spell on the hearts of man, and a more penetrating displacement in his genes. Even when its atmosphere
was transformed into a muffled breathability, it remained
an alien world; against logic, its opportunities, its possibili-
ties, were its own. It shaped men, just as Earth had shaped
them. On Venus, men bred themselves anew.

And they bred the so-called Impures. They bred new
plants, new fruits, new creatures—original ones, and dupli-
cations of creatures not seen on Earth for aeons past. From
one line of these familiar strangers Dandi's baluchitherium
was descended. So, for that matter, was Dandi.

The huge creature came now to the Involute, or as

near as it cared to get. Again it began to crop at thistles, thrusting its nose through dewy spiders' webs and ground mist.

"Like you, I'm a vegetarian," Dandi said, climbing down to the ground. A grove of low fruit trees grew nearby; she reached up into the branches, gathered and ate, before turning to inspect the Involute. Already her spine tingled at the nearness of it; awe, loathing and love made a part-pleasant sensation near her heart.

The Involute was not beautiful. True, its colours changed with the changing light, yet the colours were fish-cold, for they belonged to another universe. Though they reacted to dusk and dawn, Earth had no stronger power over them. They pricked the eyes. Perhaps too they were painful because they were the last signs of materialist man. Even Lass moved uneasily before that ill-defined lattice, the upper limits of which were lost in thickening gloom.

"Don't fear," Dandi said. "There's an explanation for this, old girl." She added sadly, "There's an explanation for everything, if we can find it."

She could feel all the personalities in the Involute. It was a frozen screen of personality. All over the old planet the structures stood, to shed their awe on those who were left behind. They were the essence of man. They were man—all that remained of him.

When the first flint, the first shell, was shaped into a weapon, that action shaped man. As he moulded and complicated his tools, so they moulded and complicated him. He became the first scientific animal. And at last, via information theory and great computers, he gained knowledge of all his parts. He formed the Laws of Intergration, which reveal all beings as part of a pattern and show them their part in the pattern. There is only the pattern, the pattern is all the universe, creator and created. For the first time, it became possible to duplicate that pattern artificially; the transubstantio-spatializers were built.

All mankind left their strange hobbies on Earth and Venus and projected themselves into the pattern. Their entire personalities were merged with the texture of space itself. Through science, they reached immortality.

It was a one-way passage.

They did not return. Each Involute carried thousands or even millions of people. There they were, not dead, not living. How they exulted or wept in their transubstantiation, nobody left could say. Only this could be said: man had gone, and a great emptiness was fallen over the Earth.

"Your thoughts are heavy, Dandi Lashadusa. Get you home." Her mentor was back in her mind. She caught the feeling of his moving round and round in his coral-formed cell.

"I must think of man," she said.

"Your thoughts mean nothing, do nothing."

"Man created us; I want to consider him in peace."

"He only shaped a stream of life that was always entirely out of his control. Forget him. Get on to your mare and ride home."

"Mentor—"

"Get home, woman. Moping does not become you. I want to hear no more of your swan song, for I've given you my final word on that. Use a theme of your own, not of man's. I've said it a million times and I say it again."

"I wasn't going to mention my music. I was only going to tell you that. . . ."

"What then?" His thought was querulous. She felt his powerful tail tremble, disturbing the quiet water of his cell.

"I don't know. . . ."

"Get home then."

"I'm lonely."

He shot her a picture from another of his wards before leaving her. Dandi had seen this ward before in similar dreamlike glimpses. It was a huge mole creature, still boring underground as it had been for the last twenty years. Occasionally it crawled through vast caves; once it swam in a subterranean lake; most of the while it just bored through rock. Its motivations were obscure to Dandi, although her mentor referred to it as "a geologer." Doubtless if the mole was vouchsafed occasional glimpses of Dandi and her musicolumnology, it would find her as baffling. At least the mentor's point was made: loneliness was psychological, not statistical.

Why, a million personalities glittered almost before her eyes!

She mounted the great baluchitherium mare and headed for home. Time and old monuments made glum company.

Twilight now, with just one streak of antique gold left in the sky, Venus sweetly bright, and stars peppering the purple. A fine night for being alive on, particularly with one's last bedtime close at hand.

And yes, for all her mentor said, she was going to turn into that old little piece derived from one of the tunes in the 1540 *Souter Liedekens,* that splendid source of Netherlands folk music. For a moment, Dandi Lashadusa chuckled almost as eruditely as her mentor. The sixteenth-century Old Time, with the virtual death of plainsong and virtual birth of the violin, was most interesting to her. Ah, the richness of facts, the texture of man's brief history! Pure joy! Then she remembered herself.

After all, she was only a megatherium, a sloth as big as an elephant, whose kind had been extinct for millions of years until man reconstituted a few of them in the Venusian experiments. Her modifications in the way of fingers and enlarged brain gave her no real qualifications to think up to man's level.

Early next morning, they arrived at the ramparts of the town Crotheria where Dandi lived. The ubiquitous goats thronged about them, some no bigger than hedgehogs, some almost as big as hippos—what madness in his last days provoked man to so many variations on one undistinguished caprine theme?—as Lass and her mistress moved up the last slope and under the archway.

It was good to be back, to push among the trails fringed with bracken, among the palms, oaks, and tree ferns. Almost all the town was deeply green and private from the sun, curtained by swathes of Spanish moss. Here and there were houses—caves, pits, crude piles of boulders or even genuine man-type buildings, grand in ruin. Dandi climbed down, walking ahead of her mount, her long hair curling in pleasure. The air was cool with the coo of doves or the occasional bleat of a merino.

As she explored familiar ways, though, disappointment overcame her. Her friends were all away, even the dreamy bison whose wallow lay at the corner of the street in which Dandi lived. Only pure animals were here, rooting happily and mindlessly in the lanes, beggars who owned the Earth. The Impures—descendants of the Venusian experimental stock—were all absent from Crotheria.

That was understandable. For obvious reasons, man had increased the abilities of herbivores rather than carnivores. After the Involution, with man gone, these Impures had taken to his towns as they took to his ways, as far as this was possible to their natures. Both Dandi and Lass, and many of the others, consumed massive amounts of vegetable matter every day. Gradually a wider and wider circle of desolation grew about each town (the greenery in the town itself was sacrosanct), forcing a semi-nomadic life on to its vegetarian inhabitants.

This thinning in its turn led to a decline in the birth rate. The travellers grew fewer, the towns greener and emptier; in time they had become little oases of forest studding the grassless plains.

"Rest here, Lass," Dandi said at last, pausing by a bank

of brightly flowering cycads. "I'm going into my house."

A giant beech grew before the stone facade of her home, so close that it was hard to determine whether it did not help support the ancient building. A crumbling balcony jutted from the first floor. Reaching up, Dandi seized the balustrade and hauled herself on to the balcony.

This was her normal way of entering her home, for the ground floor was taken over by goats and hogs, just as the second floor had been appropriated by doves and parakeets. Trampling over the greenery self-sown on the balcony, she moved into the front room. Dandi smiled. Here were her old things, the broken furniture on which she liked to sleep, the vision screens on which nothing could be seen, the heavy manuscript books in which, guided by her know-all mentor, she wrote down the outpourings of the musicolumns she had visited all over the world.

She ambled through to the next room.

She paused, her peace of mind suddenly shattered by danger.

A brown bear stood there. One of its heavy hands was clenched over the hilt of a knife.

"I am no vulgar thief," it said, curling its thick black lips over the syllables. "I am an archaeologer. If this is your place, you must grant me permission to remove the man things. Obviously you have no idea of the worth of some of the equipment here. We bears require it. We must have it."

It came towards her, panting doggy fashion with its jaw open. From under bristling eyebrows gleamed the lust to kill.

Dandi was frightened. Peaceful by nature, she feared the bears above all creatures for their fierceness and their ability to organize. The bears were few: they were the only creatures to show signs of wishing to emulate man's old aggressiveness.

She knew what the bears did. They hurled themselves

through the Involutes to increase their power; by penetrating those patterns, they nourished their psychic drive, so the Mentor said. It was forbidden. They were transgressors. They were killers.

"Mentor!" she screamed.

The bear hesitated. As far as he was concerned, the hulking creature before him was merely an obstacle in the way of progress, something to be thrust aside without hate. Killing would be pleasant but irrelevant; more important items remained to be done. Much of the equipment housed here could be used in the rebuilding of the world, the world of which bears had such high haphazard dreams. Holding the knife threateningly, he moved forward.

The Mentor was in Dandi's head, answering her cry, seeing through her eyes, though he had no sight of his own. He scanned the bear and took over her mind instantly, knifing himself into place like a guillotine.

No longer was he a blind old dolphin lurking in one cell of a cathedral pile of coral under tropical seas, a theologer, an inculcator of wisdom into feebler-minded beings. He was a killer more savage than the bear, keen to kill anything that might covet the vacant throne once held by men. The mere thought of men could send this mentor into shark-like fury at times.

Caught up in his fury, Dandi found herself advancing. For all the bear's strength, she could vanquish it. In the open, where she could have brought her heavy tail into action, it would have been an easy matter. Here, her weighty forearms must come into play. She felt them lift to her mentor's command as he planned for her to clout the bear to death.

The bear stepped back, awed by an opponent twice its size, suddenly unsure.

She advanced.

"No! Stop!" Dandi cried.

Instead of fighting the bear, she fought her mentor,

hating his hate. Her mind twisted, her dim mind full of that steely fishy one, as she blocked his resolution.

"I'm for peace!" she cried.

"Then kill the bear!"

"I'm for peace, not killing!"

She rocked back and forth. When she staggered into a wall, it shook; dust spread in the old room. The Mentor's fury was terrible to feel.

"Get out quickly!" Dandi called to the bear.

Hesitating, it stared at her. Then it turned and made for the window. For a moment it hung with its shaggy shabby hindquarters in the room. Momentarily she saw it for what it was, an old animal in an old world, without direction. It jumped. It was gone. Goats blared confusion on its retreat.

"Bitch!" screamed the Mentor. Insane with frustration, he hurled Dandi against the doorway with all the force of his mind.

Wood cracked and splintered. The lintel came crashing down. Brick and stone shifted, grumbled, fell. Powdered filth billowed up. With a great roar, one wall collapsed. Dandi struggled to get free. Her house was tumbling about her. It had never been intended to carry so much weight, so many centuries.

She reached the balcony and jumped clumsily to safety, just as the building avalanched in on itself, sending a great cloud of plaster and powdered mortar into the overhanging trees.

For a horribly long while the world was full of dust, goat bleats, and panic-stricken parakeets.

Heavily astride her baluchitherium once more, Dandi Lashadusa headed back to the empty region called Ghinomon. She fought her bitterness, trying to urge herself towards resignation.

All she had was destroyed—not that she set store by

possessions: that was a man trait. Much more terrible was the knowledge that her mentor had left her forever; she had transgressed too badly to be forgiven this time.

Suddenly she was lonely for his persnickety voice in her head, for the wisdom he fed her, for the scraps of dead knowledge he tossed her—yes, even for the love he gave her. She had never seen him, never could: yet no two beings could have been more intimate.

She missed too those other wards of his she would glimpse no more: the mole creature tunnelling in Earth's depths, the seal family that barked with laughter on a desolate coast, a senile gorilla that endlessly collected and classified spiders, and aurochs—seen only once, but then unforgettably—that lived with smaller creatures in an Arctic city it had helped build in the ice.

She was excommunicated.

Well, it was time for her to change, to disintegrate, to transubstantiate into a pattern not of flesh but music. That discipline at least the Mentor had taught and could not take away.

"This will do, Lass," she said.

Her gigantic mount stopped obediently. Lovingly she patted its neck. It was young; it would be free.

Following the dusty trail, she went ahead, alone. Somewhere far off one bird called. Coming to a mound of boulders, Dandi squatted among gorse, the points of which could not prick through her thick old coat.

Already her selected music poured through her head, already it seemed to loosen the chemical bonds of her being.

Why should she not choose an old human tune? She was an antiquarian. Things that were gone solaced her for things that were to come.

In her dim way, she had always stood out against her mentor's absolute hatred of men. The thing to hate was hatred. Men in their finer moments had risen above hate. Her death psalm was an instance of that—a multiple

instance, for it had been fingered and changed over the
ages, as the Mentor himself insisted, by men of a variety
of races, all with their minds directed to worship rather
than hate.

Locking herself into thought disciplines, Dandi began
to dissolve. Man had needed machines to help him to do
it, to fit into the Involutes. She was a lesser animal: she
could unbutton herself into the humbler shape of a musicolumn. It was just a matter of *rearranging*—and without
pain she formed into a pattern that was not a shaggy megatherium body . . . but an indigo column, hardly visible. . . .

Lass for a long while cropped thistle and cacti. Then
she ambled forward to seek the hairy creature she fondly
—and a little condescendingly—regarded as her equal. But
of the sloth there was no sign.

Almost the only landmark was a faint violet-blue dye
in the air. As the baluchitherium mare approached, a sweet
old music grew in volume from the dye. It was a music
almost as old as the landscape itself and certainly as much
travelled, a tune once known to men as The Old Hundredth.
And there were voices singing: "All creatures that on Earth
do dwell. . . ."

THE SIGNALLER

Keith Roberts

Keith Roberts, author of Pavane *and* The Chalk Giants, *is generally recognized as the best of that crop of new British SF writers who sprouted up during the last half of the sixties. Although he has already been compared to authors as diverse as Heinlein and Kipling and Aldiss, he indomitably manages to remain his own man, producing stories that vary widely in mood, style, and content—in everything, in fact, except quality.*

In "The Signaller" he takes us sideways in time to an alternate England where Queen Elizabeth was cut down by an assassin's bullet, and England itself fell to the Spanish Armada—a twentieth-century England where the deep shadow of the Church Militant stretches across a still-medieval land of forests and castles and little huddled towns; an England where travelers in the bleak winter forests or on the desolate, windswept expanses of the heath must fear wolves and brigands and routiers; *an England where it is yet possible to encounter specters of a darker and more elemental kind.*

⊙ ON EITHER SIDE of the knoll the land stretched in long, speckled sweeps, paling in the frost smoke until the outlines of distant hills blended with the curdled milk of the sky. Across the waste a bitter wind moaned, steady and chill, driving before it quick flurries of snow. The snow squalls flickered and vanished like ghosts, the only moving things in a vista of emptiness.

What trees there were grew in clusters, little coppices that leaned with the wind, their twigs meshed together as if for protection, their outlines sculpted into the smooth, blunt shapes of ploughshares. One such copse crowned the summit of the knoll; under the first of its branches, and sheltered by them from the wind, a boy lay face down in the snow. He was motionless but not wholly unconscious; from time to time his body quivered with spasms of shock. He was maybe sixteen or seventeen, blond-haired, and dressed from head to feet in a uniform of dark green leather. The uniform was slit in many places; from the shoulders down the back to the waist, across the hips and thighs. Through the rents could be seen the cream-brown of his skin and the brilliant slow twinkling of blood. The leather was soaked with it, and the long hair matted. Beside the boy lay the case of a pair of binoculars, the Zeiss lenses without which no man or apprentice of the Guild of Signallers ever moved, and a dagger. The blade of the weapon was red-stained; its pommel rested a few inches beyond his outflung right hand. The hand itself was injured, slashed across the backs of the fingers and deeply through the base of the thumb. Round it blood had diffused in a thin pink halo into the snow.

A heavier gust rattled the branches overhead, raised from somewhere a long creak of protest. The boy shivered again and began, with infinite slowness, to move. The outstretched hand crept forward, an inch at a time, to take his weight beneath his chest. The fingers traced an arc in the snow, its ridges red-tipped. He made a noise halfway between a grunt and a moan, levered himself onto his elbows, waited gathering strength. Threshed, half turned over, leaned on the undamaged left hand. He hung his head, eyes closed; his heavy breathing sounded through the copse. Another heave, a convulsive effort, and he was sitting upright, propped against the trunk of a tree. Snow stung his face, bringing back a little more awareness.

He opened his eyes. They were terrified and wild, glazed with pain. He looked up into the tree, swallowed, tried to lick his mouth, turned his head to stare at the empty snow round him. His left hand clutched his stomach; his right was crossed over it, wrist pressing, injured palm held clear of contact. He shut his eyes again briefly; then he made his hand go down, grip, lift the wet leather away from his thigh. He fell back, started to sob harshly at what he had seen. His hand, dropping slack, brushed tree bark. A snag probed the open wound below the thumb; the disgusting surge of pain brought him round again.

From where he lay the knife was out of reach. He leaned forward ponderously, wanting not to move, just stay quiet and be dead, quickly. His fingers touched the blade; he worked his way back to the tree, made himself sit up again. He rested, gasping; then he slipped his left hand under his knee, drew upward till the half-paralysed leg was crooked. Concentrating, steering the knife with both hands, he placed the tip of its blade against his trews, forced down slowly to the ankle cutting the garment apart. Then round behind his thigh till the piece of leather came clear.

He was very weak now; it seemed he could feel the strength ebbing out of him, faintness flickered in front of his eyes like the movements of a black wing. He pulled the leather toward him, got its edge between his teeth, gripped, and began to cut the material into strips. It was slow, clumsy work; he gashed himself twice, not feeling the extra pain. He finished at last and began to knot the strips round his leg, trying to tighten them enough to close the long wounds in the thigh. The wind howled steadily; there was no other sound but the quick panting of his breath. His face, beaded with sweat, was nearly as white as the sky.

He did all he could for himself, finally. His back was a bright torment, and behind him the bark of the tree was streaked with red, but he couldn't reach the lacerations there. He made his fingers tie the last of the knots, shuddered at the blood still weeping through the strappings. He dropped the knife and tried to get up.

After minutes of heaving and grunting his legs still refused to take his weight. He reached up painfully, fingers exploring the rough bole of the tree. Two feet above his head they touched the low, snapped-off stump of a branch. The hand was soapy with blood; it slipped, skidded off, groped back. He pulled, feeling the tingling as the gashes in the palm closed and opened. His arms and shoulders were strong, ribboned with muscle from hours spent at the semaphores; he hung tensed for a moment, head thrust back against the trunk, body arced and quivering; then his heel found a purchase in the snow, pushed him upright.

He stood swaying, not noticing the wind, seeing the blackness surge round him and ebb back. His head was pounding now, in time with the pulsing of his blood. He felt fresh warmth trickling on stomach and thighs, and the rise of a deadly sickness. He turned away, head bent, and started to walk, moving with the slow ponderousness of a diver. Six paces off he stopped, still swaying, edged round clumsily. The binocular case lay on the snow where it had fallen. He went back awkwardly, each step requiring now a separate effort of his brain, a bunching of the will to force the body to obey. He knew foggily that he daren't stoop for the case; if he tried he would fall headlong, and likely never move again. He worked his foot into the loop of the shoulder strap. It was the best he could do; the leather tightened as he moved, riding up round his instep. The case bumped along behind him as he headed down the hill away from the trees.

He could no longer lift his eyes. He saw a circle of snow, six feet or so across, black-fringed at its edges from his impaired vision. The snow moved as he walked, jerking toward him, falling away behind. Across it ran a line of faint impressions, footprints he himself had made. The boy followed them blindly. Some spark buried at the back of his brain kept him moving; the rest of his consciousness was gone now, numbed with shock. He moved draggingly, the leather case jerking and slithering behind his heel. With his left hand he held himself, low down over the groin; his right waved slowly, keeping his precarious balance. He left behind him a thin trail of blood spots; each drop splashed pimpernel-bright against the snow, faded and spread to a wider pink stain before freezing itself into the crystals. The blood marks and the footprints reached back in a ragged line to the copse. In front of him the wind skirled across the land; the snow whipped at his face, clung thinly to his jerkin.

Slowly, with endless pain, the moving speck separated itself from the trees. They loomed behind it, seeming through some trick of the fading light to increase in height as they receded. As the wind chilled the boy the pain ebbed fractionally; he raised his head, saw before him the tower of a semaphore station topping its low cabin. The station stood on a slight eminence of rising ground; his body felt the drag of the slope, reacted with a gale of breathing. He trudged slower. He was crying again now with little whimperings, meaningless animal noises, and a sheen of saliva showed on his chin. When he reached the cabin the copse was still visible behind him, grey against the sky. He leaned against the plank door gulping, seeing faintly the texture of the wood. His hand fumbled for the lanyard of the catch, pulled; the door opened, plunging him forward onto his knees.

After the snow light outside, the interior of the hut was dark. The boy worked his way on all fours across the board floor. There was a cupboard; he searched it blindly, sweeping glasses and cups aside, dimly hearing them shatter. He found what he needed, drew the cork from the bottle with his teeth, slumped against the wall and attempted to drink. The spirit ran down his chin, spilled across chest and belly. Enough went down his throat to wake him momentarily. He coughed and tried to vomit. He pulled himself to his feet, found a knife to replace the one he'd dropped. A wooden chest by the wall held blankets and bed linen; he pulled a sheet free and haggled it into strips, longer and broader this time, to wrap round his thigh. He couldn't bring himself to touch the leather tourniquets. The white cloth marked through instantly with blood; the patches elongated, joined and began to glisten. The rest of the sheet he made into a pad to hold against his groin.

The nausea came again; he retched, lost his balance and sprawled on the floor. Above his eye level, his bunk loomed like a haven. If he could just reach it, lie quiet till the sickness went away. . . . He crossed the cabin somehow, lay across the edge of the bunk, rolled into it. A wave of blackness lifted to meet him, deep as a sea.

He lay a long time; then the fragment of remaining will reasserted itself. Reluctantly, he forced open gummy eyelids. It was nearly dark now; the far window of the hut showed in the gloom, a vague rectangle of greyness. In front of it the handles of the semaphore seemed to swim, glinting where the light caught the polished smoothness of wood. He stared, realizing his foolishness; then he tried to roll off the bunk. The blankets, glued to his back, prevented him. He tried again, shivering now with the cold. The stove was unlit; the cabin door stood ajar, white crystals fanning in across the planking of the floor. Outside, the howling of the wind was relentless. The boy struggled; the efforts woke pain again and the sickness, the thudding and roaring. Images of the semaphore handles doubled, sextupled, rolled apart to make a glistening silver sheaf. He panted, tears running into his mouth; then his eyes slid closed. He fell into a noisy void shot with colours, sparks, and gleams and washes of light. He lay watching the lights, teeth bared, feeling the throb in his back where fresh blood pumped into the bed. After a while, the roaring went away.

The child lay couched in long grass, feeling the heat of the sun strike through his jerkin to burn his shoulders. In front of him, at the conical crest of the hill, the magic thing flapped slowly, its wings proud and lazy as those of a bird. Very high it was, on its pole on top of its hill; the faint wooden clattering it made fell remote from the blueness of the summer sky. The movements of the arms had half hypnotized him; he lay nodding and blinking, chin propped on his hands, absorbed in his watching. Up and down, up and down, *clap* . . . then down again and round, up and back, pausing, gesticulating, never staying wholly still. The semaphore seemed alive, an animate thing perched there talking strange words nobody could understand. Yet words they were, replete with meanings and mysteries like the words in his *Modern English Primer*. The child's brain spun. Words made stories; what stories was the tower telling, all alone there on its hill? Tales of kings and shipwrecks, fights and pursuits, Fairies, buried gold. . . . It was talking he knew that without a doubt; whispering and clacking, giving messages and taking them from the others in the lines, the great lines that stretched across England everywhere you could think, every direction you could see.

He watched the control rods sliding like bright muscles in their oiled guides. From Avebury, where he lived, many other towers were visible; they marched southwards across the Great Plain, climbed the westward heights of the Marlborough Downs. Though those were bigger, huge things staffed by teams of men whose signals might be visible on a clear day for ten miles or more. When they moved it was majestically and slowly, with a thundering from their jointed arms; these others, the little local towers, were friendlier somehow, chatting and pecking away from dawn to sunset.

There were many games the child played by himself in the long hours of summer; stolen hours usually, for there was always work to be found for him. School lessons, home study, chores about the house or down at his brothers' small-holding on the other side of the village; he must sneak off evenings or in the early dawn, if he wanted to be alone to dream. The stones beckoned him sometimes, the great gambolling diamond-shapes of them circling the little town. The boy would scud along the ditches of what had been an ancient temple, climb the terraced scarps to where the stones danced against the morning sun; or walk the long processional avenue that stretched eastward across the fields, imagine himself a priest or a god come to do old sacrifice to rain and sun. No one knew who first placed the stones. Some said the Fairies, in the days of their strength; others the old gods, they whose names it was a sin to whisper. Others said the Devil.

Mother Church winked at the destruction of Satanic relics, and that the villagers knew full well. Father Donovan disapproved, but he could do very little; the people went to it with a will. Their ploughs gnawed the bases of the markers, they broke the megaliths with water and fire and used the bits for patching dry stone walls; they'd been doing it for centuries now, and the rings were depleted and show-ing gaps. But there were many stones; the circles remained, and barrows crowning the windy tops of hills, *hows* where the old dead lay patient with their broken bones. The child would climb the mounds, and dream of kings in fur and jewels; but always, when he tired, he was drawn back to the semaphores and their mysterious life. He lay quiet, chin sunk on his hands, eyes sleepy, while above him Silbury 973 chipped and clattered on its hill.

The hand, falling on his shoulder, startled him from dreams. He tensed, whipped round and wanted to bolt; but there was nowhere to run. He was caught; he stared

up gulping, a chubby little boy, long hair falling across
his forehead.

The man was tall, enormously tall it seemed to the child.
His face was brown, tanned by sun and wind, and at the
corners of his eyes were networks of wrinkles. The eyes
were deep-set and very blue, startling against the colour of
the skin; to the boy they seemed to be of exactly the hue one
sees at the very top of the sky. His father's eyes had long
since bolted into hiding behind pebble-thick glasses; these
eyes were different. They had about them an appearance of
power, as if they were used to looking very long distances
and seeing clearly things that other men might miss. Their
owner was dressed all in green, with the faded shoulder
lacings and lanyard of a Serjeant of Signals. At his hip he
carried the Zeiss glasses that were the badge of any Signaller;
the flap of the case was only half secured and beneath it the
boy could see the big eyepieces, the worn brassy sheen of
the barrels.

The Guildsman was smiling; his voice when he spoke
was drawling and slow. It was the voice of a man who
knows about Time, that Time is forever and scurry and
bustle can wait. Someone who might know about the old
stones in the way the child's father did not.

"Well," he said, "I do believe we've caught a little spy.
Who be you, lad?"

The boy licked his mouth and squeaked, looking hunted.
"R-Rafe Bigland, sir. . . ."

"And what be 'ee doin'?"

Rafe wetted his lips again, looked at the tower, pouted
miserably, stared at the grass beside him, looked back
to the Signaller and quickly away. "I . . . I . . ."

He stopped, unable to explain. On top of the hill the
tower creaked and flapped. The Serjeant squatted down,
waiting patiently, still with the little half-smile, eyes twinkling at the boy. The satchel he'd been carrying he'd set on
the grass. Rafe knew he'd been to the village to pick up the

afternoon meal; one of the old ladies of Avebury was con-
tracted to supply food to the Signallers on duty. There was
little he didn't know about the working of the Silbury
station.

The seconds became a minute, and an answer had to be
made. Rafe drew himself up a trifle desperately; he heard
his own voice speaking as if it was the voice of a stranger,
and wondered with a part of his mind at the words that
found themselves on his tongue without it seemed the conscious intervention of thought. "If you please, sir," he said
pipingly, "I was watching the t-tower. . . ."

"Why?"

"I . . ."

Again the difficulty. How explain? The mysteries of the
Guild were not to be revealed to any casual stranger. The
codes of the Signallers and other deeper secrets were handed
down, jealousy, through the families privileged to wear the
Green. The Serjeant's accusation of spying had had some
truth to it; it had sounded ominous.

The Guildsman helped him. "Canst thou read the signals,
Rafe?"

Rafe shook his head, violently. No commoner could read
the towers. No commoner ever would. He felt a trembling
start in the pit of his stomach, but again his voice used itself
without his will. "No, sir," it said in a firm treble. "But I
would fain learn. . . ."

The Serjeant's eyebrows rose. He sat back on his heels,
hands lying easy across his knees, and started to laugh.
When he had finished he shook his head. "So you would
learn. . . . Aye, and a dozen kings, and many a high-placed
gentleman, would lie easier abed for the reading of the
towers." His face changed itself abruptly into a scowl.
"Boy," he said, "you mock us. . . ."

Rafe could only shake his head again, silently. The
Serjeant stared over him into space, still sitting on his heels.
Rafe wanted to explain how he had never, in his most

secret dreams, ever imagined himself a Signaller; how his tongue had moved of its own, blurting out the impossible and absurd. But he couldn't speak any more; before the Green, he was dumb. The pause lengthened while he watched inattentively the lurching progress of a rain beetle through the stems of grass. Then, "Who's thy father, boy?"

Rafe gulped. There would be a beating, he was sure of that now; and he would be forbidden ever to go near the towers or watch them again. He felt the stinging behind his eyes that meant tears were very close, ready to well and trickle. "Thomas Bigland of Avebury, sir," he said. "A clerk to Sir William M-Marshall."

The Serjeant nodded. "And thou wouldst learn the towers? Thou wouldst be a Signaller?"

"Aye, sir. . . ." The tongue was Modern English of course, the language of artisans and tradesmen, not the guttural clacking of the landless churls; Rafe slipped easily into the old-fashioned usage of it the Signallers employed sometimes among themselves.

The Serjeant said abruptly, "Canst thou read in books, Rafe?"

"Aye, sir. . . ." Then falteringly, "If the words be not too long. . . ."

The Guildsman laughed again, and clapped the boy on the back. "Well, Master Rafe Bigland, thou who would be a Signaller, and can read books if the words be but short, my book learning is slim enough as God He knows; but it may be I can help thee, if thou hast given me no lies. Come." And he rose and began to walk away toward the tower. Rafe hesitated, blinked, then roused himself and trotted along behind, head whirling with wonders.

They climbed the path that ran slantingly round the hill. As they moved, the Serjeant talked. Silbury 973 was part of the C class chain that ran from near Londinium, from the great relay station at Pontes, along the line of the road to Aquae Sulis. Its complement . . . but Rafe knew the complement well enough. Five men including the Serjeant; their cottages stood apart from the main village, on a little rise of ground that gave them seclusion. Signallers' homes were always situated like that, it helped preserve the Guild mysteries. Guildsmen paid no tithes to local demesnes, obeyed none but their own hierarchy; and though in theory they were answerable under common law, in practice they were immune. They governed themselves according to their own high code; and it was a brave man, or a fool, who squared with the richest Guild in England. There had been deadly accuracy in what the Serjeant said; when kings waited on their messages as eagerly as commoners they had little need to fear. The Popes might cavil, jealous of their independence, but Rome herself leaned too heavily on the continent-wide networks of the semaphore towers to do more than adjure and complain. Insofar as such a thing was possible in a hemisphere dominated by the Church Militant, the Guildsmen were free.

Although Rafe had seen the inside of a signal station often enough in dreams he had never physically set foot in one. He stopped short at the wooden step, feeling awe rise in him like a tangible barrier. He caught his breath. He had never been this close to a semaphore tower before; the rush and thudding of the arms, the clatter of dozens of tiny joints, sounded in his ears like music. From here only the tip of the signal was in sight, looming over the roof of the hut. The varnished wooden spars shone orange like the masts of a boat; the semaphore arms rose and dipped, black against the sky. He could see the bolts and loops near their tips where in bad weather or at night when some message of vital importance had to be passed, cressets could be attached to them. He'd seen such fires once, miles out over the Plain, the night the old King died.

The Serjeant opened the door and urged him through it. He stood rooted just beyond the sill. The place had a clean smell that was somehow also masculine, a compound of polishes and oils and the fumes of tobacco; and inside too it had something of the appearance of a ship. The cabin was airy and low, roomier than it had looked from the front of the hill. There was a stove, empty now and gleaming with blacking, its brasswork brightly polished. Inside its mouth a sheet of red crepe paper had been stretched tightly; the doors were parted a little to show the smartness. The plank walls were painted a light grey; on the breast that enclosed the chimney of the stove rosters were pinned neatly. In one corner of the room was a group of diplomas, framed and richly coloured; below them an old daguerreotype, badly faded, showing a group of men standing in front of a very tall signal tower. In one corner of the cabin was a bunk, blankets folded into a neat cube at its foot; above it a hand-coloured pinup of a smiling girl wearing a cap of Guild green and very little else. Rafe's eyes passed over it with the faintly embarrassed indifference of childhood.

In the centre of the room, white-painted and square, was the base of the signal mast; round it a little podium of smooth, scrubbed wood, on which stood two Guildsmen. In their hands were the long levers that worked the sema-phore arms overhead; the control rods reached up from them, encased where they passed through the ceiling in white canvas grommets. Skylights, opened to either side, let in the warm July air. The third duty Signaller stood at the eastern window of the cabin, glasses to his eyes, speaking quietly and continuously. "Five . . . eleven . . . thirteen . . . nine . . ." The operators repeated the combinations, working the big handles, leaning the weight of their bodies against the pull of the signal arms overhead, letting each downward rush of the semaphores help them into position for their next cypher. There was an air of concentration but not of strain; it all seemed very easy and practised. In front of the men, supported by struts from the roof, a tell-tale repeated the positions of the arms, but the Signallers rarely glanced at it. Years of training had given a fluidness to their movements that made them seem almost like the steps and posturings of a ballet. The bodies swung, checked, moved through their arabesques; the creaking of wood and the faint rumbling of the signals filled the place, as steady and lulling as the drone of bees.

No one paid any attention to Rafe or the Serjeant. The Guildsman began talking again quietly, explaining what was happening. The long message that had been going through now for nearly an hour was a list of current grain and fatstock prices from Londinium. The Guild system was invaluable for regulating the complex economy of the country; farmers and merchants, taking the Londinium prices as a yardstick, knew exactly what to pay when buying and selling for themselves. Rafe forgot to be disappointed; his mind heard the words, recording them and storing them away, while his eyes watched the changing patterns made by the Guildsmen, so much a part of the squeaking, clacking machine they controlled.

The actual transmitted information, what the Serjeant called the payspeech, occupied only a part of the signalling; a message was often almost swamped by the codings necessary to secure its distribution. The current figures for instance had to reach certain centres, Aquae Sulis among them, by nightfall. How they arrived, their routing on the way, was very much the concern of the branch Signallers through whose stations the cyphers passed. It took years of experience coupled with a certain degree of intuition to route signals in such a way as to avoid lines already congested with information; and of course while a line was in use in one direction, as in the present case with a complex message being moved from east to west, it was very difficult to employ it in reverse. It was in fact possible to pass two messages in different directions at the same time, and it was often done on the A Class towers. When that happened every third cypher of a north-bound might be part of

another signal moving south; the stations transmitted in
bursts, swapping the messages forward and back. But
coaxial signalling was detested even by the Guildsmen. The
line had to be cleared first, and a suitable code agreed on;
two lookouts were employed, chanting their directions alternately to the Signallers, and even in the best-run station
total confusion could result from the smallest slip, neces-
sitating reclearing of the route and a fresh start.

With his hands, the Serjeant described the washout
signal a fouled-up tower would use; the three horizontal
extensions of the semaphores from the sides of their mast.
If that happened, he said, chuckling grimly, a head would
roll somewhere; for a Class A would be under the command
of a Major of Signals at least, a man of twenty or more
years experience. He would be expected not to make
mistakes, and to see in turn that none were made by his
subordinates. Rafe's head began to whirl again; he looked
with fresh respect at the worn green leather of the Serjeant's
uniform. He was beginning to see now, dimly, just what sort
of thing it was to be a Signaller.

The message ended at last, with a great clapping of the
semaphore arms. The lookout remained at his post but
the operators got down, showing an interest in Rafe for
the first time. Away from the semaphore levers they seemed
far more normal and unfrightening. Rafe knew them well;
Robin Wheeler, who often spoke to him on his way to and
from the station, and Bob Camus, who's split a good many
heads in his time at the feastday cudgel playing in the
village. They showed him the code books, all the scores
of cyphers printed in red on numbered black squares. He
stayed to share their meal; his mother would be concerned
and his father annoyed, but home was almost forgotten.
Toward evening another message came from the west;
they told him it was police business, and sent it winging and
clapping on its way. It was dusk when Rafe finally left
the station, head in the clouds, two unbelievable pennies

jinking in his pocket. It was only later, in bed and trying
to sleep, he realized a long-submerged dream had come
true. He did sleep finally, only to dream again of signal
towers at night, the cressets on their arms roaring against
the blueness of the sky. He never spent the coins.

Once it had become a real possibility, his ambition to be
a Signaller grew steadily; he spent all the time he could at
the Silbury Station, perched high on its weird prehistoric
hill. His absences met with his father's keenest disapproval.
Mr. Bigland's wage as an estate clerk barely brought in
enough to support his brood of seven boys; the family had
of necessity to grow most of its own food, and for that
every pair of hands that could be mustered was valuable.
But nobody guessed the reason for Rafe's frequent disap-
pearances; and for his part he didn't say a word.

He learned, in illicit hours, the thirty-odd basic positions
of the signal arms, and something of the commonest se-
quences of grouping; after that he could lie out near Silbury
Hill and mouth off most of the numbers to himself, though
without the codes that informed them he was still dumb.
Once Serjeant Gray let him take the observer's place for a
glorious half hour while a message was coming in over the
Marlborough Downs. Rafe stood stiffly, hands sweating on
the big barrels of the Zeiss glasses, and read off the cyphers
as high and clear as he could for the Signallers at his back.
The Serjeant checked his reporting unobtrusively from the
other end of the hut, but he made no mistakes.

By the time he was ten Rafe had received as much formal
education as a child of his class could expect. The great
question of a career was raised. The family sat in conclave;
father, mother, and the three eldest sons. Rafe was unim-
pressed; he knew, and had known for weeks, the fate they
had selected for him. He was to be apprenticed to one of
the four tailors of the village, little bent old men who sat
like cross-legged hermits behind bulwarks of cloth bales
and stitched their lives away by the light of penny dips. He

hardly expected to be consulted on the matter; however he was sent for, formally, and asked what he wished to do. That was the time for the bombshell. "I know exactly what I want to be," said Rafe firmly. "A Signaller."

There was a moment of shocked silence; then the laughing started and swelled. The Guilds were closely guarded; Rafe's father would pay dearly even for his entry into the tailoring trade. As for the Signallers . . . no Bigland had ever been a Signaller, no Bigland ever would. Why, that . . . it would raise the family status! The whole village would have to look up to them, with a son wearing the Green. Preposterous . . .

Rafe sat quietly until they were finished, lips compressed, cheekbones glowing. He'd known it would be like this, he knew just what he had to do. His composure discomfited the family; they quietened down enough to ask him, with mock seriousness, how he intended to set about achieving his ambition. It was time for the second bomb. "By approaching the Guild with regard to a Common Entrance Examination," he said, mouthing words that had been learned by rote. "Serjeant Gray, of the Silbury Station, will speak for me."

Into the fresh silence came his father's embarrassed coughing. Mr. Bigland looked like an old sheep, sitting blinking through his glasses, nibbling at his thin moustache. "Well," he said, "Well, I don't know. . . . *Well.* . . ." But Rafe had already seen the glint in his eyes at the dizzying prospect of prestige. That a son of his should wear the Green. . . .

Before their minds could change Rafe wrote a formal letter which he delivered in person to the Silbury Station; it asked Serjeant Gray, very correctly, if he would be kind enough to call on Mr. Bigland with a view of discussing his son's entry to the College of Signals in Londinium.

The Serjeant was as good as his word. He was a widower, and childless; maybe Rafe made up in part for the son he'd never had, maybe he saw the reflection of his own youthful enthusiasm in the boy. He came the next evening, strolling quietly down the village street to rap at the Biglands' door; Rafe, watching from his shared bedroom over the porch, grinned at the gaping and craning of the neighbours. The family was all a-flutter; the household budget had been scraped for wine and candles, silverware and fresh linen were laid out in the parlour, everybody was anxious to make the best possible impression. Mr. Bigland of course was only too agreeable; when the Serjeant left, an hour later, he had his signed permission in his belt. Rafe himself saw the signal originated asking Londinium for the necessary entrance papers for the College's annual examination.

The Guild gave just twelve places per year, and they were keenly contested. In the few weeks at his disposal Rafe was crammed mercilessly; the Serjeant coached him in all aspects of Signalling he might reasonably be expected to know while the village dominie, impressed in spite of himself, brushed up Rafe's bookwork, even trying to instill into his aching head the rudiments of Norman French. Rafe won admittance; he had never considered the possibility of failure, mainly because such a thought was unbearable. He sat the examination in Sorviodunum, the nearest regional centre to his home; a week later a message came through offering him his place, listing the clothes and books he would need and instructing him to be ready to present himself at the College of Signals in just under a month's time. When he left for Londinium, well muffled in a new cloak, riding a horse provided by the Guild and with two russet-coated Guild servants in attendance, he was followed by the envy of a whole village. The arms of the Silbury tower were quiet; but as he passed they flipped quickly to Attention, followed at once by the cyphers for Origination and Immediate Locality. Rafe turned in the saddle, tears stinging his eyes, and watched the letters quickly spelled out in plaintalk. "Good luck. . . ."

After Avebury, Londinium seemed dingy, noisy, and old. The College was housed in an ancient, ramshackle building just inside the City walls; though Londinium had long since over-spilled its former limits, sprawling south across the river and north nearly as far as Tyburn Tree. The Guild children were the usual crowd of brawling, snotty-nosed brats that comprised the apprentices of any trade. Hereditary sons of the Green, they looked down on the Common Entrants from the heights of an unbearable and imaginary eminence; Rafe had a bad time till a series of dormitory fights, all more or less bloody, proved to his fellows once and for all that young Bigland at least was better left alone. He settled down as an accepted member of the community.

The Guild, particularly of recent years, had been tending to place more and more value on theoretical knowledge, and the two year course was intensive. The apprentices had to become adept in Norman French, for their further training would take them inevitably into the houses of the rich. A working knowledge of the other tongues of the land, the Cornish, Gaelic, and Middle English, was also a requisite; no Guildsman ever knew where he would finally be posted. Guild history was taught too, and the elements of mechanics and coding, though most of the practical work in those directions would be done in the field, at the training stations scattered along the south and west coasts of England and through the Welsh Marches. The students were even required to have a nodding acquaintance with thaumaturgy; though Rafe for one was unable to see how the attraction of scraps of paper to a polished stick of amber could ever have an application to Signalling.

He worked well nonetheless, and passed out with a mark high enough to satisfy even his professors. He was posted directly to his training station, the A Class complex atop Saint Adhelm's Head in Dorset. To his intense pleasure he was accompanied by the one real friend he had made

at College; Josh Cope, a wild, black-haired boy, a Common
Entrant and the son of a Durham mining family.

They arrived at Saint Adhelm's in the time-honored way,
thumbing a lift from a road train drawn by a labouring
Fowler compound. Rafe never forgot his first sight of the
station. It was far bigger than he'd imagined, sprawling
across the top of the great blunt promontory. For conve-
nience, stations were rated in accordance with the heaviest
towers they carried; but Saint Adhelm's was a clearing
centre for B, C, and D lines as well, and round the huge
paired structures of the A Class towers ranged a circle
of smaller semaphores, all twirling and clacking in the sun.
Beside them, establishing rigs displayed the codes the towers
spoke in a series of bright-coloured circles and rectangles;
Rafe, staring, saw one of them rotate, displaying to the west
a yellow Bend Sinister as the semaphore above it switched
in midmessage from plaintalk to the complex Code Twenty-
Three. He glanced sidelong at Josh, got from the other lad
a jaunty thumbs-up; they swung their satchels onto their
shoulders and headed up toward the main gate to report
themselves for duty.

For the first few weeks both boys were glad enough of
each other's company. They found the atmosphere of a
major field station very different from that of the College;
by comparison the latter, noisy and brawling as it had been,
came to seem positively monastic. A training in the Guild
of Signallers was like a continuous game of ladders and
snakes; and Rafe and Josh had slid back once more to the
bottom of the stack. Their life was a near-endless round of
canteen fatigues, of polishing and burnishing, scrubbing
and holystoning. There were the cabins to clean, gravel
paths to weed, what seemed like miles of brass rail to
scour till it gleamed. Saint Adhelm's was a show station,
always prone to inspection. Once it suffered a visit from the
Grand Master of Signallers himself, and his Lord Lieutenant; the spitting and polishing before that went on

for weeks. And there was the maintenance of the towers themselves; the canvas grommets on the great control rods to renew and pipe-clay, the semaphore arms to be painted, their bearings cleaned and packed with grease, spars to be sent down and re-rigged, always in darkness when the day's signalling was done and generally in the foullest of weathers. The semi-military nature of the Guild made necessary side-arms practice and shooting with the longbow and cross-bow, obsolescent weapons now but still occasionally employed in the European wars.

The station itself surpassed Rafe's wildest dreams. Its standing complement, including the dozen or so apprentices always in training, was well over a hundred, of whom some sixty or eighty were always on duty or on call. The big semaphores, the Class A's, were each worked by teams of a dozen men, six to each great lever, with a Signal Master to control coordination and pass on the cyphers from the observers. With the station running at near capacity the scene was impressive; the lines of men at the controls, as synchronised as troupes of dancers; the shouts of the Signal Masters, scuffle of feet on the white planking, rumble and creak of the control rods, the high thunder of the signals a hundred feet above the roofs. Though that, according to the embittered Officer in Charge, was not Signalling but "unscientific bloody timber-hauling." Major Stone had spent most of his working life on the little Class C's of the Pennine Chain before an unlooked-for promotion had given him his present position of trust.

The A messages short-hopped from Saint Adhelm's to Swyre Head and from thence to Gad Cliff, built on the high land overlooking Warbarrow Bay. From there along the coast to Golden Cap, the station poised six hundred sheer feet above the fishing village of Lymes, to fling themselves in giant strides into the west, to Somerset and Devon and far-off Cornwall, or northwards again over the heights of the Great Plain en route for Wales. Up there Rafe knew they passed in sight of the old stone rings of Avebury. He often thought with affection of his parents and Serjeant Gray; but he was long past homesickness. His days were too full for that.

Twelve months after their arrival at Saint Adhelm's, and three years after their induction into the Guild, the apprentices were first allowed to lay hands on the semaphore bars. Josh in fact had found it impossible to wait and had salved his ego some months before by spelling out a frisky message on one of the little local towers in what he hoped was the dead of night. For that fall from grace he had made intimate and painful contact with the buckle on the end of a green leather belt, wielded by none other than Major Stone himself. Two burly Corporals of Signals held the miners' lad down while he threshed and howled; the end result had convinced even Josh that on certain points of discipline the Guild stood adamant.

To learn to signal was like yet another beginning. Rafe found rapidly that a semaphore lever was no passive thing to be pulled and hauled at pleasure; with the wind under the great black sails of the arms an operator stood a good chance of being bowled completely off the rostrum by the back-whip of even a thirty foot unit, while to the teams on the A Class towers lack of coordination could prove, and had proved in the past, fatal. There was a trick to the thing, only learned after bruising hours of practice; to lean the weight of the body against the levers rather than just using the muscles of back and arms, employ the jounce and swing of the semaphores to position them automatically for their next cypher. Trying to fight them instead of working with the recoil would reduce a strong man to a sweat-soaked rag within minutes; but a trained Signaller could work half the day and feel very little strain. Rafe approached the task assiduously; six months and one broken collarbone later he felt able to pride himself on mastery of

his craft. It was then he first encountered the murderous
intricacies of coaxial signalling. . . .

After two years on the station the apprentices were
finally deemed ready to graduate as full Signallers. Then
came the hardest test of all. The site of it, the arena, was
a bare hillock of ground some half mile from Saint Adhelm's
Head. Built onto it, and facing each other about forty yards
apart, were two Class D towers with their cabins. Josh was
to be Rafe's partner in the test. They were taken to the
place in the early morning, and given their problem; to
transmit to each other in plaintalk the entire of the Book
of Nehemiah in alternate verses, with appropriate Attention,
Acknowledgement, and End-of-Message cyphers at the head
and tail of each. Several ten minute breaks were allowed,
though they had been warned privately it would be better
not to take them; once they left the rostrums they might
be unable to force their tired bodies back to the bars.

Round the little hill would be placed observers who would
check the work minute by minute for inaccuracies and
sloppiness. When the messages were finished to their satisfaction the apprentices might leave, and call themselves
Signallers; but not before. Nothing would prevent them
deserting their task if they desired before it was done.
Nobody would speak a word of blame, and there would be
no punishment; but they would leave the Guild the same
day, and never return. Some boys, a few, did leave. Others
collapsed; for them, there would be another chance.

Rafe neither collapsed nor left, though there were times
when he longed to do both. When he started, the sun had
barely risen; when he left it was sinking toward the western
rim of the horizon. The first two hours, the first three, were
nothing; then the pain began. In the shoulders, in the back,
in the buttocks and calves. His world narrowed; he saw
neither the sun nor the distant sea. There was only the
semaphore, the handles of it, the text in front of his eyes,

the window. Across the space separating the huts he could see Josh staring as he engaged in his endless, useless task. Rafe came by degrees to hate the towers, the Guild, himself, all he had done, the memory of Silbury and old Serjeant Gray; and to hate Josh most of all, with his stupid white blob of a face, the signals clacking above him like some absurd extension of himself. With fatigue came a trance-like state in which logic was suspended, the reasons for actions lost. There was nothing to do in life, had never been anything to do but stand on the rostrum, work the levers, feel the jounce of the signals, check with the body, feel the jounce. . . . His vision doubled and trebled till the lines of copy in front of him shimmered unreadably; and still the test ground on.

At any time in the afternoon Rafe would have killed his friend had he been able to reach him. But he couldn't get to him; his feet were rooted to the podium, his hands glued to the levers of the semaphore. The signals grumbled and creaked; his breath sounded in his ears harshly, like an engine. His sight blackened; the text and the opposing semaphore swam in a void. He felt disembodied; he could sense his limbs only as a dim and confused burning. And somehow, agonizingly, the transmission came to an end. He clattered off the last verse of the book, signed End of Message, leaned on the handles while the part of him that could still think realized dully that he could stop. And then, in black rage, he did the thing only one other apprentice had done in the history of the station; flipped the handles to Attention again, spelled out with terrible exactness and letter by letter the message *"God Save the Queen."* Signed End of Message, got no acknowledgement, swung the levers up and locked them into position for Emergency-Contact Broken. In a signalling chain the alarm would be flashed back to the originating station, further information rerouted and a squad sent to investigate the breakdown.

Rafe stared blankly at the levers. He saw now the

puzzling bright streaks on them were his own blood. He
forced his raw hands to unclamp themselves, elbowed his
way through the door, shoved past the men who had come
for him and collapsed twenty yards away on the grass.
He was taken back to Saint Adhelm's in a cart and put to
bed. He slept the clock round; when he woke it was with
the knowledge that Josh and he now had the right to put
aside the cowled russet jerkins of apprentices for the full
green of the Guild of Signallers. They drank beer that
night, awkwardly, gripping the tankards in both bandaged
paws; and for the second and last time, the station cart
had to be called into service to get them home.

The next part of training was a sheer pleasure. Rafe
made his farewells to Josh and went home on a two month
leave; at the end of his furlough he was posted to the
household of the Fitzgibbons, one of the old families of
the Southwest, to serve twelve months as Signaller-Page.
The job was mainly ceremonial, though in times of national
crisis it could obviously carry its share of responsibility.
Most well-bred families, if they could afford to do so,
bought rights from the Guild and erected their own tiny
stations somewhere in the grounds of their estate; the little
Class E towers were even smaller than the Class D's on
which Rafe had graduated.

In places where no signal line ran within easy sighting
distance, one or more stations might be erected across the
surrounding country and staffed by Journeyman-Signallers
without access to coding; but the Fitzgibbons' great aitch-
shaped house lay almost below Swyre Head, in a sloping
coombe open to the sea. Rafe, looking down on the roofs of
the place the morning he arrived, started to grin. He could
see his semaphore perched up among the chimney stacks;
above it a bare mile away was the A repeater, the short-
hop tower for his old station of Saint Adhelm's just over
the hill. He touched heels to his horse, pushing it into a
canter. He would be signalling direct to the A Class, there

was no other outroute; he couldn't help chuckling at the thought of its Major's face when asked to hurl to Saint Adhelm's or Golden Cap requests for butter, six dozen eggs, or the services of a cobbler. He paid his formal respects to the station and rode down into the valley to take up his new duties.

They proved if anything easier than he had anticipated. Fitzgibbon himself moved in high circles at Court and was rarely home, the running of the house being left to his wife and two teen-age daughters. As Rafe had expected, most of the messages he was required to pass were of an intensely domestic nature. And he enjoyed the privileges of any young Guildsman in his position; he could always be sure of a warm place in the kitchen at nights, the first cut off the roast, the prettiest serving wenches to mend his clothes and trim his hair. There was sea bathing within a stone's throw, and feast day trips to Durnovaria and Bourne Mouth. Once a little fair established itself in the grounds, an annual occurrence apparently; and Rafe spent a delicious half hour signalling the A Class for oil for its steam engines, and meat for a dancing bear.

The year passed quickly; in late autumn the boy, promoted now to Signaller-Corporal, was reposted, and another took his place. Rafe rode west, into the hills that crowd the southern corner of Dorset, to take up what would be his first real command.

The station was part of a D Class chain that wound west over the high ground into Somerset. In winter, with the short days and bad seeing conditions, the towers would be unused; Rafe knew that well enough. He would be totally isolated; winters in the hills could be severe, with snow making travel next to impossible and frosts for weeks on end. He would have little to fear from the *routiers,* the footpads who legend claimed haunted the West in the cold months; the station lay far from any road and there was nothing in the cabins, save perhaps the Zeiss glasses carried

by the Signaller, to tempt a desperate man. He would be
in more danger from wolves and Fairies, though the former
were virtually extinct in the south and he was young enough
to laugh at the latter. He took over from the bored Corporal just finishing his term, signalled his arrival back
through the chain, and settled down to take stock of things.

By all reports this first winter on a one-man station
was a worse trial than the endurance test. For a trial it
was, certainly. At some time through the dark months
ahead, some hour of the day, a message would come along
the dead line, from the west or from the east; and Rafe
would have to be there to take it and pass it on. A minute
late with his acknowledgement and a formal reprimand
would be issued from Londinium; that might peg his promotion for years, maybe for good. The standards of the
Guild were high, and they were never relaxed; if it was
easy for a Major in charge of an A Class station to fall from
grace, how much easier for an unknown and untried Corporal! The duty period of each day was short, a bare six
hours, five through the darkest months of December and
January; but during that time, except for one short break,
Rafe would have to be continually on the alert.

One of his first acts on being left alone was to climb to
the diminutive operating gantry. The construction of the
station was unusual. To compensate for its lack of elevation
a catwalk had been built across under the roof; the operating
rostrum was located centrally on it, while at each end
double-glazed windows commanded views to west and east.
Between them, past the handles of the semaphore, a track
had been worn half an inch deep in the wooden boards. In
the next few months Rafe would wear it deeper, moving
from one window to the other checking the arms of the next
towers in line. The matchsticks of the semaphores were
barely visible; he judged them to be a good two miles
distant. He would need all his eyesight, plus the keenness of
the Zeiss lenses, to make them out at all on a dull day;

but they would have to be watched minute by minute
through every duty period because sooner or later one of
them would move. He grinned and touched the handles of
his own machine. When that happened, his acknowledgement would be clattering before the tower had stopped
calling for Attention.

He examined the stations critically through his glasses.
In the spring, riding out to take up a new tour, he might
meet one of their operators; but not before. In the hours of
daylight they as well as he would be tied to their gantries,
and on foot in the dark it might be dangerous to try to reach
them. Anyway it would not be expected of him; that was
an unwritten law. In case of need, desperate need, he could
call help through the semaphores; but for no other reason.
This was the true life of the Guildsman; the bustle of Londinium, the warmth and comfort of the Fitzgibbons' home,
had been episodes only. Here was the end result of it all;
the silence, the desolation, the ancient, endless communion
of the hills. He had come full circle.

His life settled into a pattern of sleeping and waking and
watching. As the days grew shorter the weather worsened;
freezing mists swirled round the station, and the first snow
fell. For hours on end the towers to east and west were
lost in the haze; if a message was to come now, the Signallers would have to light their cressets. Rafe prepared
the bundles of faggots anxiously, wiring them into their
iron cages, setting them beside the door with the paraffin
that would soak them, make them blaze. He became ob-
sessed by the idea that the message had in fact come, and
he had missed it in the gloom. In time the fear ebbed. The
Guild was hard, but it was fair; no Signaller, in winter of
all times, was expected to be a superman. If a Captain rode
suddenly to the station demanding why he had not answered
this or that he would see the torches and the oil laid and
ready and know at least that Rafe had done his best.

Nobody came; and when the weather cleared the towers were still stationary.

Each night after the light had gone Rafe tested his signals, swinging the arms to free them from their wind-driven coating of ice; it was good to feel the pull and flap of the thin wings up in the dark. The messages he sent into blackness were fanciful in the extreme; notes to his parents and old Serjeant Gray, lurid suggestions to a little girl in the household of the Fitzgibbons to whom he had taken more than a passing fancy. Twice a week he used the lunch-time break to climb the tower, check the spindles in their packings of grease. On one such inspection he was appalled to see a hairline crack in one of the control rods, the first sign that the metal had become fatigued. He replaced the entire section that night, breaking out fresh parts from store, hauling them up and fitting them by the improvised light of a hand lamp. It was an awkward, dangerous job with his fingers freezing and the wind plucking at his back, trying to tug him from his perch onto the roof below. He could have pulled the station out of line in daytime, sig-nalled Repairs and given himself the benefit of light, but pride forbade him. He finished the job two hours before dawn, tested the tower, made his entry in the log and went to sleep, trusting in his Signaller's sense to wake him at first light. It didn't let him down.

The long hours of darkness began to pall. Mending and laundering only filled a small proportion of his off-duty time; he read through his stock of books, re-read them, put them aside and began devising tasks for himself, checking and rechecking his inventories of food and fuel. In the black-ness, with the long crying of the wind over the roof, the stories of Fairies and were-things on the heath didn't seem quite so fanciful. Difficult now even to imagine summer, the slow clicking of the towers against skies bright blue and burning with light. There were two pistols in the hut;

Rafe saw to it their mechanisms were in order, loaded and primed them both. Twice after that he woke to crashings on the roof, as if some dark thing was scrabbling to get in; but each time it was only the wind in the skylights. He padded them with strips of canvas; then the frost came back, icing them shut, and he wasn't disturbed again.

He moved a portable stove up onto the observation gallery and discovered the remarkable number of operations that could be carried out with one eye on the windows. The brewing of coffee and tea were easy enough; in time he could even manage the production of hot snacks. His lunch hours he preferred to use for things other than cooking. Above all else he was afraid of inaction making him fat; there was no sign of it happening but he still preferred to take no chances. When snow conditions permitted he would make quick expeditions from the shack into the surrounding country. On one of these the hillock with its smoothly shaped crown of trees attracted his eye. He walked toward it jauntily, breath steaming in the air, the glasses as ever bumping his hip. In the copse, his Fate was waiting.

The catamount clung to the bole of a fir, watching the advance of the boy with eyes that were slits of hate in the vicious mask of its face. No one could have read its thoughts. Perhaps it imagined itself about to be attacked; perhaps it was true what they said about such creatures, that the cold of winter sent them mad. There were few of them now in the west; mostly they had retreated to the hills of Wales, the rocky peaks of the far north. The survival of this one was in itself a freak, an anachronism.

The tree in which it crouched leaned over the path Rafe must take. He ploughed forward, head bent a little, intent only on picking his way. As he approached the catamount drew back its lips in a huge and silent snarl, showing the wide pink vee of its mouth, the long needle-sharp teeth. The eyes blazed; the ears flattened, making the skull a

round, furry ball. Rafe never saw the wildcat, its stripes
blending perfectly with the harshness of branches and snow.
As he stepped beneath the tree it launched itself onto him,
landed across his shoulders like a spitting shawl; his neck
and back were flayed before the pain had travelled to his
brain.

The shock and the impact sent him staggering. He
reeled, yelling; the reaction dislodged the cat but it spun
in a flash, tearing upward at his stomach. He felt the hot
spurting of blood, and the world became a red haze of
horror. The air was full of the creature's screaming. He
reached his knife but teeth met in his hand and he dropped
it. He grovelled blindly, found the weapon again, slashed
out, felt the blade strike home. The cat screeched, writhing
on the snow. He forced himself to push his streaming knee
into the creature's back, pinning the animal while the knife
flailed down, biting into its mad life; until the thing with
a final convulsion burst free, fled limping and splashing
blood, died maybe somewhere off in the trees. Then there
was the time of blackness, the hideous crawl back to the
signal station; and now he lay dying too, unable to reach
the semaphore, knowing that finally he had failed. He
wheezed hopelessly, settled back farther into the crowding
dark.

In the blackness were sounds. Homely sounds. A regular
scrape-clink, scrape-clink; the morning noise of a rake being
drawn across the bars of a grate. Rafe tossed muttering,
relaxed in the spreading warmth. There was light now,
orange and flickering; he kept his eyes closed, seeing the
glow of it against the insides of the lids. Soon his mother
would call. It would be time to get up and go to school,
or out into the fields.

A tinkling, pleasantly musical, made him turn his head.
His body still ached, right down the length of it, but somehow the pain was not quite so intense. He blinked. He'd

expected to see his old room in the cottage at Avebury; the
curtains stirring in the breeze perhaps, sunshine coming
through open windows. It took him a moment to readjust to
the signal hut; then memory came back with a rush. He
stared; he saw the gantry under the semaphore handles, the
rods reaching out through the roof; the whiteness of their
grommets, pipe-clayed by himself the day before. The tar-
paulin squares had been hooked across the windows, shut-
ting out the night. The door was barred, both lamps were
burning; the stove was alight, its doors open and spreading
warmth. Above it, pots and pans simmered; and bending
over them was a girl.

She turned when he moved his head and he looked into
deep eyes, black-fringed, with a quick nervousness about
them that was somehow like an animal. Her long hair was
restrained from falling round her face by a band or ribbon
drawn behind the little pointed ears; she wore a rustling
dress of an odd light blue, and she was brown. Brown as a
nut, though God knew there had been no sun for weeks
to tan her like that. Rafe recoiled when she looked at him,
and something deep in him twisted and needed to scream.
He knew she shouldn't be here in this wilderness, amber-
skinned and with her strange summery dress; that she was
one of the Old Ones, the half-believed, the Haunters of the
Heath, the possessors of men's souls if Mother Church spoke
truth. His lips tried to form the word "Fairy" and could
not. Blood-smeared, they barely moved.

His vision was failing again. She walked toward him
lightly, swaying, seeming to his dazed mind to shimmer
like a flame; some unnatural flame that a breath might
extinguish. But there was nothing ethereal about her touch.
Her hands were firm and hard; they wiped his mouth,
stroked his hot face. Coolness remained after she had gone
away and he realized she had laid a damp cloth across his
forehead. He tried to cry out to her again; she turned to
smile at him, or he thought she smiled, and he realized

she was singing. There were no words; the sound made itself in her throat, goldenly, like the song a spinning wheel might hum in the ears of a sleepy child, the words always nearly there ready to well up through the surface of the colour and never coming. He wanted badly to talk now, tell her about the cat and his fear of it and its paws full of glass, but it seemed she knew already the things that were in his mind. When she came back it was with a steaming pan of water that she set on a chair beside the bunk. She stopped the humming, or the singing, then and spoke to him; but the words made no sense, they banged and splattered like water falling over rocks. He was afraid again, for that was the talk of the Old Ones; but the defect must have been in his ears because the syllables changed of themselves into the Modern English of the Guild. They were sweet and rushing, filled with a meaning that was not a meaning, hinting at deeper things beneath themselves that his tired mind couldn't grasp. They talked about the Fate that had waited for him in the wood, fallen on him so suddenly from the tree. *"The Norns spin the Fate of a man or of a cat,"* sang the voice. *"Sitting beneth Yggdrasil, great World Ash, they work; one Sister to make the yarn, the next to measure, the third to cut it at its end. . . ."* and all the time the hands were busy, touching and soothing.

Rafe knew the girl was mad, or possessed. She spoke of Old things, the things banished by Mother Church, pushed out forever into the dark and cold. With a great effort he lifted his hand, held it before her to make the sign of the Cross; but she gripped the wrist, giggling, and forced it down, started to work delicately on the ragged palm, cleaning the blood from round the base of the fingers. She unfastened the belt across his stomach, eased the trews apart; cutting the leather, soaking it, pulling it away in little twitches from the deep tears in groin and thighs. *"Ah . . . ,"* he said, *"ah . . ."* She stopped at that, frowning, brought something from the stove, lifted his head gently to let him drink. The liquid soothed, seeming to run from his throat down into body and limbs like a trickling anaesthesia. He relapsed into a warmness shot through with little coloured stabs of pain, heard her crooning again as she dressed his legs. Slid deeper, into sleep.

Day came slowly, faded slower into night that turned to day again, and darkness. He seemed to be apart from Time, lying dozing and waking, feeling the comfort of bandages on his body and fresh linen tucked round him, seeing the handles of the semaphores gleam a hundred miles away, wanting to go to them, not able to move. Sometimes he thought when the girl came to him he pulled her close, pressed his face into the mother-warmth of her thighs while she stroked his hair, and talked, and sang. All the time it seemed, through the sleeping and the waking, the voice went on. Sometimes he knew he heard it with his ears, sometimes in fever dreams the words rang in his mind. They made a mighty saga; such a story as had never been told, never imagined in all the lives of men.

It was the tale of Earth; Earth and a land, the place her folk called Angle-Land. Only once there had been no Angle-Land because there had been no planets, no sun. Nothing had existed but Time; Time, and a void. Only Time was the void, and the void was Time itself. Through it moved colours, twinklings, sudden shafts of light. There were hummings, shoutings, perhaps, musical tones like the notes of organs that thrummed in his body until it shook with them and became a melting part. Sometimes in the dream he wanted to cry out; but still he couldn't speak, and the beautiful blasphemy ground on. He saw the brown mists lift back waving and whispering, and through them the shine of water; a harsh sea, cold and limitless, ocean of a new world. But the dream itself was fluid; the images shone and altered, melding each smoothly into each, yielding place majestically, fading into dark. The hills came, rolling, tentative, squirming, pushing up dripping flanks that shuddered, sank back, returned to silt. The silt, the sea bed, enriched itself with a million year snowstorm of little dying creatures. The piping of the tiny snails as they fell was a part of the chorus and the song, a thin, sweet harmonic.

And already there were Gods; the Old Gods, powerful and vast, looking down, watching, stirring with their fingers at the silt, waving the swirling brownness back across the sea. It was all done in a dim light, the cold glow of dawn. The hills shuddered, drew back, thrust up again like golden, humped animals, shaking the water from their sides. The sun stood over them, warming, adding steam to the fogs, making multiple and shimmering reflections dance from the sea. The Gods laughed; and over and again, uncertainly, unsurely, springing from the silt, sinking back to silt again, the hills writhed, shaping the shapeless land. The voice sang, whirring like a wheel; there was no "forward," no "back"; only a sense of continuity, of massive development, of the huge Everness of Time. The hills fell and rose; leaves brushed away the sun, their reflections waved in water, the trees themselves sank, rolled and heaved, were thrust down to rise once more dripping, grow afresh. The rocks formed, broke, re-formed, became solid, melted again until from the formlessness somehow the land was made; Angle-Land, nameless still, with its long pastures, its fields, and silent hills of grass. Rafe saw the endless herds of animals that crossed it, wheeling under the wheeling sun; and the first shadowy Men. Rage possessed them; they hacked and hewed, rearing their stone circles in the wind and emptiness, finding again the bodies of the Gods in the chalky flanks of downs. Until all ended, the Gods grew tired; and the ice came flailing and crying from the north, the sun sank dying in its blood and there was coldness and blackness and nothingness and winter.

Into the void, He came; only He was not the Christos, the God of Mother Church. He was Balder, Balder the

Lovely, Balder the Young. He strode across the land, face
burning as the sun, and the Old Ones grovelled and adored.
The wind touched the stone circles, burning them with
frost; in the darkness men cried for spring. So he came to
the Tree Yggdrasil—*What Tree,* Rafe's mind cried despairingly, and the voice checked and laughed and said without
anger *"Yggdrasil, great World Ash, whose branches pierce
the layers of heaven, whose roots wind through all Hells.
. . ."* Balder came to the Tree, on which he must die for
the sins of Gods and Men; and to the Tree they nailed him,
hung him by the palms. And there they came to adore while
His blood ran and trickled and gouted bright, while he
hung above the Hells of the Trolls and of the Giants of
Frost and Fire and Mountain, below the Seven Heavens
where Tiw and Thunor and old Wo-Tan trembled in Val-
halla at the mightiness of what was done.

And from His blood sprang warmth again and grass
and sunlight, the meadow flowers and the calling, mating
birds. And the Church came at last, stamping and jingling,
out of the east, lifting the brass wedding cakes of her altars
while men fought and roiled and made the ground black
with their blood, while they raised their cities and their
signal towers and their glaring castles. The Old Ones moved
back, the Fairies, the Haunters of the Heath, the People of
the Stones, taking with them their lovely bleeding Lord; and
the priests called despairingly to Him, calling Him the
Christos, saying he did die on a tree, at the Place Golgotha,
the Place of the Skull. Rome's navies sailed the world; and
England woke up, steam jetted in every tiny hamlet, and
clattering and noise; while Balder's blood, still raining down,
made afresh each spring. And so after days in the telling,
after weeks, the huge legend paused, and turned in on
itself, and ended.

The stove was out, the hut smelled fresh and cool. Rafe
lay quiet, knowing he had been very ill. The cabin was a

place of browns and clean bright blues. Deep brown of woodwork, orange brown of the control handles, creamy brown of planking. The blue came from the sky, shafting in through windows and door, reflecting from the long-dead semaphore in pale spindles of light. And the girl herself was brown and blue; brown of skin, frosted blue of ribbon and dress. She leaned over him smiling, all nervousness gone. *"Better,"* sang the voice. *"You're better now. You're well."*

He sat up. He was very weak. She eased the blankets aside, letting the air tingle like cool water on his skin. He swung his legs down over the edge of the bunk and she helped him stand. He sagged, laughed, stood again swaying, feeling the texture of the hut floor under his feet, looking down at his body, seeing the pink criss-crossing of scars on stomach and thighs, the jaunty penis thrusting from its nest of hair. She found him a tunic, helped him into it laughing at him, twitching and pulling. She fetched him a cloak, fastened it round his neck, knelt to push sandals on his feet. He leaned against the bunk panting a little, feeling stronger. His eye caught the semaphore; she shook her head and teased him, urging him toward the door. *"Come,"* said the voice. *"Just for a little while."*

She knelt again outside, touched the snow while the wind blustered wetly from the west. Round about, the warming hills were brilliant and still. *"Balder is dead,"* she sang. *"Balder is dead. . . ."* And instantly it seemed Rafe could hear the million chuckling voices of the thaw, see the very flowers pushing coloured points against the translucency of snow. He looked up at the signals on the tower. They seemed strange to him now, like the winter a thing of the past. Surely they too would melt and run, and leave no trace. They were part of the old life and the old way; for the first time he could turn his back on them without distress. The girl moved from him, low shoes showing her ankles against the snow; and Rafe followed, hesitant

at first then more surely, gaining strength with every step.
Behind him, the signal hut stood forlorn.

The two horsemen moved steadily, letting their mounts
pick their way. The younger rode a few paces ahead,
muffled in his cloak, eyes beneath the brim of his hat
watching the horizon. His companion sat his horse quietly,
with an easy slouch; he was grizzled and brown-faced, skin
tanned by the wind. In front of him, over the pommel of the
saddle, was hooked the case of a pair of Zeiss binoculars.
On the other side was the holster of a musket; the barrel
lay along the neck of the horse, the butt thrust into the air
just below the rider's hand.

Away on the left a little knoll of land lifted its crown
of trees into the sky. Ahead, in the swooping bowl of the
valley, was the black speck of a signal hut, its tower showing
thinly above it. The officer reined in quietly, took the glasses
from their case and studied the place. Nothing moved, and
no smoke came from the chimney. Through the lenses the
shuttered windows stared back at him; he saw the black
vee of the Semaphore arms folded down like the wings of
a dead bird. The Corporal waited impatiently, his horse
fretting and blowing steam, but the Captain of Signals was
not to be hurried. He lowered the glasses finally, and clicked
to his mount. The animal moved forward again at a walk,
picking its hooves up and setting them down with care.

The snow here was thicker; the valley had trapped it,
and the day's thaw had left the drifts filmed with a brittle
skin of ice. The horses floundered as they climbed the slope
to the hut. At its door the Captain dismounted, leaving the
reins hanging slack. He walked forward, eyes on the lintel
and the boards.

The mark. It was everywhere, over the door, on its
frame, stamped along the walls. The circle, with the crab
pattern inside it; rebus or pictograph, the only thing the
People of the Heath knew, the only message it seemed they
had for men. The Captain had seen it before, many times;

it had no power left to surprise him. The Corporal had not. The older man heard the sharp intake of breath, the click as a pistol was cocked; saw the quick, instinctive movement of the hand, the gesture that wards off the Evil Eye. He smiled faintly, almost absentmindedly, and pushed at the door. He knew what he would find, and that there was no danger.

The inside of the hut was cool and dark. The Guildsman looked round slowly, hands at his sides, feet apart on the boards. Outside a horse champed, jangling its bit, and snorted into the cold. He saw the glasses on their hook, the swept floor, the polished stove, the fire laid neat and ready on the bars; everywhere, the Fairy mark danced across the wood.

He walked forward and looked down at the thing on the bunk. The blood it had shed had blackened with the frost; the wounds on its stomach showed like leafshaped mouths, the eyes were sunken now and dull; one hand was still extended to the signal levers eight feet above.

Behind him the Corporal spoke harshly, using anger as a bulwark against fear. "The . . . People that were here. They done this. . . ."

The Captain shook his head. "No," he said slowly. " 'Twas a wildcat."

The Corporal said thickly, "They were here though. . . ." The anger surged again as he remembered the unmarked snow. "There weren't no tracks, sir. *How could they come?* . . ."

"How comes the wind?" asked the Captain, half to himself. He looked down again at the corpse in the bunk. He knew a little of the history of this boy, and of his record. The Guild had lost a good man.

How did they come? The People of the Heath. . . . His mind twitched away from using the names the commoners had for them. What did they look like, when they came? What did they talk of, in locked cabins to dying men? Why did they leave their mark. . . .

It seemed the answers shaped themselves in his brain. It was as if they crystallized from the cold, faintly sweet air of the place, blew in with the soughing of the wind. *All this would pass,* came the thoughts, *and vanish like a dream. No more hands would bleed on the signal bars, no more children freeze in their lonely watchings. The Signals would leap continents and seas, winged as thought. All this would pass, for better or for ill. . . .*

He shook his head, bearlike, as if to free it from the clinging spell of the place. He knew, with a flash of inner sight, that he would know no more. The People of the Heath, the Old Ones; they moved back, with their magic and their lore. Always back, into the yet remaining dark. Until one day they themselves would vanish away. They who were, and yet were not. . . .

He took the pad from his belt, scribbled, tore off the top sheet. "Corporal," he said quietly. "If you please. . . . Route through Golden Cap."

He walked to the door, stood looking out across the hills at the matchstick of the eastern tower just visible against the sky. In his mind's eye a map unrolled; he saw the message flashing down the chain, each station picking it up, routing it, clattering it on its way. Down to Golden Cap, where the great signals stood gaunt against the cold crawl of the sea; north up the A line to Aquae Sulis, back again along the Great West Road. Within the hour it would reach its destination at Silbury Hill; and a grave-faced man in green would walk down the village street of Avebury, knock at a door. . . .

The Corporal climbed to the gantry, clipped the message in the rack, eased the handles forward lightly testing against the casing ice. He flexed his shoulders, pulled sharply. The dead tower woke up, arms clacking in the quiet. *Attention, Attention.* . . . Then the signal for Origination, the cypher for the eastern line. The movements dislodged a little cloud of ice crystals; they fell quietly, sparkling against the greyness of the sky.

READER'S GUIDE TO SF

○ THIS READER'S GUIDE is primarily intended for those encountering the complex SF genre for the first time and for those living in small towns and rural areas where many SF books never penetrate. But it may also be useful to those occasional readers—bookstore browsers and bus-trip readers—of randomly selected SF who now want to gain a more systematic knowledge of the field. This guide may even prove helpful to some who already consider themselves confirmed devotees. I am thinking in particular of college- and high-school-age readers who may lack knowledge of the history of SF, of the existence of certain out-of-print books, or of the structure of SF as both genre and micro-cosmic society, even though they religiously buy each month's new paperback selections.

The guide consists of two parts: a perspective of the field and a list of recommended books. It is a sort of eclectic catalog and overview that I hope will give even the most isolated reader the chance to become more familiar with the SF world.

PERSPECTIVE

The hardest thing for the novice to acquire, something no list of books alone will provide, is a sense of the history of the genre, which is either half a century or thousands of years old, depending on whom you ask. Fortunately, two excellent formal histories have recently been published: *Alternate Worlds*, by James Gunn, and *Billion Year Spree*, by Brian W. Aldiss. Although these two histories often differ sharply in emphasis and sometimes come to contradictory conclusions, together they represent the best history of SF currently available. Here are some other books that may help you acquire a feel for the fiction of various historical periods.

For pre-1930 SF, I recommend: *Science Fiction by Gaslight* and *Under the Moons of Mars*, both edited by Sam Moskowitz; *The Battle of the Monsters and Other Stories*, edited by David G. Hartwell and L. W. Currey; *The Light Fantastic*, edited by Harry Harrison; *Perchance to Dream*, edited by Damon Knight; *The Science Fiction of Jack London*, edited by Richard Gid Powers; and *The Science Fiction of Rudyard Kipling*, edited by Frederik Pohl. If you can afford them (or get library access to them), various series of quality reprint editions are also excellent for this period and, indeed, for most periods. Gregg Press, Garland Press, Arno, Dragon Press, and Hyperion offer hundreds of rare volumes that are printed on acid-free paper and are handsomely bound. Some libraries, especially college libraries, have collections of pulp SF magazines from the late twenties to the present. Some of these collections are available on microfilm.

For SF of the late twenties and thirties, the definitive anthologies to date are *Before the Golden Age*, edited by Isaac Asimov, and *Science Fiction of the 30's*, edited by Damon Knight. Also useful are the retrospective single-author collections published by Doubleday, *The Early*

*Asimov, The Early del Rey, The Early Long, The Early
Williamson, The Early Pohl;* and books such as *The Best
of Stanley G. Weinbaum, The Best of John W. Campbell,*
and *The Best of C. L. Moore.*

The last thirty years—the "Golden Age" and beyond—
are covered in dozens of volumes: *Adventures in Time and
Space,* edited by Raymond J. Healy and J. Francis Mc-
Comas; *The Astounding-Analog Reader,* vols. 1 & 2, edited
by Brian W. Aldiss and Harry Harrison; *A Treasury of
Great Science Fiction,* vols. 1 & 2, edited by Anthony
Boucher; *The Worlds of Science Fiction,* edited by Robert
P. Mills; *New Dreams This Morning,* edited by James Blish;
Dangerous Visions and *Again, Dangerous Visions,* edited
by Harlan Ellison; *SF: The Great Years,* vols. 1 & 2, and
Jupiter, edited by Carol and Frederik Pohl; and in an-
thologies edited by Groff Conklin, Damon Knight, and
Robert Silverberg, too numerous to name individually.
Frederik Pohl's *Star* anthology series is also valuable, as is
the *Spectrum* series, edited by Kingsley Amis and Robert
Conquest, and *The Best of Planet Stories,* edited by Leigh
Brackett.

Overviews of SF's evolution are provided by a number
of books: *The Hugo Winners,* vols. 1 & 2, edited by Isaac
Asimov; *The Science Fiction Hall of Fame,* vol. 1, edited
by Robert Silverberg; *The Science Fiction Hall of Fame,*
vols. 2A & 2B, edited by Ben Bova; *Science Fiction Argosy,*
edited by Damon Knight; *Modern Science Fiction,* edited
by Norman Spinrad; *The Mirror of Infinity,* edited by Robert Silverberg; *A Decade of Fantasy and Science Fiction,*
edited by Robert P. Mills, and *Twenty Years of Fantasy
and Science Fiction,* edited by Robert P. Mills and Edward
L. Ferman; *A Spectrum of Worlds,* edited by Thomas D.
Clareson; *The Ruins of Earth,* edited by Thomas M. Disch;
*A Century of Science Fiction, One Hundred Years of Sci-
ence Fiction,* and *A Century of Great Short Science Fiction
Novels,* all edited by Damon Knight; *Where Do We Go*

from Here, edited by Isaac Asimov; *Time Probe,* edited by Arthur C. Clarke; and *SF: Authors' Choice,* vols. 1–4, edited by Harry Harrison.

One of the best retrospective reprint series available is the *Alpha* series, edited by Robert Silverberg, currently up to volume 6. Also valuable are the *Nebula Award Stories* volumes, by varying editors, now up to volume 10. You may also want to check out *The Best from Fantasy and Science Fiction,* now in 18 volumes; the derivative *Analog* series, now up to volume 9; and the *Galaxy Readers,* also in 9 volumes. Some of these titles may be difficult to find in paperback, especially the *Galaxy Readers* and the early numbers of the *F&SF* series, but many libraries will have at least some, and possibly all, of them.

Also outstanding was the *World's Best Science Fiction* series of anthologies, edited by Terry Carr and Donald A. Wollheim. This series ran to 7 volumes before Carr and Wollheim parted forces, and most of those volumes are still available in paperback, although you may have to visit used paperback stores or bookstores specializing in SF to find them. Also excellent was Judith Merrill's *The Year's Best S-F* series. This series ran to 12 volumes plus a retrospective *Best of the Best* anthology. You probably will not be able to find them in paperback even in SF bookstores —with the possible exception of the *Best of the Best.* Many libraries, however, will have the complete run in hardcover. After a lapse of some years, there is again a derivative *Galaxy* series: *The Best from Galaxy,* vols. 1–3, and a companion series, *The Best from If,* vols. 1–3. Also published recently are *The Best from Amazing* and *The Best from Fantastic,* edited by Ted White.

A number of "Best of the Year" anthologies continue to be published annually. Consistently the most popular has been Terry Carr's *Best Science Fiction of the Year* series, now up to volume 5. Others include Donald A. Wollheim's *Annual World's Best SF* series, also in 5 volumes; Brian W.

Aldiss and Harry Harrison's *Best SF* series (now apparently defunct), in 7 volumes; and the *Best Science Fiction Stories of the Year* series, in 6 volumes, the first five edited by Lester del Rey and the sixth edited by Gardner Dozois.

But books are not all that ties the SF world together. A large number of SF magazines are published each year —some monthly, some quarterly, and some on more erratic schedules. Often these magazines contain some of the year's best short fiction. The healthiest and most successful SF magazine, in terms of circulation and financial stability, is *Analog* (published monthly by Conde Nast Publications, Inc., Conde Nast Building, 350 Madison Avenue, New York, N.Y.; subscriptions: Box 5205, Boulder, Colo. 80302; editor, Ben Bova); followed by *The Magazine of Fantasy and Science Fiction* (published monthly by Mercury Press, Inc., Box 56, Cornwall, Conn. 06753; editor, Edward L. Ferman), a monthly with a lower circulation rate but a good deal of literary prestige. Other magazines include *Galaxy* (published monthly by UPD Publishing Corporation, 235 East 45th St., New York, N.Y. 10017; editor, James Baen), which seems to have steadied down on a monthly schedule again after a spate of bimonthly issues; and the sister magazines *Amazing* and *Fantastic* (Ultimate Publishing Co., Box 7, Oakland Gardens, Flushing, N.Y. 11364; editor, Ted White), which now seem to be on quarterly schedules. A new SF magazine also entered the lists this year: *Isaac Asimov's Science Fiction Magazine* (Davis Publications, Inc., Box 13116, Philadelphia, Pa. 19101; subscriptions: 229 Park Avenue South, New York, N.Y. 10003; editor, George Scithers), a quarterly.

In recent years several original anthology series have successfully taken up some of the slack in the dwindling magazine market. The oldest of these series is *Orbit,* edited by Damon Knight, now up to volume 18. There is also a retrospective anthology drawn from the series and currently available in paperback, *The Best from Orbit.* Some of the early *Orbits* are difficult to find in paperback, but many libraries carry the entire series. Besides *Orbit*, the two most successful and firmly established original anthology series are *New Dimensions*, edited by Robert Silverberg, now up to volume 6, and *Universe*, edited by Terry Carr, also in 6 volumes. *Orbit*, *New Dimensions*, and *Universe* are all published annually. Other anthology series include *Stellar*, edited by Judy-Lynn del Rey, now up to volume 2; *Science Fiction Discoveries*, edited by Carol and Frederik Pohl, the first volume of which has just been released; and the forthcoming *Entropy*, edited by Edward Bryant. *Stellar* and *Science Fiction Discoveries* have erratic schedules, and *Entropy* is supposed to be an annual.

Critical books on SF have also proliferated in recent years. Probably the best single SF critical book is still Damon Knight's pioneering *In Search of Wonder*. Other worthwhile books include: *The Issue at Hand* and *More Issues at Hand*, both by James Blish; *Pilgrims through Time and Space*, edited by J. O. Bailey; *Turning Points*, edited by Damon Knight; *Science Fiction Today and Tomorrow* and *Modern Science Fiction: Its Meaning and Its Future*, both edited by Reginald Bretnor; *Of Worlds Beyond*, edited by Lloyd Arthur Eshbach; *The Science Fiction Novel: Imagination and Social Criticism*, edited by Basil Davenport; *The Universe Makers*, by Donald A. Wollheim; *Heinlein in Dimension*, by Alexei Panshin; and *SF: The Other Side of Realism*, edited by Thomas D. Clareson.

Of particular interest to would-be SF writers are: *Writing and Selling Science Fiction*, a collection of how-to articles by SF writers; *The Craft of Science Fiction*, a similar collection of articles edited by Reginald Bretnor; *The Science Fiction Handbook, Revised*, by L. Sprague De Camp and Catherine Crook De Camp; and *Hell's Cartographers*, edited by Brian W. Aldiss and Harry Harrison, a collection of six autobiographies by famous SF writers.

Many SF writers also produce a good deal of nonfiction, primarily on scientific subjects. Those most prolific in this area include Isaac Asimov (with more than a hundred such books to his credit), L. Sprague De Camp, Ben Bova, Poul Anderson, and Robert Silverberg. There was even an anthology of nonfiction articles by well-known SF writers, *Adventures in Discovery,* edited by Tom Purdom, a book also available in many libraries.

Hordes of amateur fan magazines (fanzines) are also published each year. They contain some of the most intimate inside glimpses available into the SF world. Among the most popular fanzines are *Locus,* edited by Charles N. and Dena Brown, published on a more-or-less monthly schedule (15 issues for $6.00, Box 3938, San Francisco, Calif. 94119); *Algol,* edited by Andrew Porter, published twice a year ($6.00 for 6 issues, P.O. Box 4175, New York, N.Y. 10017); *Science Fiction Review,* edited by Richard E. Geis, published quarterly ($4.00 for 4 issues, P.O. Box 11408, Portland, Ore. 97211); *Khatru,* edited by Jeffrey D. Smith, published quarterly (4 issues for $4.00, 1339 Weldon Ave., Baltimore, Md. 21211); *Delap's F & SF Review,* edited by Richard Delap, published monthly ($9.00 annually, 11863 W. Jefferson Blvd., Culver City, Calif. 90230); *Outworlds,* edited by William L. Bowers, published quarterly ($4.00 for 4 issues, P.O. Box 2521, North Canton, Ohio 44720). All of these fanzines are different in tone, emphasis, and thrust. Some are news-oriented, like *Locus;* some are primarily review magazines, like *Science Fiction Review* and *Delap's F & SF Review;* some feature in-depth critical essays, like *Khatru;* and some are eclectic compendiums reflecting the editors' interests, like *Algol* and *Outworlds.* None of these magazines adheres to an easily categorized niche.

Many cities across the nation—especially such population centers as New York, Boston, Chicago, Philadelphia, Los Angeles, Washington, and Denver—support SF fan clubs and annual SF conventions. Lists of these SF conventions are regularly printed in *Analog, Galaxy, Locus,* and elsewhere.

Relatively new phenomena are the SF bookstores that have suddenly mushroomed across the nation, in small towns as well as major cities. Check the Yellow Pages to see if there's one where you live. Even if there is not a specialty SF bookstore in your vicinity, SF books may still be found. Most college bookstores have extensive SF sections, and many large paperback bookstores have them, too. If there is an SF convention in your area, go to it and check out the huckster room. It is possible to find a large number of both new and out-of-print books and magazines for sale at most SF conventions.

It is possible to be actively involved in SF even if your hometown is too small and isolated to boast a bookstore or a library. Many book publishers sell by mail order, especially such large paperback houses as Ballantine, Berkley, DAW, and Ace. The Doubleday Science-Fiction Book Club (ads for the club run in most SF magazines) performs an invaluable service by putting inexpensive club editions of otherwise difficult-to-find hardcover books right into your mailbox. Several large mail-order companies specialize in SF and fantasy books. Two of the largest are The F & SF Book Company, P.O. Box 415, Staten Island, N.Y. 10302; and T-K Graphics, P.O. Box 1951, Baltimore, Md. 21203. Many SF convention hucksters will fill mail orders for you. Both SF magazines and fanzines sell subscriptions. No matter where you are in the continental United States, the chances are that at some time during the year there will be an SF convention within reasonable traveling distance. All it takes to stay in touch is motivation and a clever use of money and the mails.

BOOK LIST

It is an unfortunate and only slowly-changing fact that most SF books look alike. Cover art, blurbs, jacket copy—they are likely to be similar whether the book is the worst novel of the decade or a Hugo-and-Nebula-winning classic. This makes it difficult for a bookstore browser with no systematic knowledge of SF to make an intelligent selection. Most SF books, with their garish covers and lurid blurbs, look like sophomoric junk of the worst sort, and, indeed, a good percentage *is* sophomoric junk. How then tell the good from the bad? The browser needs to know which authors are generally considered superior, and which titles represent their best work. It's possible that SF is more name-oriented than any other kind of literature. Authors' names and book titles are of supreme importance in determining which SF book to buy. Often there simply are not other reliable criteria.

This listing is not intended to be exhaustive. A trip to any large paperback bookstore will demonstrate that most of the authors listed have more titles to their credit than those included here and that many authors, not necessarily inferior ones, are not included at all. The listing must not be considered a rundown of all the worthwhile SF ever published. Such a list, if it were possible to compile at all, would be a book in itself.

The list below *is* intended to aid you in building a basic SF library of some depth, scope, and variety, and to help you acquire the beginnings of an intelligent overview of a complex field. Although none of the books listed here is a failure on its own terms, there are some that I dislike, and some that you will dislike as well. *But it is extremely unlikely that our tastes will agree exactly, if they coincide at all.* Only by including a wide range of SF can one hint at the incredible diversity and richness of the field.

As a rule, I have not included fantasy, except fantasy by a major SF author or a book that has had a wide impact on the field. Neither have I included sword-and-sorcery, horror, or occult titles, or series such as Perry Rhodan, Cap Kennedy, or Doc Savage. One must draw the line somewhere, and many bookstores now shelve each of these types separately. I have not listed the classics—books by H. G. Wells, Jules Verne, George Orwell, Aldous Huxley, or Olaf Stapledon. These books are listed in many dozens, if not hundreds, of college textbooks and anthologies aimed at the school market and are taught in so many SF courses that it would be redundant to list them here. They are readily available in the bookstores and libraries of all but the smallest hamlets and are therefore the books most likely familiar to the SF novice. For similar reasons, I have not listed the works of J. R. R. Tolkien, Kurt Vonnegut, Jr., H. P. Lovecraft, Robert E. Howard, or the four-foot shelf of Edgar Rice Burroughs titles. All these gentlemen have been "discovered" by the literary establishment and do not need to be called to the attention of the general reading public. Their books are readily available even in bookstores that do not otherwise carry much SF.

The listing below also has a built-in bias toward the SF of the last forty years, particularly that of the fifties, sixties, and seventies. Most SF prior to the so-called Golden Age (the late thirties and forties)—and even some fifties SF— is long out-of-print or available only in very high-priced editions aimed at collectors and libraries.

There are signs that this situation is changing, however. Ballantine, Avon, and Ace have been particularly active in recent years in reissuing out-of-print books. As a result, there are many books on the paperback racks today that have not been available for a decade or more. There are recent editions, for instance, of once-rare books by Dick, Piper, Pangborn, Kornbluth, Leiber, Vance, and many others. My advice is to buy them before they go out of print again, especially if you are trying to collect the complete works of certain authors.

When I have listed out-of-print books, they are usually titles that you are still fairly likely to come across in used paperback bookstores, SF bookstores, huckster rooms at SF conventions, or in most libraries.

Although some hardcover books are mentioned, the listing includes mostly paperback books currently in print. Throughout, the most recent paperback edition is given.

Single-author short-story collections are indicated by (ss).

Omissions are the result either of oversight or prejudice. I apologize for both but cannot do much about either.

Aldiss, Brian W. *Barefoot in the Head*. New York: Ace, 1972.
———. *Billion Year Spree*. New York: Shocken, 1974.
———. *Cryptozoic!* New York: Avon, 1969.
———. *Earthworks*. New York: Signet, 1967.
———. *Frankenstein Unbound*. Greenwich, Conn.: Fawcett, 1975.
———. *Greybeard*. New York: Signet, 1965.
———. *The Long Afternoon of Earth*. New York: Signet, 1962.
———. *The Moment of Eclipse*. New York: Doubleday, 1972. (ss)
———. *Starship*. New York: Avon, 1975.
———. *Starswarm*. New York: Signet, 1964. (ss)
———. *Who Can Replace a Man?* New York: Signet, 1976. (ss)
———, and Harrison, Harry, eds. *Annual World's Best SF*, vols. 1–8. New York: Berkley, 1968–73.
———, and Harrison, Harry, eds. *The Astounding-Analog Reader*, vols. 1 & 2. New York: Doubleday, 1972–73.
———, and Harrison, Harry, eds. *Hell's Cartographers*. New York: Harper & Row, 1976.

Amis, Kingsley, and Conquest, Robert, eds. *Spectrum*, vols. 1–5. New York: Berkley, 1963–1968.

Anderson, Poul. *The Best of Poul Anderson*. New York: Pocket Books, 1976. (ss)
———. *Brain Wave*. New York: Ballantine, 1954.

————. *The Broken Sword.* New York: Ballantine, 1971.

————. *The Enemy Stars.* New York: Ballantine, 1965.

————. *Guardians of Time.* New York: Ballantine, 1960. (ss)

————. *The High Crusade.* New York: Manor Books, 1975.

————. *Homeward and Beyond.* New York: Berkley, 1976, (ss)

————. *A Midsummer Tempest.* New York: Ballantine, 1975.

————. *People of the Wind.* New York: Signet, 1973.

————. *The Queen of Air and Darkness.* New York: Signet, 1973. (ss)

————. *Tau Zero.* New York: Berkley, 1976.

————. *Three Hearts and Three Lions.* New York: Avon, 1961.

————. *War of the Wing-Men.* New York: Ace, 1973.

Asimov, Isaac. *The Best of Isaac Asimov.* Greenwich, Conn.: Fawcett, 1976. (ss)

————. *The Caves of Steel.* Greenwich, Conn.: Fawcett, 1974.

————. *The Early Asimov.* Greenwich, Conn.: Fawcett, 1972. (ss)

————. *Earth Is Room Enough.* Greenwich, Conn.: Fawcett, 1974.

————. *The Foundation Trilogy.* New York: Avon, 1974.

————. *I, Robot.* Greenwich, Conn.: Fawcett, 1973.

————. *The Martian Way.* Greenwich, Conn.: Fawcett, 1975. (ss)

————. *The Naked Sun.* Greenwich, Conn.: Fawcett, 1972.

————. *Nightfall & Other Stories.* Greenwich, Conn.: Fawcett, 1974. (ss)

————. *Nine Tomorrows.* Greenwich, Conn.: Fawcett, 1972. (ss)

————. *Pebble in the Sky.* Greenwich, Conn.: Fawcett, 1973.

————, ed. *Before the Golden Age,* vols. 1–3. Greenwich, Conn.: Fawcett, 1975.

————, ed. *The Hugo Winners,* vols. 1–3, abridged. Greenwich, Conn.: Fawcett, 1974.

————, ed. *Where Do We Go from Here?* Greenwich, Conn.: Fawcett, 1972.

Bailey, J. O. *Pilgrims through Space and Time: Trends and Patterns in Scientific and Utopian Fiction.* Westport, Conn.: Greenwood Press, 1972.

Ballard, J. G. *Chronopolis.* New York: Berkley, 1971. (ss)
———. *Crystal World.* New York: Avon, 1976.

Bass, T. J. *The Godwhale.* New York: Ballantine, 1975.
———. *Half-Past Human.* New York: Ballantine, 1975.

Benford, Gregory. *Deeper than the Darkness.* New York: Ace, 1970.
———, and Eklund, Gordon. *If the Stars Are Gods.* New York: Putnam, 1977.
———. *Jupiter Project.* Nashville, Tenn.: Thomas Nelson, 1975.

Best From Amazing. Edited by Ted White. New York: Manor Books, 1973.

Best From Fantastic. Edited by Ted White. New York: Manor Books, 1973.

Best From Fantasy and Science Fiction, vols. 1–8. Edited by Anthony Boucher. New York: Ace, 1952–58.
———, vols. 9–11. Edited by Robert P. Mills. New York: Ace, 1960–62.
———, vols. 12–14. Edited by Avram Davidson. New York: Ace, 1963–64.
———, vols. 15–20. Edited by Edward L. Ferman. New York: Ace, 1965–73.

Best from Galaxy, vols. 1–3. Edited by the editors of *Galaxy* magazine. New York: Award Books, 1972–75.

Best from If, vols. 1–3. Edited by the editors of *If* magazine. New York: Award Books, 1973–75.

Best from Planet Stories. Edited by Leigh Brackett. New York: Ballantine, 1975.

Bester, Alfred. *The Computer Connection.* New York: Berkley, 1976.
———. *The Demolished Man.* New York: Signet, 1959.
———. *The Light Fantastic.* New York: Berkley, 1976. (ss)
———. *Star Light, Star Bright.* New York: Putnam, 1976. (ss)
———. *The Stars My Destination.* New York: Berkley, 1975.

Bishop, Michael. *A Funeral for the Eyes of Fire.* New York: Ballantine, 1975.

————. *A Little Knowledge.* New York: Putnam, 1977.
————. *Stolen Faces.* New York: Harper & Row, 1977.
————. *And Strange at Ecbatan the Trees.* New York: Harper & Row, 1976.

Blish, James. *And All the Stars a Stage.* New York: Avon, 1974.
————. *A Case of Conscience.* New York: Ballantine, 1975.
————. *Cities in Flight.* New York: Avon, 1970.
————. *Galactic Cluster.* New York: Signet, 1972. (ss)
————. *The Issue at Hand.* Chicago: Advent, 1964.
————. *Jack of Eagles.* New York: Avon, 1952.
————. *Midsummer Century.* New York: DAW, 1974.
————. *More Issues at Hand.* Chicago: Advent, 1972.
————, ed. *New Dreams This Morning.* New York: Ballantine, 1966.

Boucher, Anthony, ed. *A Treasury of Great Science Fiction,* vols. 1 & 2. New York: Doubleday, 1959.

Bova, Ben. *As on a Darkling Plain.* New York: Walker, 1972.
————. *Millennium.* New York: Random House, 1976.
————, ed. *The Science Fiction Hall of Fame,* vols. 2A & 2B. New York: Avon, 1974.

Brackett, Leigh. *The Long Tomorrow.* New York: Ballantine, 1974.

Bradbury, Ray. *I Sing the Body Electric.* New York: Bantam, 1971. (ss)
————. *The Martian Chronicles.* New York: Bantam, 1974. (ss)
————. *The October Country.* New York: Ballantine, 1972. (ss)
————. *Something Wicked This Way Comes.* New York: Bantam, 1972.
————. *The Vintage Bradbury.* New York: Vintage, 1965. (ss)

Bretnor, Reginald, ed. *The Craft of Science Fiction.* New York: Harper & Row, 1976.
————, ed. *Modern Science Fiction, Its Meaning and Its Future.* New York: Coward-McCann, 1953.
————, ed. *Science Fiction Today and Tomorrow.* New York: Penguin, 1975.

Brown, Frederic. *Martians, Go Home.* New York: Ballantine, 1976.

Brunner, John. *The Book of John Brunner.* New York: DAW, 1976. (ss)

————. *The Jagged Orbit.* New York: Ace, 1969.

————. *Polymath.* New York: DAW, 1974.

————. *Quicksand.* New York: DAW, 1976.

————. *The Sheep Look Up.* New York: Ballantine, 1976.

————. *The Shockwave Rider.* New York: Ballantine, 1976.

————. *Squares of the City.* New York: Ballantine, 1973.

————. *Stand on Zanzibar.* New York: Ballantine, 1976.

Bryant, Edward. *Among the Dead.* New York: Collier, 1974. (ss)

————. *Cinnabar.* New York: Macmillan, 1976. (ss)

————, ed. *Entropy.* Los Angeles: Pegana Press, 1977.

Budrys, Algis. *Budrys' Inferno.* New York: Berkley, 1963. (ss)

————. *The Falling Torch.* New York: Pyramid, 1974.

————. *Rogue Moon.* New York: Avon, 1974.

————. *Who?* New York: Ballantine, 1975.

Campbell, John W. *The Best of John W. Campbell.* New York: Ballantine, 1976. (ss)

Carr, Terry, ed. *Best Science Fiction of the Year,* vols. 1–5. New York: Ballantine, 1972–76.

————, ed. *An Exaltation of Stars.* New York: Pocket Books, 1974.

————, ed. *The Fellowship of the Stars.* New York: Simon & Schuster, 1974.

————, ed. *On Our Way to the Future.* New York: Ace, 1970.

————, ed. *This Side of Infinity.* New York: Ace, 1972.

————, ed. *Universe,* vols. 1–2. New York: Ace, 1971–72.

————, ed. *Universe,* vols. 3–5. New York: Popular Library, 1973–75.

————, ed. *Universe,* vol. 6. New York: Doubleday, 1976.

————, and Wollheim, Donald A., eds. *World's Best Science Fiction,* vols. 1–7. New York: Ace, 1965–71.

Charnas, Suzy McKee. *Walk to the End of the World.* New York: Ballantine, 1975.

Clareson, Thomas D., ed. *SF: The Other Side of Realism; Essays on Modern Fantasy and Science Fiction.* Bowling Green, Ohio: Bowling Green University Press, 1972.
————, ed. *A Spectrum of Worlds.* New York: Doubleday, 1972.

Clarke, Arthur C. *Childhood's End.* New York: Ballantine, 1976.
————. *The City and the Stars.* New York: Signet, 1973.
————. *The Deep Range.* New York: Signet, 1974.
————. *Expeditions to Earth.* New York: Ballantine, 1972. (ss)
————. *A Fall of Moondust.* New York: Signet, 1974.
————. *Imperial Earth.* New York: Ballantine, 1976.
————. *Rendezvous with Rama.* New York: Ballantine, 1974.
————. *The Sands of Mars.* New York: Signet, 1974.
————. *Tales of Ten Worlds.* New York: Signet, 1973. (ss)
————, ed. *Time Probe.* New York: Dell, 1967.

Clement, Hal. *Close to Critical.* New York: Ballantine, 1975.
————. *Cycle of Fire.* New York: Ballantine, 1975.
————. *Mission of Gravity.* New York: Pyramid, 1974.
————. *Needle.* New York: Avon, 1976.

Compton, David G. *Cronicules.* New York: Ace, 1970.
————. *The Steel Crocodile.* New York: Ace, 1970.
————. *Synthajoy.* New York: Ace, 1968.
————. *The Unsleeping Eye.* New York: DAW, 1974.

Dann, Jack. *Junction.* Greenwich, Conn.: Gold Medal, 1977.
————. *Starhiker.* New York: Harper & Row, 1977.
————, and Zebrowski, George, eds. *Faster than Light.* New York: Harper & Row, 1976.
————, ed. *Immortal.* New York: Harper & Row, 1977.
————, and Harris, David, eds. *Transition.* New York: Vintage, 1977.
————, ed. *Wandering Stars.* New York: Washington Square Press, 1975.

Davenport, Basil, ed. *The Science Fiction Novel: Imagination and Social Criticism.* Chicago: Advent, 1964.

Davidson, Avram. *The Enemy of My Enemy*. New York: Berkley, 1966.
―――. *The Enquiries of Dr. Eszterhazy*. New York: Warner Books, 1975. (ss)
―――. *The Island Under the Earth*. New York: Ace, 1969.
―――, and Moore, Ward. *Joyleg*. New York: Pyramid, 1962.
―――. *Masters of the Maze*. New York: Manor Books, 1976.
―――. *Or All the Seas with Oysters*. New York: Berkley, 1962. (ss)
―――. *The Phoenix and the Mirror*. New York: Ace, 1969.
―――. *Rogue Dragon*. New York: Ace, 1965.
―――. *Rork!* New York: Berkley, 1965.
―――. *Strange Seas and Shores*. New York: Doubleday, 1971. (ss)

De Camp, L. Sprague, and Pratt, Fletcher. *The Compleat Enchanter*. New York: Ballantine, 1976.
―――. *The Continent Makers*. New York: Signet, 1971. (ss)
―――. *The Hand of Zei/The Search for Zei*. New York: Ace, 1962.
―――, and Pratt, Fletcher. *Land of Unreason*. New York: Ballantine, 1970.
―――. *Lest Darkness Fall*. New York: Ballantine, 1974.
―――. *Rogue Queen*. New York: Signet, 1972.
―――, and De Camp, Catherine C. *The Science Fiction Handbook, Revised*. Philadelphia: Owlswick Press, 1976.
―――. *The Tower of Zanid*. New York: Manor Books, 1972.

Delany, Samuel R. *Babel-17*. New York: Ace, 1973.
―――. *Dhalgren*. New York: Bantam, 1975.
―――. *Driftglass*. New York: Signet, 1971. (ss)
―――. *The Einstein Intersection*. New York: Ace, 1967.
―――. *The Fall of the Towers*. New York: Ace, 1976.
―――. *Nova*. New York: Bantam, 1975.
―――. *Triton*. New York: Bantam, 1976.

del Rey, Judy Lynn, ed. *Stellar,* vols. 1 & 2. New York: Ballantine, 1974–76.

del Rey, Lester. *The Early del Rey*. New York: Ballantine, 1976. (ss)

——. *The Eleventh Commandment*. New York: Ballantine, 1976.

——. *Nerves*. New York: Ballantine, 1974.

Dick, Philip K. *Do Androids Dream of Electric Sheep?* New York: Signet, 1968.

——. *Dr. Bloodmoney*. New York: Ace, 1976.

——. *Flow My Tears, the Policeman Said*. New York: DAW, 1975.

——. *The Man in the High Castle*. New York: Berkley, 1974.

——. *The Man Who Japed*. New York: Ace, 1975.

——. *Martian Time-Slip*. New York: Ballantine, 1976.

——. *Now Wait for Last Year*. New York: Manor Books, 1974.

——. *Our Friends from Frolix 8*. New York: Ace, 1970.

——. *The Penultimate Truth*. New York: Leisure Books, 1975.

——. *The Preserving Machine*. New York: Ace, 1976. (ss)

——. *Solar Lottery*. New York: Ace, 1975.

——. *The Three Stigmata of Palmer Eldritch*. New York: Manor Books, 1975.

——. *Time Out of Joint*. New York: Belmont, 1959.

——. *Ubik*. New York: Dell, 1970.

——. *The Variable Man & Other Stories*. New York: Ace, 1976. (ss)

——. *The World Jones Made*. New York: Ace, 1975.

Dickson, Gordon R. *Ancient, My Enemy*. New York: DAW, 1976.

——. *The Book of Gordon Dickson*. New York: DAW, 1973. (ss)

——. *Dorsai*. New York: DAW, 1976.

——. *Soldier, Ask Not*. New York: DAW, 1975.

——. *The Tactics of Mistake*. New York: DAW, 1972.

Disch, Thomas M. *Camp Concentration*. New York: Avon, 1971.

——. *Fun with Your New Head*. New York: Signet, 1972. (ss)

——. *Getting into Death*. New York: Knopf, 1976. (ss)

——. *334*. New York: Avon, 1974.

——, ed. *Bad Moon Rising*. New York: Harper & Row, 1973.

————, ed. *The New Improved Sun*. New York: Harper & Row, 1975.

————, ed. *The Ruins of Earth*. New York: Berkley, 1971.

Dozois, Gardner, and Effinger, George Alec. *Nightmare Blue*. New York: Berkley, 1975.

————. *The Visible Man*. New York: Berkley, 1977. (ss)

————, ed. *Best Science Fiction Stories of the Year,* vol. 6. New York: Dutton, 1977.

————, ed. *Beyond the Golden Age*. New York: Berkley, 1977.

————, ed. *A Day in the Life*. New York: Harper & Row, 1973.

————, and Dann, Jack, eds. *Future Power*. New York: Random House, 1976.

Edmondson, G. C. *The Aluminium Man*. New York: Berkley, 1975.

————. *Blue Face*. New York: DAW, 1972.

————. *The Ship That Sailed the Time Stream*. New York: Ace, 1965.

————. *Stranger than You Think*. New York: Ace, 1965. (ss)

Effinger, George Alec. *Irrational Numbers*. New York: Doubleday, 1976. (ss)

————. *Mixed Feelings*. New York: Harper & Row, 1974. (ss)

————. *Relatives*. New York: Dell, 1976.

————. *What Entropy Means to Me*. New York: Signet, 1973.

Eklund, Gordon. *The Eclipse of Dawn*. New York: Ace, 1971.

————, and Anderson, Poul. *Inheritors of Earth*. New York: Pyramid, 1976.

Elder, Joseph, ed. *Eros in Orbit*. New York: Pocket Books, 1974.

————, ed. *The Farthest Reaches*. New York: Pocket Books, 1968.

Ellison, Harlan. *Alone against Tomorrow*. New York: Collier, 1972. (ss)

————. *Approaching Oblivion*. New York: Signet, 1976. (ss)

————. *The Beast That Shouted Love at the Heart of the World*. New York: Signet, 1974. (ss)

————. *Deathbird Stories*. New York: Dell, 1976. (ss)

————. *Paingod and Other Delusions*. New York: Pyramid, 1975. (ss)

————, and various authors. *Partners in Wonder*. New York: Pyramid, 1975. (ss)

————, ed. *Again, Dangerous Visions*. New York: Signet, 1973.

————, ed. *Dangerous Visions*. New York: Signet, 1973.

Elwood, Roger, and Silverberg, Robert, eds. *Epoch*. New York: Putnam, 1975.

————, ed. *Future City*. New York: Pocket Books, 1974.

————, ed. *Showcase*. New York: Harper & Row, 1973.

————, and Kidd, Virginia, eds. *The Wounded Planet*. New York: Bantam, 1974.

Emshwiller, Carol. *Joy in Our Cause*. New York: Harper & Row, 1974. (ss)

Eshbach, Lloyd Arthur. *Of Worlds Beyond: The Science of Science Fiction Writing*. Chicago: Advent, 1964.

Farmer, Philip José. *The Fabulous Riverboat*. New York: Berkley, 1973.

————. *Inside, Outside*. New York: Avon, 1975.

————. *Lord Tyger*. New York: Signet, 1972.

————. *The Lovers*. New York: Ballantine, 1961.

————. *Night of Light*. New York: Berkley, 1972.

————. *Strange Relations*. New York: Avon, 1974. (ss)

————. *To Your Scattered Bodies Go*. New York: Berkley, 1973.

Ferman, Edward L., and Malzberg, Barry N., eds. *Final Stage*. New York: Penguin, 1975.

Galaxy Readers, vols. 1–2. Edited by H. L. Gold. New York: Crown, 1952–54.

————, vols. 3–6. Edited by H. L. Gold. New York: Doubleday, 1958–62.

Gotschalk, Felix C. *Growing Up in Tier 3000*. New York: Ace, 1975.

Gunn, James. *Alternate Worlds: An Illustrated History of Science Fiction*. New York: A & W Visual Library, 1976.

————. *The Listeners*. New York: Signet, 1974.

Haldeman, Joe. *The Forever War*. New York: Ballantine, 1976.

————. *Mindbridge*. New York: St. Martin's Press, 1976.
————. *War Year*. New York: Holt, Rinehart & Winston, 1972.
————, ed. *Study War No More*. New York: St. Martin's Press, 1977.

Harness, Charles L. *The Ring of Ritornel*. New York: Berkley, 1968.
————. *The Rose*. New York: Berkley, 1953.

Harrison, Harry. *The Best of Harry Harrison*. New York: Pocket Books, 1976. (ss)
————. *Bill the Galactic Hero*. New York: Avon, 1975.
————. *The Deathworld Trilogy*. New York: Berkley, 1976.
————. *Make Room! Make Room!* New York: Berkley, 1973.
————, ed. *The Light Fantastic*. New York: Scribners, 1971.
————, ed. *Nova*, vols. 1 & 2. New York: Dell, 1970–74.
————, ed. *SF: Authors' Choice*, vols. 1–4. New York: Berkley, 1970–74.
————, ed. *The Year 2000*. New York: Berkley, 1972.

Hartwell, David G., and Currey, L. W., eds. *The Battle of the Monsters and Other Stories: An Anthology of American Science Fiction*. Boston: Gregg Press, 1976.

Healy, Raymond J., and McComas, J. Francis, eds. *Adventures in Time and Space*. New York: Ballantine, 1975.

Heinlein, Robert A. *Between Planets*. New York: Ace, 1971.
————. *Beyond This Horizon*. New York: Signet, 1974.
————. *Citizen of the Galaxy*. New York: Ace, 1975.
————. *The Door into Summer*. New York: Signet, 1970.
————. *Double Star*. New York: Signet, 1956.
————. *Farmer in the Sky*. New York: Ballantine, 1975.
————. *Have Space Suit Will Travel*. New York: Ace, 1975.
————. *The Moon Is a Harsh Mistress*. New York: Berkley, 1968.
————. *The Past through Tomorrow*. New York: Berkley, 1975. (ss)
————. *The Puppet Masters*. New York: Signet, 1970.
————. *Red Planet*. New York: Ace, 1975.
————. *The Rolling Stones*. New York: Ace, 1975.
————. *Star Beast*. New York: Ace, 1975.

————. *Starman Jones*. New York: Ballantine, 1975.

————. *Starship Troopers*. New York: Berkley, 1970.

————. *Stranger in a Strange Land*. New York: Berkley, 1968.

————. *Tunnel in the Sky*. New York: Ace, 1970.

————. *The Unpleasant Profession of Jonathan Hoag*. New York: Berkley, 1976. (ss)

————. *Waldo & Magic, Inc.* New York: Signet, 1970. (ss)

Herbert, Frank. *The Book of Frank Herbert*. New York: DAW, 1973. (ss)

————. *Dune*. New York: Berkley, 1975.

————. *The Green Brain*. New York: Ace, 1974.

————. *Under Pressure*. New York: Ballantine, 1974.

————. *The Worlds of Frank Herbert*. New York: Ace, 1971. (ss)

Keyes, Daniel. *Flowers for Algernon*. New York: Bantam, 1970.

Knight, Damon. *A for Anything*. Greenwich, Conn.: Fawcett, 1965.

————. *The Best of Damon Knight*. New York: Pocket Books, 1976. (ss)

————. *Far Out*. New York: Berkley, 1962. (ss)

————. *Hell's Pavement*. Greenwich, Conn.: Fawcett, 1971.

————. *In Deep*. New York: Manor Books, 1972. (ss)

————. *In Search of Wonder*. Chicago: Advent, 1967.

————. *Off Center*. New York: Award Books, 1973. (ss)

————. *The Other Foot*. New York: Manor Books, 1971.

————. *The Rithian Terror*. New York: Award Books, 1973 .

————. *Three Novels*. New York: Berkley, 1969.

————. *Turning On*. New York: Doubleday, 1966. (ss)

————. *World without Children* and *The Earth Quarter*. New York: Lancer, 1970.

————, ed. *The Best from Orbit*. New York: Berkley, 1976.

————, ed. *A Century of Great Short Science Fiction Novels*. New York: Delacorte, 1964.

————, ed. *A Century of Science Fiction*. New York: Simon & Schuster, 1962.

————, ed. *Dimension X*. New York: Simon & Schuster, 1970.

————, ed. *One Hundred Years of Science Fiction*. New York: Simon & Schuster, 1968.

————, ed. *Orbit,* vols. 1–13. New York: Berkley, 1966–74.

————, ed. *Orbit,* vols. 14–18. New York: Harper & Row, 1974–76.

————, ed. *Perchance to Dream.* New York: Manor Books, 1973.

————, ed. *Science Fiction Argosy.* New York: Simon & Schuster, 1972.

————, ed. *Science Fiction of the 30's.* New York: Bobbs-Merrill, 1975.

————, ed. *Turning Points.* New York: Harper & Row, 1976.

Kornbluth, C. M. *The Best of C. M. Kornbluth.* New York: Ballantine, 1976. (ss)

————. *A Mile Beyond the Moon.* New York: Manor Books, 1972. (ss)

————. *Not This August.* New York: Bantam, 1956.

————. *The Syndic.* New York: Avon, 1974.

Kuttner, Henry. *The Best of Henry Kuttner.* New York: Ballantine, 1975. (ss)

————. *Bypass to Otherness.* New York: Ballantine, 1961.

————, and Moore, C. L. *Fury.* New York: Lancer, 1950.

————. *Return to Otherness.* New York: Ballantine, 1962.

————. *Robots Have No Tails.* New York: Lancer, 1973.

Lafferty, R. A. *Arrive at Easterwine.* New York: Scribners, 1971.

————. *The Devil Is Dead.* New York: Avon, 1971.

————. *Does Anyone Else Have Something Further to Add?* New York: Scribners, 1974. (ss)

————. *The Fall of Rome.* New York: Doubleday, 1973.

————. *The Flame Is Green.* New York: Walker, 1971.

————. *Fourth Mansions.* New York: Ace, 1969.

————. *Nine Hundred Grandmothers.* New York: Ace, 1970. (ss)

————. *Okla Hannali.* New York: Pocket Books, 1973.

————. *Past Master.* New York: Ace, 1968.

————. *The Reefs of Earth.* New York: Berkley, 1968.

————. *Strange Doings.* New York: DAW, 1973. (ss)

Laumer, Keith. *The Best of Keith Laumer.* New York: Pocket Books, 1976. (ss)

————. *A Plague of Demons.* New York: Warner Books, 1971.

————. *A Trace of Memory*. New York: Warner Books, 1972.

————. *Worlds of the Imperium*. New York: Ace, 1973.

Le Guin, Ursula K. *City of Illusions*. New York: Ace, 1974.

————. *The Dispossessed*. New York: Avon, 1975.

————. *The Farthest Shore*. New York: Bantam, 1975.

————. *The Lathe of Heaven*. New York: Avon, 1973.

————. *The Left Hand of Darkness*. New York: Ace, 1974.

————. *Planet of Exile*. New York: Ace, 1974.

————. *Rocannon's World*. New York: Ace, 1974.

————. *The Tombs of Atuan*. New York: Bantam, 1975.

————. *The Wind's Twelve Quarters*. New York: Bantam, 1976. (ss)

————. *The Wizard of Earthsea*. New York: Bantam, 1975.

————. *The Word for World Is Forest*. New York: Berkley, 1976.

Leiber, Fritz. *The Best of Fritz Leiber*. New York: Ballantine, 1974. (ss)

————. *The Big Time*. New York: Ace, 1972.

————. *Conjure Wife*. New York: Award Books, 1968.

————. *Gather, Darkness*. New York: Ballantine, 1975.

————. *Green Millennium*. New York: Ace, 1976.

————. *The Mind Spider*. New York: Ace, 1976. (ss)

————. *Night of the Wolf*. New York: Ballantine, 1966. (ss)

————. *Night's Black Agents*. New York: Aeonian Press, 1976. (ss)

————. *A Pail of Air*. New York: Aeonian Press, 1976. (ss)

————. *Ships to the Stars*. New York: Ace, 1976. (ss)

————. *A Specter Is Haunting Texas*. New York: Bantam, 1968.

————. *The Wanderer*. New York: Ballantine, 1976.

————. *You're All Alone*. New York: Ace, 1972. (ss)

Long, Frank Belknap. *The Early Long*. New York: Doubleday, 1975. (ss)

McCaffrey, Anne. *Dragonflight*. New York: Ballantine, 1975.

————. *Dragonquest*. New York: Ballantine, 1975.

McCauley, Kirby, ed. *Frights*. New York: St. Martin's Press, 1976.

McIntyre, Vonda N. *The Exile Waiting.* Greenwich, Conn.: Fawcett, 1976.

———, and Anderson, Susan Janice, eds. *Aurora: Beyond Equality.* Greenwich, Conn.: Fawcett, 1976.

McKenna, Richard. *Casey Agonistes and Other Stories.* New York: Harper & Row, 1974. (ss)

Malzberg, Barry N. *The Best of Barry N. Malzberg.* New York: Pocket Books, 1976. (ss)

———. *Beyond Apollo.* New York: Pocket Books, 1974.

———. *Herovit's World.* New York: Pocket Books, 1974.

Martin, George R. R. *After the Festival.* New York: Avon, 1977.

———. *A Song for Lya.* New York: Avon, 1976. (ss)

Merril, Judith. *The Best of Judith Merril.* New York: Warner, 1976. (ss)

———, ed. *SF: The Best of the Best.* New York: Dell, 1967.

———, ed. *The Year's Best S-F,* vols. 1–12. New York: Dell, 1956–69.

Miller, Walter M., Jr. *A Canticle for Leibowitz.* New York: Bantam, 1969.

———. *The View from the Stars.* New York: Ballantine, 1964. (ss)

Mills, Robert P., ed. *A Decade of Fantasy and Science Fiction.* New York: Doubleday, 1960.

———, and Ferman, Edward L., eds. *Twenty Years of Fantasy and Science Fiction.* New York: Berkley, 1970.

———, ed. *The Worlds of Science Fiction.* New York: Paperback Library, 1970.

Moorcock, Michael. *An Alien Heat.* New York: Harper & Row, 1973.

———. *Behold the Man.* New York: Avon, 1976.

———. *The End of All Songs.* New York: Harper & Row, 1976.

———. *The Hollow Lands.* New York: Harper & Row, 1974.

———. *Legends from the End of Time.* New York: Harper & Row, 1976. (ss)

————, ed. *New Worlds Quarterly,* vols. 1–4. New York: Berkley, 1971–72.

Moore, C. L. *The Best of C. L. Moore.* New York: Ballantine, 1976. (ss)

Moore, Ward. *Bring the Jubilee.* New York: Avon, 1976.

Moskowitz, Sam, ed. *Science Fiction by Gaslight.* Westport, Conn.: Hyperion Press, 1974.
————, ed. *Under the Moons of Mars: A History and Anthology of "The Scientific Romance" in the Munsey Magazines, 1912–1920.* Westport, Conn.: Hyperion Press, 1970.

Nebula Award Stories, vol. 1. Edited by Damon Knight. New York: Pocket Books, 1970.
————, vol. 2. Edited by Brian W. Aldiss and Harry Harrison. New York: Pocket Books, 1970.
————, vol. 3. Edited by Roger Zelazny. New York: Pocket Books, 1970.
————, vol. 4. Edited by Poul Anderson. New York: Pocket Books, 1971.
————, vol. 5. Edited by James Blish. New York: Pocket Books, 1972.
————, vol. 6. Edited by Clifford D. Simak. New York: Pocket Books, 1972.
————, vol. 7. Edited by Lloyd Biggle, Jr. New York: Harper & Row, 1974.
————, vol. 8. Edited by Isaac Asimov. New York: Berkley, 1975.
————, vol. 9. Edited by Kate Wilhelm. New York: Harper & Row, 1974.
————, vol. 10. Edited by James Gunn. New York: Harper & Row, 1975.

Niven, Larry. *All the Myriad Ways.* New York: Ballantine, 1975. (ss)
————. *A Gift from Earth.* New York: Ballantine, 1975.
————. *A Hole in Space.* New York: Ballantine, 1974. (ss)
————. *The Long Arm of Gil Hamilton.* New York: Ballantine, 1976. (ss)

————, and Pournelle, J. E. *The Mote in God's Eye.* New York: Pocket Books, 1975.

————. *Neutron Star.* New York: Ballantine, 1973. (ss)

————. *Protector.* New York: Ballantine, 1973.

————. *Ringworld.* New York: Ballantine, 1972.

————. *Tales of Known Space.* New York: Ballantine, 1975. (ss)

————. *World of Ptavvs.* New York: Ballantine, 1975.

————. *A World Out of Time.* New York: Holt, Rinehart & Winston, 1976.

Norton, Andre. *The Beast Master.* New York: Ace, 1972.

————. *Galactic Derelict.* New York: Ace, 1974.

————. *Greeneye.* New York: Ace, 1971.

————. *The Time Traders.* New York: Ace, 1974.

————. *Witch World.* New York: Ace, 1974.

Pangborn, Edgar. *The Company of Glory.* New York: Pyramid, 1975.

————. *Davy.* New York: Ballantine, 1976.

————. *Good Neighbors and Other Strangers.* New York: Collier, 1973. (ss)

————. *The Judgement of Eve.* New York: Avon, 1976.

————. *A Mirror for Observers.* New York: Avon, 1976.

————. *West of the Sun.* New York: Dell, 1966.

Panshin, Alexei. *Heinlein in Dimension.* Chicago: Advent, 1968.

Piper, H. Beam. *Fuzzy Sapiens.* New York: Ace, 1976.

————. *Little Fuzzy.* New York: Ace, 1976.

————. *Lord Kalvan of Otherwhen.* New York: Ace, 1977.

————. *Space Viking.* New York: Ace, 1977.

Pohl, Frederik. *The Best of Frederik Pohl.* New York: Ballantine, 1975. (ss)

————. *The Early Pohl.* New York: Doubleday, 1976. (ss)

————. *The Gold at the Starbow's End.* New York: Ballantine, 1972. (ss)

————. *In the Problem Pit.* New York: Bantam, 1976. (ss)

————. *Man Plus.* New York: Random House, 1976.

————. *A Plague of Pythons.* New York: Ballantine, 1973.

————. *Slave Ship.* New York: Ballantine, 1975.

————, and Kornbluth, C. M. *Gladiator-at-Law.* New York: Bantam, 1977.

————, and Kornbluth, C. M. *The Space Merchants.* New York: Ballantine, 1953.

————, and Kornbluth, C. M. *Wolfbane.* New York: Bantam, 1976.

————, and Pohl, Carol, eds. *Jupiter.* New York: Ballantine, 1973.

————, ed. *Nightmare Age.* New York: Ballantine, 1972.

————, and Pohl, Carol, eds. *Science Fiction Discoveries.* New York: Bantam, 1976.

————, ed. *The Science Fiction of Rudyard Kipling.* New York: Doubleday, 1977.

————, and Pohl, Carol, eds. *SF: The Great Years,* vols. 1–2. New York: Ace, 1973–76.

————, ed. *Star,* vols. 1–6. New York: Ballantine, 1953–60; reissued 1972.

————, ed. *Star of Stars.* New York: Doubleday, 1960.

————, ed. *Star Short Novels.* New York: Ballantine, 1954.

Pournelle, J. E., ed. *20–20 Vision.* New York: Avon, 1974.

Powers, Richard Gid, ed. *The Science Fiction of Jack London.* Boston: Gregg Press, 1976.

Purdom, Tom. *The Barons of Behavior.* New York: Ace, 1972.
————. *Reduction in Arms.* New York: Berkley, 1971.
————, ed. *Adventures in Discovery.* New York: Doubleday, 1969.

Reynolds, Mack. *The Best of Mack Reynolds.* New York: Pocket Books, 1976. (ss)

Roberts, Keith. *The Chalk Giants.* New York: Berkley, 1976.
————. *Pavane.* New York: Berkley, 1976.

Russ, Joanna. *Alyx.* Boston: Gregg Press, 1976. (ss)
————. *And Chaos Died.* New York: Ace, 1975.
————. *The Female Man.* New York: Bantam, 1975.
————. *Picnic on Paradise.* New York: Ace, 1974.

Russell, Eric Frank. *Wasp.* New York: Bantam, 1971.

Saberhagen, Fred. *Berserker*. New York: Ballantine, 1967. (ss)

Sallis, James. *A Few Last Words*. New York: Collier, 1971. (ss)

――――, ed. *The Shores Beneath*. New York: Avon, 1971.

Sargent, Pamela. *Cloned Lives*. Greenwich, Conn.: Fawcett, 1976.

――――, ed. *Bio-Futures*. New York: Vintage, 1976.

――――, ed. *More Women of Wonder*. New York: Vintage, 1976.

――――, ed. *Women of Wonder*. New York: Vintage, 1975.

Schmitz, James H. *Agent of Vega*. New York: Grosset & Dunlap, 1972.

――――. *The Demon Breed*. New York: Ace, 1968.

――――. *A Pride of Monsters*. New York: Macmillan, 1973.

――――. *The Witches of Karres*. New York: Ace, 1977.

Science Fiction Writers of America, eds. *Writing and Selling Science Fiction*. Cincinnati: Writer's Digest Press, 1976.

Scortia, Thomas N. *Artery of Fire*. New York: Popular Library, 1974.

――――, ed. *Strange Bedfellows*. New York: Pocket Books, 1974.

Shaw, Bob. *Other Days, Other Eyes*. New York: Ace, 1972.

――――. *The Two-Timers*. New York: Ace, 1968.

Sheckley, Robert. *Can You Feel Anything When I Do This?* New York: DAW, 1974. (ss)

――――. *The Status Civilization*. New York: Dell, 1960.

Silverberg, Robert. *The Best of Robert Silverberg*. New York: Pocket Books, 1976. (ss)

――――. *The Book of Skulls*. New York: Signet, 1972.

――――. *Born with the Dead*. New York: Vintage, 1975. (ss)

――――. *Capricorn Games*. New York: Random House, 1976. (ss)

――――. *Downward to the Earth*. New York: Signet, 1971.

――――. *Dying Inside*. New York: Ballantine, 1973.

――――. *The Man in the Maze*. New York: Avon, 1975.

————. *The Masks of Time*. New York: Ballantine, 1973.

————. *Nightwings*. New York: Avon, 1976.

————. *The Reality Trip*. New York: Ballantine, 1972. (ss)

————. *The Second Trip*. New York: Signet, 1973.

————. *Shadrack in the Furnace*. New York: Bobbs-Merrill, 1976.

————. *The Stochastic Man*. Greenwich, Conn.: Fawcett, 1976.

————. *A Time of Changes*. New York: Signet, 1971.

————. *Tower of Glass*. New York: Signet, 1970.

————. *Unfamiliar Territory*. New York: Scribners, 1973. (ss)

————. *Up the Line*. New York: Ballantine, 1973.

————. *The World Inside*. New York: Signet, 1974.

————, ed. *Dark Stars*. New York: Ballantine, 1969.

————, ed. *Deep Space*. New York: Dell, 1974.

————, ed. *The Ends of Time*. New York: Dell, 1971.

————, ed. *The Mirror of Infinity*. New York: Harper & Row, 1970.

————, ed. *New Dimensions,* vol. 1–2. New York: Avon, 1971–74.

————, ed. *New Dimensions,* vols. 3–4. New York: Signet, 1974.

————, ed. *New Dimensions,* vols. 5–6. New York: Harper & Row, 1975–76.

————, ed. *The Science Fiction Hall of Fame,* vol. 1. New York: Avon, 1974.

Simak, Clifford D. *The Best of Clifford D. Simak*. New York: Doubleday, 1963. (ss)

————. *City*. New York: Ace, 1973.

————. *Time and Again*. New York: Ace, 1975.

————. *Time Is the Simplest Thing*. New York: Leisure, 1974.

————. *Way Station*. New York: Manor Books, 1975.

Sladek, John T. *The Müller-Fokker Effect*. New York: Pocket Books, 1973.

————. *The Reproductive System*. New York: Avon, 1974.

Smith, Cordwainer. *The Best of Cordwainer Smith*. New York: Ballantine, 1975. (ss)

————. *Norstrilia*. New York: Ballantine, 1975.

————. *Quest of the Three Worlds*. New York: Ace, 1966. (ss)

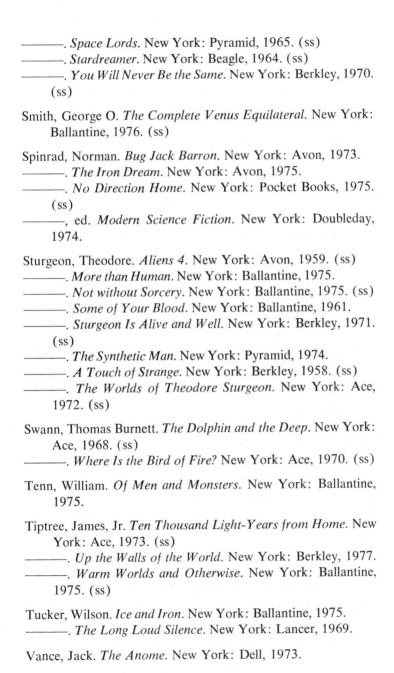

————. *Space Lords*. New York: Pyramid, 1965. (ss)
————. *Stardreamer*. New York: Beagle, 1964. (ss)
————. *You Will Never Be the Same*. New York: Berkley, 1970.
(ss)

Smith, George O. *The Complete Venus Equilateral*. New York:
Ballantine, 1976. (ss)

Spinrad, Norman. *Bug Jack Barron*. New York: Avon, 1973.
————. *The Iron Dream*. New York: Avon, 1975.
————. *No Direction Home*. New York: Pocket Books, 1975.
(ss)
————, ed. *Modern Science Fiction*. New York: Doubleday,
1974.

Sturgeon, Theodore. *Aliens 4*. New York: Avon, 1959. (ss)
————. *More than Human*. New York: Ballantine, 1975.
————. *Not without Sorcery*. New York: Ballantine, 1975. (ss)
————. *Some of Your Blood*. New York: Ballantine, 1961.
————. *Sturgeon Is Alive and Well*. New York: Berkley, 1971.
(ss)
————. *The Synthetic Man*. New York: Pyramid, 1974.
————. *A Touch of Strange*. New York: Berkley, 1958. (ss)
————. *The Worlds of Theodore Sturgeon*. New York: Ace,
1972. (ss)

Swann, Thomas Burnett. *The Dolphin and the Deep*. New York:
Ace, 1968. (ss)
————. *Where Is the Bird of Fire?* New York: Ace, 1970. (ss)

Tenn, William. *Of Men and Monsters*. New York: Ballantine,
1975.

Tiptree, James, Jr. *Ten Thousand Light-Years from Home*. New
York: Ace, 1973. (ss)
————. *Up the Walls of the World*. New York: Berkley, 1977.
————. *Warm Worlds and Otherwise*. New York: Ballantine,
1975. (ss)

Tucker, Wilson. *Ice and Iron*. New York: Ballantine, 1975.
————. *The Long Loud Silence*. New York: Lancer, 1969.

Vance, Jack. *The Anome*. New York: Dell, 1973.

———. *The Asutra*. New York: Dell, 1974.

———. *The Best of Jack Vance*. New York: Pocket Books, 1976. (ss)

———. *Big Planet*. New York: Ace, 1957.

———. *The Blue World*. New York: Ballantine, 1966.

———. *The Brave Free Men*. New York: Dell, 1973.

———. *The Dragon Masters*. New York: Ace, 1975.

———. *The Dying Earth*. New York: Lancer, 1962. (ss)

———. *Eight Fantasms and Magics*. New York: Collier, 1970. (ss)

———. *Emphyric*. New York: Dell, 1970.

———. *The Killing Machine*. New York: Berkley, 1964.

———. *The Languages of Pao*. New York: Ace, 1974.

———. *The Last Castle*. New York: Ace, 1975.

———. *To Live Forever*. New York: Ballantine, 1976.

———. *Marune: Alastor 933*. New York: Ballantine, 1975.

———. *The Palace of Love*. New York: Berkley, 1967.

———. *Showboat World*. New York: Pyramid, 1975.

———. *The Star Kings*. New York: Berkley, 1963.

———. *Trullion: Alastor 2262*. New York: Ballantine, 1973.

———. *The Worlds of Jack Vance*. New York: Ace, 1973. (ss)

Van Vogt, A. E. *The Best of A. E. Van Vogt*. New York: Pocket Books, 1976. (ss)

———. *The Players of Null-A*. New York: Berkley, 1974.

———. *Slan*. New York: Berkley, 1975.

———. *The War against the Rull*. New York: Ace, 1972.

———. *The Weapon Shops of Isher*. New York: Ace, 1973.

———. *The World of Null-A*. New York: Berkley, 1974.

———. *The Worlds of A. E. Van Vogt*. New York: Ace, 1973. (ss)

Varley, John. *Ophiuchi Hotline*. New York: Dial, 1977.

Vinge, Vernor. *The Witling*. New York: DAW, 1976.

Weinbaum, Stanley G. *The Best of Stanley G. Weinbaum*. New York: Ballantine, 1974. (ss)

Wilhelm, Kate. *Abyss*. New York: Bantam, 1973.

———. *City of Cain*. Boston: Little, Brown, 1974.

————. *The Clewiston Test.* New York: Pocket Books, 1977.

————. *The Downstairs Room.* New York: Dell, 1970. (ss)

————. *The Infinity Box.* New York: Pocket Books, 1977. (ss)

————. *The Killer Thing.* New York: Ace, 1969.

————. *Let the Fire Fall.* New York: Lancer, 1969.

————. *Margaret and I.* New York: Pocket Books, 1977.

————. *Where Late the Sweet Birds Sang.* New York: Pocket Books, 1977.

Williamson, Jack. *The Early Williamson.* New York: Doubleday, 1975. (ss)

————. *The Humanoids.* New York: Avon, 1975.

Wolfe, Gene. *The Devil in a Forest.* Chicago: Follett, 1976.

————. *The Fifth Head of Cerberus.* New York: Ace, 1976.

————. *Peace.* New York: Harper & Row, 1975.

Zebrowski, George. *Macrolife.* New York: Harper & Row, 1977.

————, and Scortia, Thomas N., eds. *Human-Machines.* New York: Vintage, 1976.

Zelazny, Roger. *The Doors of His Face, the Lamps of His Mouth.* New York: Avon, 1974. (ss)

————. *Doorways in the Sand.* New York: Harper & Row, 1976.

————. *The Dream Master.* New York: Ace, 1973.

————. *Four for Tomorrow.* New York: Ace, 1973. (ss)

————. *Isle of the Dead.* New York: Ace, 1969.

————. *Lord of Light.* New York: Avon, 1971.

————. *My Name Is Legion.* New York: Ballantine, 1976. (ss)

————. *This Immortal.* New York: Ace, 1973.

ABOUT THE AUTHORS

BRIAN W. ALDISS was born in East Dereham, Norfolk, in 1925. He is the author of two non-SF novels that were best sellers in England—*The Hand-Reared Boy* and *A Soldier Erect*—as well as a number of SF novels, among them *Starship, The Long Afternoon of Earth, Cryptozoic!, Frankenstein Unbound,* and *Barefoot in the Head.* He won the Hugo Award for his "Hothouse" series (later incorporated into *The Long Afternoon of Earth*), and the Nebula Award for his novella, "The Saliva Tree." He was formerly literary editor of the *Oxford Mail* and is the author of a critical history of science fiction, *Billion Year Spree.* He presently lives in Oxford with his wife, Margaret, and their children.

DAMON KNIGHT was born in Baker, Oregon, in 1922. He is the author of many SF novels and short story collections, among them *Hell's Pavement, Beyond the Barrier, Mind Switch, Three Novels, A for Anything, The Best of Damon*

Knight, and *In Deep.* His anthologies include *A Century of Science Fiction, The Dark Side, Dimension X, Cities of Wonder, First Flight,* and the *Orbit* series. He won the Hugo Award for *In Search of Wonder,* a book of critical essays. He also founded the Science Fiction Writers of America and became its first president. He lives in Eugene, Oregon, with his wife, writer Kate Wilhelm.

R. A. LAFFERTY is a retired electrical engineer who resides in Oklahoma, where he has spent most of his life, except for a number of years in Australia, the Dutch East Indies, and New Guinea as a staff sergeant during World War II. His novels include *Past Master, The Reefs of Earth, Fourth Mansions, The Devil is Dead, Arrive at Easterwine,* and *Okla Hannali.* He has three short story collections: *Nine Hundred Grandmothers, Strange Doings,* and *Does Anyone Else Have Something Further to Add?* He won the Hugo Award for his short story "Eurema's Dam."

URSULA K. LE GUIN received her B.A. from Radcliffe College and her M.A. in French and Italian Renaissance Literature from Columbia University. Her novels include *The Left Hand of Darkness, The Dispossessed, Planets of Exile, The Lathe of Heaven, City of Illusions, The Wizard of Earthsea, The Tombs of Atuan,* and *The Farthest Shore.* She has two short story collections, *The Wind's Twelve Quarters and Orsinian Tales. The Left Hand of Darkness* won both the Hugo and the Nebula awards, as did *The Dispossessed.* She also won the Hugo Award for her novella, "The Word for World Is Forest," and for her short story, "The Ones Who Walk Away from Omelas," and the Nebula Award for her short story, "The Day After the Revolution." *The Farthest Shore* received the National Book Award for Children's Literature. She lives in Portland, Oregon, with her husband, historian Charles A. Le Guin.

FRITZ LEIBER was born in Chicago in 1910 and is a graduate of the University of Chicago (Philosophy, Phi Beta Kappa). He has worked as an actor both in films and on the stage, toured with a Shakespeare Company, and for a number of years was editor of *Science Digest*. His books include *The Big Time; The Wanderer; Conjure Wife; The Green Millennium; A Spectre Is Haunting Texas; Gather, Darkness; Night of the Wolf;* and *The Best of Fritz Leiber*. He won the Hugo Award for his novels, *The Big Time* and *The Wanderer,* for his novella, *Ship of Shadows,* and for his novelette, *Gonna Roll the Bones.* He won the Nebula Award for *Gonna Roll the Bones,* for his novelette, *Ill Met in Lankhmar,* and for his short story, "Catch That Zeppelin!" He lives in San Francisco, California.

KEITH ROBERTS was born in Kettering, Northamptonshire. Artist as well as author, he has worked in the British film industry as a cartoon animator and as an illustrator and cover artist for a number of SF magazines. He was associate editor of the British SF magazine *Science Fantasy* for a number of years and editor of *Impulse* in 1966. His books include *Pavane, The Chalk Giants, The Furies, The Inner Wheel,* and a historical novel, *The Boat of Fate.* He lives in Henley-on-Thames, Oxfordshire.

JOANNA RUSS was born in The Bronx, New York, in 1937. She attended Cornell University, where she received a B.A. in English Literature, and Yale University, where she studied playwriting and received her M.A. Her books include *Picnic on Paradise, And Chaos Died,* and *The Female Man.* She won the Nebula Award for her short story, "When It Changed." She lives in Boulder, Colorado, where she teaches at the University of Colorado.

ROBERT SILVERBERG was born in Brooklyn, New York, in 1935, and is a graduate of Columbia University. One of the most prolific authors alive, he is the author of more than 450 fiction and nonfiction books and 3,000 magazine pieces. His novels and short story collections include *Dying Inside, The Book of Skulls, Downward to the Earth, Tower of Glass, The World Inside, The Stochastic Man, Shadrach in the Furnace, Born with the Dead, Unfamiliar Territory,* and *The Best of Robert Silverberg.* His anthologies include *Dark Stars, The Mirror of Infinity, The Science Fiction Bestiary, Worlds of Maybe, Beyond Control,* the *New Dimensions* series, and the *Alpha* series. He won the Nebula Award for his novel, *A Time of Changes,* and for his short stories, "Good News from the Vatican" and "Passengers." He won the Hugo Award for his novella, *Nightwings,* and another Hugo in 1956 as Most Promising New Writer of the Year. He lives in Oakland, California, with his wife, Barbara.

CORDWAINER SMITH was the pseudonym of the late Dr. Paul M.A. Linebarger, Professor of Asiatic Politics at the Johns Hopkins School of Advanced International Studies. Born in Milwaukee, Wisconsin, in 1913, Linebarger entered George Washington University in Washington at the age of fourteen, later attended Oxford University and North China University in Peking, and received his Ph.D. from Johns Hopkins University when he was twenty-two. A civilian advisor to the military in three wars, he was the author of *Psychological Warfare,* which remains a classic text on that subject, and a number of books on Far Eastern and Southeast Asian politics. His SF books include *Nostrilla, Space Lords, Quest of the Three Worlds, You Will Never Be the Same, Stardreamer,* and *The Best of Cordwainer Smith.* He died in 1966.

JAMES TIPTREE, JR., is the author of numerous science fiction stories that have appeared in most of the leading magazines and anthologies. He won the Nebula Award for his short story, "Love Is the Plan the Plan Is Death," and the Hugo Award for his novella, *The Girl Who Was Plugged In*. He has two short story collections, *Ten Thousand Light Years from Home* and *Warm Worlds and Otherwise*. He is currently working on a novel, tentatively entitled *Up the Walls of the World*. Nothing definite is known about his private life, but he operates out of a post office box address in McLean, Virginia.

GENE WOLFE was born in Brooklyn, New York, in 1931. His stories have appeared in most of the leading SF magazines and anthologies, and his books include *The Fifth Head of Cerberus, Peace,* and *The Devil in a Forest*. He won the Nebula Award for his novella, *The Death of Doctor Island*. He lives in Barrington, Illinois, with his wife, Rosemary, and their children. He edits the trade publication, *Plant Engineering*.

ABOUT THE EDITOR

GARDNER DOZOIS was born and raised in Salem, Massachusetts. He sold his first science fiction story in 1966 and entered the Army almost immediately thereafter, spending the next three years overseas as a military journalist. He has been a full-time writer since his discharge from the service in 1969. His short fiction has appeared in *Orbit, New Dimensions, Analog, Quark, Generation, Amazing, Worlds of If, Chains of the Sea,* and other magazines and anthologies. He has been a Nebula Award finalist five times, a Hugo Award finalist four times, and a Jupiter Award finalist twice. He is the editor of a number of anthologies, among them *A Day in the Life, Future Power* (with Jack Dann), and *Beyond the Golden Age.* He is also the editor of Dutton's *Best Science Fiction Stories of the Year* series, and associate editor of *Isaac Asimov's Science Fiction Magazine.* He is coauthor, with George Alec Effinger, of the novel *Nightmare Blue,* and is currently at work on another novel. A collection of his short fiction, *The Visible*

Man and Other Stories, is forthcoming. He is a member of the Science Fiction Writers of America, the SFWA Credentials Committee, the SFWA Speakers' Bureau, and the Professional Advisory Committee to the Special Collections Department of the Paley Library at Temple University. Mr. Dozois lives in Philadelphia.